this

darkness

mine

Also by Mindy McGinnis
The Female of the Species
A Madness So Discreet
In a Handful of Dust
Not a Drop to Drink
Given to the Sea

MINDY McGINNIS

this

darkness

mine

KATHERINE TEGEN BOOKS
An Imprint of HarperCollins *Publishers*

Katherine Tegen Books is an imprint of HarperCollins Publishers.

This Darkness Mine
Copyright © 2017 by Mindy McGinnis

Library of Congress Control Number: 2017932878
ISBN 978-0-06-256159-6

Typography by Erin Fitzsimmons
17 18 19 20 21   PC/LSCH 10 9 8 7 6 5 4 3 2 1

First Edition

For my sister.
She's the nice one.

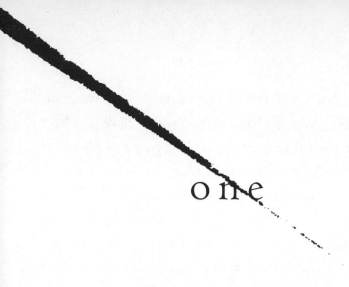

one

I'm digging splinters out of my gums again.

The closest music store carries only cheap reeds, and Mom and Dad won't pay shipping for something that weighs practically nothing. The end result is me leaning over the girls' bathroom sink with Brooke's tweezers, trying to focus on the sliver by my canine rather than on my best friend's morbid fascination with the process.

"Some space?" I ask, pulling back from the mirror. It's hard enough to do this without her shoulder rubbing against mine.

"Sorry, Sasha," she says. "It's just so gross."

Which is exactly why she's leaning in. That's the kind of girl Brooke is. She'll pop the zits you can't reach and offer to skin everyone else's cat in bio, but the downside of having that for a friend is that she's also intensely interested in any open wounds you might have. I'm back up against the mirror, my breath fogging exactly where I need to see before she speaks again.

"I've never even heard of people getting reed splinters in their gums. . . ." She lets her sentence die out, like I'm supposed to provide a more likely explanation for the slivers of bone-white wood that work their way out of my gums.

"Reeds break." I shrug. "And no one else practices as much as I do."

Brooke nods in the mirror, because there's no point arguing about that. I arch an eyebrow at her and she shrugs, letting me know she won't interrupt again.

I pull down my lower lip, resting the tweezers on the callus that's developed on the inside. The latest splinter is barely poking through, a hard white tip in a sea of soft pink. Getting a good grip on them is always the worst part. Each near miss creates a scraping noise I can feel as well as hear, a tiny vibration that passes through the roots of my teeth. But leaving it there isn't an option. The last time I ignored one I got an infection and couldn't play for a week, after which Charity Newell challenged me for first chair. I retained my seat, but she looked oddly hopeful afterward—so I hadn't crushed her.

I pinch down on the tweezers at the right moment, the tip of the splinter flattening under the pressure. Behind me I hear Brooke taking a deep breath as I pull, the end finally coming free, the tiny round hole in my gum filling with a dot of blood. I run my tongue over it, the tang of copper fading quickly. Brooke takes her tweezers back from me, inspecting the tiny fleck of wood still stuck on the end.

"Does it hurt?" she asks.

I rinse my mouth out with water and do a quick check to see if there are more. "No," I tell her, which is sort of true.

Like a lot of things, it only hurts if you let it.

Brooke keeps an eye on me throughout lunch, like she thinks I'm going to cough up a femur or something. We're at our normal table, tucked into a corner where the band geeks and literal drama queens find a measure of peace. We can talk about wet versus dry embouchure without any unwanted sexual innuendo from idiots, and the word *thespian* gets by without giggles. Which is not to say that we don't have our own brand of shortcomings. If I hear one more joke about Heath's trombone . . .

"God, take a shower, Harver," Lilly says, but her eyes show something less than disgust as they follow Isaac Harver across the cafeteria. Brooke's too.

"That's easily three days no-wash, maybe five," Brooke says.

"You would know," Lilly says, rubbing the tips of her squeaky-clean blond curls between her fingers.

"Two weeks, baby." Brooke flips double *V*s for victory toward the football players' table. She hasn't let them live down the eighth-grade bet to see who could go the longest without showering. They ignore her, so she decides to pester Lilly instead.

"Like you'd pass up the chance to shower with Isaac," she says.

Lilly's narrowed eyes are still on him as he flops into his seat at the table by the window, the one that all the stoners claimed at the beginning of the year and no one had the guts to oust them from.

"Is there a prerinse involved?" Lilly asks, and Brooke busts out laughing.

"Omigod, you whore."

I smack down my spoon, not caring that chili splatters across Brooke's sweater. "Do you mind?"

"What?" Her eyes are wide and confused, but Brooke can't quite pull off total innocence. She knows exactly what she did.

"You should watch your language," I tell her. "One day it's going to bite you in the butt."

"I think you mean ass," Brooke says, and Lilly ducks

her head so I can't see her smiling. But I know she is.

"Seriously, Brooke. Remember when Miss Upton dropped the f-bomb at band camp?"

"That one time?" Brooke adds, and Lilly can't smother her laugh.

That joke needs to die already.

"She was almost fired over it," I remind them.

Summer band camp doesn't exactly bring out the best in people, especially by midweek. Hauling heavy instruments in hundred-degree weather, blowing every breath you've got into music you haven't learned yet, and fresh breakouts around your lips as your mouthpiece jams every drop of sweat right back into your pores makes you cranky. It's not ideal, but it still wasn't okay for the flag instructor to toss out the big no-no when a girl lost her pole grip and Miss Upton took one in the face.

"I think you'd swear if your nose was broken too," Lilly says. She sneaks a glance at me and adds, "Maybe."

"Yeah, and anyway, she didn't actually say *fuck*," Brooke goes on, ignoring my wince. "It was more like—" She dumps some milk into her palm, huffs it up her nose, covers her face with her hands, and makes an inarticulate noise that might or might not be a swear. I can't tell because I'm already pushing back from the table to avoid the white froth Brooke is spewing everywhere.

"What?" she asks. "Too much?"

"No wonder you don't have a boyfriend," Lilly says.

Brooke waves her off as she wipes her face with a napkin. "Who cares? Unlike Sasha, I can survive without a trom . . . boner."

And there it is. At least once a week. Why couldn't I date a drummer?

I wad up my own napkin, tossing it into my chili, where it immediately starts to soak up grease and sink.

"Seriously. Why are we even friends?"

Brooke stops laughing, managing to look dignified even with twin rivers of milk flowing from her nostrils. "I really don't know," she says.

And somehow, I feel like I didn't win that one.

There is nothing as beautiful as silver against black.

My clarinet rests in its case, but not for long. It's time to practice, time to smell wet cork and my own breath, time for my brain to disconnect and my fingers to move of their own volition, music seeping out from under my bedroom door until Mom calls me down to dinner. And maybe even after that, if I play softly enough that they can't hear.

Six years ago Mr. Hunter brought us into the high school band room, our little sixth-grade bodies small enough to fit into the instrument cages. He showed us every instrument, played a B flat major scale on each one, sent little slips home to our parents explaining financing options and the pros and cons of new versus used.

I knew what I wanted, even then. An unswerving dedication fired in my soul at the sight of the clarinet. I'm not like Lilly, who started out on trumpet, said it hurt her lips too much and tried a sax, flaked out and switched over to the flute, which she's stayed with for two years—but I've seen her casting looks at the oboes lately. I'm not like Brooke either, happy to stand in the back and hit bells, drums, timpani, freshmen, anything that gets close to her mallets.

They chose music because we always did things together, from dressing up like triplet bunnies at Halloween to making a pact that our boyfriends always had to get along with one another or it was a deal breaker. Lilly's talents extended from the orchestra pit to the stage, even if she had yet to snag a lead role, while Brooke had transposed her penchant for hitting things into a decent softball career.

Me, I live by one thing. And I do it well.

I snap the joints together and tighten the ligature, ignoring the slight scream in my wrist as I do. My hands have crackled since seventh grade, the tendons forever swollen and stiff. Mom keeps warning me that I'm doing permanent damage. Dad doesn't comment because he always has earplugs in.

It's together now, resting on my lap, the last rays of the evening sun slipping through my window and bouncing off the keys. I love how it looks so complicated, spikes of silver flaring, empty holes of nothingness, a mass of wood and metal that almost seems vicious until you hear its voice. Low. Melodic. Lulling. It can convince you of anything if you listen to it long enough. My hands find their place and do their work. They must want Brahms tonight because that's what my ears get.

There's nothing better than letting your brain go dead. I use it so much, taxing it to the limit with facts, theories, definitions—whatever I need to regurgitate for the next test. Then I push everything I dedicated my mind to for the week out the back door to make room for the next batch, the next test, a red A+ bleeding onto the white of whatever paper I wrote last.

It's my hands that know the clarinet, not my brain. It unclenches, resting lightly in a fluid bed as Brahms rocks it to sleep, the curtains of my eyelids drawing shut to give it peace from the daylight.

My phone goes off.

I jolt, knocking my teeth against the mouthpiece. The reed cracks and I suck back a word that I'd yell at Brooke for saying. I settle for growling deep in my throat as I dig through the mass of covers on my bed for the phone. It dings at me again, lighting up enough for me to see it under the pillow where it slipped when I tossed it on the bed.

There's a text from an unfamiliar number, with a monosyllabic message.

hey

I don't hesitate with my response. A few years ago Kate Gulland accidentally sexted with her boyfriend's dad because of a single-digit mix-up. She said it made Christmas dinner incredibly awkward.

Who is this?

There's no answer. I stare at the screen until the opening bars of Beethoven's Eighth that I use as my background begin to blur into each other. I roll onto my belly, phone still in hand but composure shattered. Full-on practice mode is my favorite place to be, but it's not an easy one to get to. Recapturing the semiconscious state that I prefer will take a full ten minutes, only to be interrupted again as soon as dinner is ready.

The phone vibrates in my hand, light bouncing off my palm.

Isaac

I roll my eyes.

Whatever, B. Give your little bro his phone back.

Brooke's time would be better spent perfecting the new cadence on her quads than screwing with me over text, or next week the woodwinds are going to march right into the brass when we try to pregame. I turn off my phone as Mom's voice sails up the stairs.

Dad likes to say the only things you can count on in life are death and taxes, but I'll add our seating arrangement at dinner to that. Dad at the head, Mom at the foot, me to his right. There are scuff marks on the wall behind me where I've shoved away from the table too hard, the back of my chair scraping away slivers of wallpaper and digging into the drywall underneath. Seventeen years' worth of minor arguments and a few dashes for the bathroom are imprinted there, marking my place.

I've charted the conversation while staring at the empty chair across from me. I know what to expect the moment my butt is in my spot, so I have my answers preloaded, my mouth ready to convince them I'm present and accounted for while my hands work through some fingering, tapping on the dead silence of fork and spoon.

"How was school today?" from Mom is a middle E, simple and sweet, a good warm-up for more complicated things to come.

"Fine. We played *insert current band piece here* and Brooke said, '*fill in with best friend's witticism of the day.*'" One note up, the F, all throat, which is fitting, since this is the most I'll say in the dinner hour.

Mom says, "How was work?" This is my cue to launch into the A flat major scale, because I'm not needed here. Dad will talk about foreign and domestic taxes, 529 payouts and offshore banking, then complain about people who don't understand these things. He fills his plate while he talks, making sure none of his food touches.

Much like the chairs around the table, safe distance is always assured.

He'll ask how her day was next, and Mom will talk about a long phone call with a friend, reiterating it almost word for word. I once made it through all twelve major scales while she informed us about someone's spinal fusion. I don't remember whose.

Sometimes I wonder what Mom's day is like once Dad and I are gone, if she's relieved to see our backs or if the house feels empty without us. Her coffee cups have permanent rings on the inside, her levels of determination rising as they drop. I imagine her day, starting with getting everyone else moving, ending with turning out bedroom lights. Though she always has something to say at dinner, I've noticed that Mom's stories are never about her.

My fingers have stopped moving, a spoonful of mashed potatoes paused halfway to my mouth.

"Sasha?" Mom asks. "Everything okay?"

"My day was fine," I say, and a line of worry forms between her eyebrows. I've interrupted the flow of dinner, said a line from the beginning here at the end, where it doesn't belong.

"How are you?" I ask, and the line deepens into confusion. Dad always asks how her day was, which is something else entirely.

"I'm . . ." Mom shakes her head, not able to improvise an answer to an unscripted question. "I'm fine," she says. But her voice goes up at the end, turning it into an uncertainty.

Dad clears his throat. "Sasha."

"I'm fine too," I say.

And my chair smacks the wall as I leave.

Homework waits for me, reliable as ever. I turn on my phone so that I can have some Pachelbel in the background while I work. Everyone else in the world might prefer the Canon, but his Ciaccona in F minor blows it out of the water. Brooke says I only listen to it to be elitist.

I smirk while my phone powers up, thinking about Brooke. I'm sure I've got either an apology or a long line of texts from her still trying to convince me she's Isaac. Instead I get this:

WTF you gave me your #

U want me to txt you or not?

A new one comes in just as I'm about to crack some sass.

THIS DARKNESS MINE 13

Whatever

Brooke may be my best friend, but she knows better than to whatever me, over text or otherwise. My phone shakes in my hands as I consider the alternatives. There aren't many. Either someone who doesn't like me is screwing with me—and I'll admit, that list is long—or this actually is Isaac. Which puts me in an odd place because I have nothing to say to him. I settle for

I think you have the wrong number

Then I mute my phone and fire up the Pachelbel.

Brooke says life is easier in the key of F.

Of course she always adds "you."

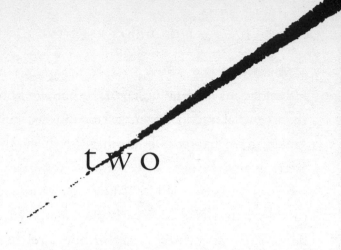

two

School is a process, a series of hoops to be jumped through, set at the appropriate heights for whoever the jumper is. Mine are high, and while there are days that I resent the mental acrobatics necessary for me to clear them, I also realize that they've been positioned there for a reason. It has been determined that I am capable of performing at that level. All I have to do is prove it.

Senior year has been no more taxing than the others. Assigned novels are longer and the equations more convoluted, but nothing has set me back yet. Colleges have been courting me since I was a junior, but my sights have been set on Oberlin since I picked up a pamphlet from the band director as a sixth grader. I can get a degree in psychology as well as a performance degree from their conservatory, something that Dad thinks is hilarious. He told me if my goal was to drive people crazy with my constant playing, I'd already accomplished it.

That's when Mom bought him the earplugs.

Dad tried to steer me toward an economics major, telling me that music might be my passion but I needed to think rationally about employment. He said taxes only sound boring and can provide a reliable income. I sat through an hour lecture about how there's a sense of calm to be found in columns of integers, and that numbers never lie. So I found a copy of our cell phone bill and highlighted all the calls from his account to an unfamiliar number that always happened right around the time he got off work. I mailed it to his office with a Post-it attached that said, "You're right, Dad! Numbers don't lie. Love, Sasha."

He left me alone after that. Like pretty much all the time.

My fingers fly through my locker combination without thought, my mind idly following the junior high band as they murder our fight song, its agonizing death floating down the hallway. They've pounded through the first sixteen measures, and I'm bracing myself for the bridge when my locker is slammed shut, my index finger two inches from losing some length.

"What the hell?"

"That's what I'm thinking," Isaac Harver says as he leans against the wall.

My heart hits at least a hundred beats per minute as I glance up and down the hall, but there's hardly anyone here this early. Just me, the sixth-grade morning class using the shared band room, and the only person in the world I know who actually owns a black leather jacket.

And somehow Isaac wears it like it's any other coat, as if he could take it off and still look like a badass. I glance at the tattoo trailing down his neck into his white T-shirt and the scabs on his knuckles from where—the word is—he punched out Jade McCarren's dad last week when he shorted him on weed.

Intimidating or not he almost took off one of my fingers, and I need all ten if I'm going to Oberlin.

"Thinking," I say. "Not your normal mode of operation is it?"

He smiles and I stop breathing for a second, either because he might be about to stab me or because he has dimples.

"So, what?" he says. "You came over to the dark side for a minute when you gave me your number?"

I yank my locker open for the second time. "I did not give you my number," I say between clenched teeth, and my anger makes him take a step back. People are always surprised when roses have a few thorns, like the girls who wear khakis and live with our natural hair color aren't ever going to bite.

"Yeah . . ." Isaac's eyes narrow as he watches me fish a copy of *Great Expectations* out of my locker, even though I have no idea why I need it, since English isn't until after lunch. "Except you did."

It's my turn to slam the locker, and I'm about to say something nasty when there's a hand on my shoulder, heavy, cool, and calm.

"Everything okay?" Heath asks, his voice as steady as his pulse.

Isaac doesn't look at my boyfriend. I can feel his eyes on me even though I'm staring at my locker.

"Yeah, man," Isaac says. "Everything's peaches." Then he flicks a strand of my hair over my shoulder as he walks away.

Heath's grip on me tightens. "What was that?"

I turn into him, switching my view from the numbers on my locker to the steady, sensible third buttonhole on Heath's shirt. It's Tuesday, so he's wearing his blue oxford.

"Nothing," I tell him, my eyes slipping slightly upward to the collar of his new tee, crisp and white, barely stretched. I remember that Isaac's was worn out, with the tiniest drop of rust on the edge that was probably blood.

"Just a psycho being a psycho," I add, because Heath hasn't let go of my shoulder, and I can feel the tips of his manicured nails through my sweater.

I head toward the band room, Heath in my wake as the sixth graders spill out to get to their wing before the rest of the high schoolers fill the halls. I swear I can feel the strand of hair that Isaac touched burning right through my clothes.

Which makes no sense because we've barely exchanged ten words our entire lives, even in a school this small. The only memory I have of him is from third grade, when he wrote the f-word in red crayon on the bottom of the tube slide, and we all dared each other to go look at it.

He's at the end of the hall, headed for the back door where smokers sneak one before first period. I watch him take the turn, part of me hoping I never see him again and another part willing him to look back at me. Then he's gone, and my heart stops.

It actually stops.

I make the oddest noise, the slightest *oooh*, as I lose the beat, my hands clamping to my chest as if I can reset the metronome there with my fingers. Heath is at my side, hands tight on both arms now, forcing my arms deeper into their sockets, my collarbone protesting. I can't speak, can't tell him to stop. My heart has left me. I felt it go, slipping down the hall to follow Isaac.

Like a rubber band stretched too far it comes back to me, slamming into my rib cage just as I crumple to the floor.

One beat.

Two.

A thread of regularity.

"I'm fine," I say to Heath, who came down to the floor with me. "Not enough to eat this morning, I think."

He digs in his pocket and pulls out a package of granola, which should be some kind of heroism in this moment but instead all I can think is that he'll be a great dad and somehow that's unsexy as hell right now.

"Just get me off the floor before anybody sees me," I say, waving away the granola. He's a gentleman, hand on my elbow, counting to three, saying "careful," as I come to my feet.

Heath holds the door to the band room open for me, and I get to my chair without falling, snapping together my clarinet and trying to reclaim the steps of this day, the ones that need to accumulate to get me through the week, the month, the year. Everything that needs to pass to land me where I deserve to be—the first clarinet chair in a bigger room than this, surrounded by real musicians.

Isaac Harver is not going to distract me from that.

And if my heart stops first, I'll find a way to keep going without it.

I monitor my pulse throughout the day, slipping my fingers onto my wrist and counting, well aware that if I collapse again Heath will call 911 and I'll spend my evening explaining that my heart travels with Isaac Harver now. Which is just as ridiculous as it sounds, even taken symbolically.

How he got my number I don't know, but I definitely didn't give it to him, I reassure myself as I pull the cuff of my sweater back down over my wrist in sixth period. My pulse is right where it's supposed to be, my heart behaving instead of traipsing toward certain doom. Lilly flops into the seat next to mine, her hair ballooning up into a mushroom cloud that carries nothing more lethal than an overdose of lavender vanilla.

"Hey," she says. "When you get a chance I need a baby picture for the yearbook."

I'm still counting heartbeats, so she clarifies.

"The senior baby pictures?" she goes on. "Cole Vance gave us one of him in the tub, but you could totally see his dick. I had to photoshop some bubbles in. They were really small bubbles. But I guess he was a baby then, so he gets a waiver on that one. Although, maybe it matters even on babies? Do some boy babies have bigger—"

I stop her with my hand in the air.

"You need a baby picture of me?"

"Yes."

"For the layout of senior baby pictures?"

"Yes."

I nod. "Got it. Stories of Cole Vance's prepubescent penis not necessary."

"Brooke thought it was funny," she huffs.

"Brooke would," I shoot back. "Just give me the bare minimums of what I need to know. I'm operating on overload as it is."

And while this is certainly true, I don't know why it's suddenly getting to me. Pressure is my environment, like a creature three miles underneath the sea. If you took all the expectations away, the shock would kill me, my lungs flattening and refusing to reinflate.

"You okay?" Lilly asks.

I'm not used to hearing this question. I am always okay. That's when I realize both my hands are to my chest, shielding my heart from an unseen threat.

"I'm fine," I snap, dropping my arms to my side.

I love Lilly but Charity Newell is her cousin, and I can't say for sure that she was entirely happy for me when I defended first chair successfully. She might actually care if I'm okay. She might be checking for cracks in my veneer.

"Did you finish?" I ask, waving *Great Expectations* in the air to change the subject.

"You bet," she says, flashing her phone with highlighted SparkNotes.

"Nice," I say. "Slacker."

Lilly shrugs. She's always been this way, smart enough to skate by but not really caring. She'll be married in five years, have three kids before thirty and call herself happy.

Great expectations, indeed.

Her eyes are glued on Cole as he walks in the room, and I'm guessing her mind might still be on baby pictures, but probably not mine. I roll my eyes and schedule a reminder in my phone to ding the second I walk in the door. If I don't grab Mom as soon as I get home, I'll forget. There are bigger things on my mind, and the last thing I need is Lilly hassling me about it if it slips through the cracks.

Heath comes in and gives me a smile, but takes his usual seat at the front. I study the back of his shirt, the precise cut of his hair—always even because he gets it trimmed on schedule. Next to me, Lilly is teasing Cole about bubbles. Legs crossed, body at an angle, eyes cast upward, fingers twisting in her hair. Everything about her is screaming at him to notice her and it's working.

Meanwhile I'm ramrod straight staring at Heath's back, well aware that he'd be irritated if he knew his tag was sticking up.

I don't tell him.

three

All the stupid people I know are happy.

A fresh set of nails. The release of a new video game. Mascara that doesn't run. Shiny rims on a car. These are the things I hear people gushing about as I walk out of school, their momentary elation at the simplest things serving as a reminder that I have higher ideals, bigger goals, a reward in my sights that won't chip, wash off, wear down, or become boring. Sometimes I think I should borrow Dad's earplugs to get through the day.

I drive home, ignoring the ache of my hands as they clench on the steering wheel. I'm squeezing more than necessary, thinking about Cole and Lilly in English. A cloud of pheromones surrounded them by the time Mrs. Walker started class, their eyes on each other's mouths

when they talked, straying to other body parts as if they
lacked the willpower to control their gaze.

Heath and I aren't like that, never have been. There's
a calm assurance in our relationship: he is my boyfriend; I am his girlfriend. We've been together since
eighth grade, a slow escalation from texts that held
nothing more than casual information (*I'm home. Going
skiing. Your hair is pretty.*) to mild groping in his parents'
den that came about more from curiosity than passion.
We make out because we're supposed to. That's what
couples do.

The clinical nature of our relationship doesn't bother
me, the hard and fast definitions of what we are to each
other reading more like a contractual agreement than
anything bordering on affection. We're cutouts on top
of a wedding cake, fingers interlaced but bodies permanently frozen far apart from each other, our smiles
painted on. And who cares, really? Wedding cakes are
supposed to have toppers. Girls like me are supposed to
have boyfriends. Checkmark.

My phone dings at me as I walk in the door, right on
schedule. *Picture*, it says.

"Mom," I yell, kicking off my shoes. "I need one of
my baby pictures."

I flip through the mail on the table, adding to the pile
of acceptance letters from colleges I have no intention

of going to. Still, they look nice padding the bottom drawer of my desk.

"Mom," I call again, raising my voice to be heard over the ice dispenser as I get a drink. There's no answer. I gulp down half the glass of water and pour the rest on the aloe plant she keeps on the kitchen windowsill. Its leaves are trimmed back, the tips brittle and brown from where she's had to clip it so many times to treat the little burns she always manages to accumulate in the kitchen. She's had the same plant for ten years; it's one of the more useful things we own. So I water it when I've got anything left in my glass, one hard worker to another.

"*Mom,*" I try for a third time, irritated now. I've got homework, studying, and hopefully at least two hours of practice ahead of me. Taking care of this baby-picture business was supposed to be a quick chore, a box to checkmark. But she's not home, which means I'm going to lose time digging through plastic bins jammed at the back of the hall closet.

I open the door and flop to the ground, dragging out an old globe, a pair of waders that fit no one, a shower mat that ended up in here for some reason, and a shoe rack with zero pairs of shoes on it. The photo bins are stacked nicely on top of one another, the only thing in here with any semblance of order.

But that's on the outside. Once I pop the top off the first one, I realize I've signed up for more than a few minutes of browsing. Mom's never been the neatest person, but the tubs aren't even sorted by decade. There's a shot of my mom in the nineties wearing plaid and drinking beer out of a Styrofoam cup in the same bin as a sepia-toned shot of someone I don't know and don't have a timeline's chance of ever having met.

"Seriously?" I mutter under my breath as I toss a picture of Dad proudly displaying his first cell phone. I jam my hand to the bottom of the pile and close my eyes, counting on dumb luck to deliver me from this mess of undated, unnamed, unorganized people. A sharp edge slides under my thumbnail and I yank back, dragging it with me.

The paper is thin, the corner jammed a couple millimeters under my nail, angry red dots of trapped blood welling around it. I pull it free and unroll it, expecting to see the receipt from when Mom bought the plastic bins.

But it's a picture. Specifically, an ultrasound.

"Wonder what Lilly would make of that," I say to myself. I don't know if fetal-me would be more interesting to her than Cole Vance's tiny penis.

Except . . . it's not me. Or rather, it's not *just* me.

I scan panel to panel, analyzing what I see, separating

black from gray, sound bouncing back off solid versus liquid. The shapes are difficult to distinguish, more white noise than picture. But the neatly printed text at the bottom cannot be misinterpreted, my mother's name and the date—when she would've been pregnant with me.

But I'm not alone in there.

A paradigm shift is defined as a fundamental change in approach or underlying assumptions, and people often come unmoored when they occur. The Catholic Church persecuted Galileo when he argued for a heliocentric universe; people didn't know germs caused illnesses until the nineteenth century.

And I thought I was an only child until just now.

I take it well, all things considered. That is to say I fall over, crumpling the photos I'd tossed aside. A thousand sharp-edged corners dig into my skin as all the blood leaves my head, my fingers and toes tingling as every drop concentrates to my center. To my engorged heart.

I felt it swell at the sight of two amorphous blobs, vague outline of limbs entwined with one another, heads inclined as if sharing a secret. My heart beats to tear through my chest, my collarbone pounding with the rhythm of it. I am no longer flesh and bone; I am one organ only.

And it will have its way.

I didn't know I stopped breathing until I take a deep gasp, the black spots on my vision fading with the action. My hands come back to life, curling around the ultrasound as my mind grapples with the new information, scanning the tidy columns of known things it has acquired and not finding a spot to fit this particular fact.

It's in the shape of a question mark, and I don't allow for those. There is no place for this, so I stare until the feeling is back in my hands and feet, until I'm able to slowly sit up, the world righted again though so much in it has gone wrong.

I fold the picture, taking care to crease only the white lines separating the pictures, as if the yet-to-be-born could be harmed. It makes a perfect rectangle, a life-changing fact that fits neatly in my pocket. I put the rest of the pictures back, stack the bins, toss all the useless things no one ever sees back where they were, relegated once again to nonexistence.

Like my twin sister.

I. *Things I Know*

    A. *Ultrasound*

        1. *According to date and name of mother, one of the fetuses is me.*

        2. *Both of the fetuses are female.*

   3. This has been kept from me on purpose.
 II. *Things I Don't Know*
   A. *Sister*
     1. *If she was born*
     2. *If she died*
     3. *If she was adopted*
   B. *How Isaac Harver got my number*

  I shake my head and erase out the last line as irrelevant. I don't like not knowing things, but that list has suddenly become longer than I imagined possible, and I need to prioritize. I write *unlikely* next to *adopted*. We're not rich but definitely comfortable enough to afford two kids. I've chewed the eraser off my pencil, spitting out the soft pink nub and crunching the metal that held it between my teeth while I think.

  Mom came home half an hour ago, Dad shortly after. She's banging pots and pans around in the kitchen, his earplugs are doing overtime, so neither one of them knows I'm not playing clarinet up here. Instead I'm weighing my options.

  I can walk downstairs, the ultrasound trailing behind me like a ticker-tape parade celebrating the dawn of a new world, one in which I'm aware of my anonymous sibling. I know how that will play out. Mom will cry; Dad will yell; I will stand like a pillar in a storm, demanding truth. I spit out the metal casing from the eraser and chomp down on the wet wood of the pencil, appreciating the give in it when everything else seems to be pushing back at me.

I fold up my list, blowing away the last bits of eraser that linger from eradicating Isaac Harver's name. If only I could drag one across my brain, ridding myself of him up there too. My heart gives a little shudder at the thought, and I look down at my chest.

"Shut up," I say.

Mom's voice floats up the stairs, hitting the same notes as always. Din—ner. It's an F sharp followed by a half step down to the F, the normalcy of our routine inked out in notes of black and white. I can shatter this, sweep everything to the side in a discordant crash, but then I'll have to deal with Dad's bullish baritone, Mom's panic in a jarring soprano. My blank stare, whole rests of nothingness, can only bear so much.

Or, I can do what I do best.

Figure things out on my own.

four

Our courthouse looks like what you'd expect in a small Ohio town; someone started with ambition and then ran out of energy. Or money. Or both.

The front does everything a courthouse should. It looks serious, imposing, like a brick bastion of justice that fell from the sky. But once I walk through the double doors on Wednesday after school, all the trappings of glory fall away. I'm hit with a mix of mildew and ancient cigarette smoke that only a demolition is going to address. The plaster walls have cracks like varicose veins, small explosions of age. One last holdout of nobility—a grand old wooden staircase—is stripped of its dignity by the orange traffic cone on the landing, draped with caution tape of no specific nature. I can only assume I'm supposed to watch out for the water dripping from the ceiling.

There's a directory mounted on the wall, white peg letters canted at angles that make me want to reach out and straighten them. The office of vital statistics is in the addition, a polite word for the pressboard square attached to the back of the building. I walk in, worried that my feet might punch right through the linoleum floor, or that my voice will blow the wood paneling from the studs. The waiting room looks sick, badly lit by fluorescent lights, the mismatched set of chairs all clear castoffs. The lady behind the counter glances up at me, her fingers still moving across her keyboard.

"What do you need?"

Mom would call her rude. I call it efficient. This woman speaks my language.

"Birth certificate," I say.

Her eyes go back to her screen. "Yours or someone else's?"

"Someone else's."

She doesn't glance back at me. "Birth certificates can only be issued to the parent or spouse. I'm betting you're neither of those."

"What about a sister?"

The word feels weird on my tongue, one I'm not sure I've said before.

"Sure," she says, still looking at the screen. "What's her name?"

I pause too long, and she prompts me. "Your sister's name?"

"I'm not sure," I admit, and she looks up at me. I only have her attention for a split second before she's back on the computer again, our business together finished.

"Adoption records are sealed," she says.

"Look"—I scan the piles of papers on her desk and finally locate a name plaque—"Jane, I don't think she was adopted. I don't even know if she was born."

The keys stop clicking and I've got her. I don't think Jane gets a lot of high excitement or mystery here in the addition, so I whip out the ultrasound.

"This is me . . . well, one of them is," I tell her.

"So you're a twin," Jane says. "Or you were supposed to be, anyway." She takes it from me, unfurling the thin paper and holding it up to the light. "Don't want to ask Mom?"

"No."

"What about Dad?"

I let silence answer that one.

She sighs and hands the ultrasound back to me. "Like I said, birth certificates can be issued only to parents." I'm about to argue when she puts her hand up to stop me. "But vital statistics are public record."

Jane motions me to follow her as she pulls open a flimsy door, a puff of stale air greeting us. She flips a switch and the lights bubble to life, flickering as if they resent it. Racks of heavy books surround us, but Jane goes right for the one she wants, tossing it onto a wide wooden table in the center of the room.

"Name?"

"Mine?"

"Yeah. She's your twin. She'll have the same last name and birthdate."

"Sasha Stone," I say, more than a little embarrassed I didn't think of that on my own. My brain has always been a sharp instrument, a pencil with lead that tears through paper. But on this subject I've been dull, barely leaving a mark behind.

"Birthdate?"

I tell her, and Jane's finger trails down a column of *S*s. "There," she taps my name. "Found you."

I lean over the table, fascinated by this stark representation of my existence. There I am, Sasha Stone, daughter of Patricia (Hall) Stone and Mark Stone. I feel a ridiculous bloom of relief in my chest to see that information, as if I needed proof that I was indeed born.

"No sister, though," Jane says, her finger moving over to the birthdate column. "See? No other Stones born on November twenty-first of that year."

"So she was stillborn?"

"Maybe," Jane says, disappearing in the racks of books for a second, and returning with one titled *Deaths 2000—*

I don't like all the possibilities encapsulated after the dash, an endless stream of deaths with no definitive cut-off point.

"If she died at birth, she'll be in here," Jane says, finger once again slicing through columns of ink. I wonder if she has calluses on her fingertips like I do, mine from making music, hers from trailing over lives begun and ended.

"She's not here," Jane announces.

My hand goes back to my pocket to reassure myself that the ultrasound is still there, the only thing in the world that says I have—or had—a sister.

A sister who wasn't born and never died.

When I see Isaac in the hallway I take an impulsive step backward, the heels of my shoes knocking against the door of the vital records office. He looks up from the bench he's sitting on, a solid expanse of wood that belongs in a church, not a common hall with pictures of child-support nonpayers posted above it. Still, he looks comfortable, arms spread across the rolled back like he belongs here. Our eyes meet and he smiles like there's nothing surprising about the situation.

I look away quickly, to the words on the door next to him. *Parole Officer.* So I guess he does belong here.

"I'm starting to think you might be following me," Isaac says.

"You wish," I say, anything more cutting than that lost to me. I've been demoted to monosyllabic words.

He smiles again, gaze traveling over me in a way I definitely don't like . . . except I feel a subtle shift, muscles loosening or tensing ever so slightly, and somehow I'm angled toward him, like Lilly was with Cole, one shoulder dropped just enough that my shirt gapes a little. Isaac senses it, rising from the bench to cut the space between us, his body a knife that mine wants to be cut by. Because I'm moving forward too, and soon we're indecently close, my heart hammering so hard I've got spots in my vision again.

"I got your text," he says.

"I didn't text you," I shoot back, my mouth the only thing I still have control of. But even that feels slippery, as if it might jump the last few inches between mine and his without permission.

"Huh . . . ," he says. "That's funny 'cause . . ." and he holds up his phone, showing me a text that came in early this morning at three fifteen—

What r u doing?

"One"—I hold up an index finger, hoping it's an effective barrier between us—"I was asleep at three.

Two"—another finger goes up, adding a board to the wall I'm building—"I use real words when I text. And three"—last one, to hold it all in place—"that text came from someone named Lady, not me."

He flips it back open, pulls up his contacts and shows me the entry for "Lady." It's my number, sure and true, a dark rendering of facts as concrete as the books in Jane's office.

"You're a lady, all right," Isaac says, his voice husky in my ear as he leans closer.

"I . . ." My voice fails me, my hand trailing up to his neck to touch the tattoo there rather than push him back like I told it to.

"Something's wrong," I say, sidestepping away from him, my hand leaving his chest and going to mine to feel the pace of my heart. Very allegro.

"Yep," he agrees. "And I know what it is. You like me . . . but you don't like that you like me."

"Based only on that sentence, you're an idiot," I say just as the parole officer's door opens and a man sticks his head out.

"Sounds like she's got your number, Harver," he says, gesturing for Isaac to come inside.

"Uh-huh . . . ," Isaac says. "And I've got hers."

And then he winks at me.

And I like it.

five

"I asked Melanie if she knew what color the carpet was in her brother's room, and she said green." Brooke brings the wooden mallet down on the skull of our fetal pig, sending some cartilage onto my safety goggles.

"So taking that and the toe of the shoe I spotted in the pic, I'm guessing that *is* Cole's dick. Hardly worth Instagramming." She gives the pig another whack.

Lilly perches on a stool, elbows resting on the black countertop of the biology room. "Dammit," she says. "It *is* a little dick."

My friends have been plumbing the depths of the mysteries of the size of Cole Vance's dick for a few days, not coming up with any solid evidence as of yet.

"Hmmmm . . ." Brooke watches Lilly carefully. "You

could always ask Charity."

Lilly flushes. "No way."

"I can find out for sure," Brooke says, pressing her thumb on the cranium.

"Excuse me?" Lilly says, her embarrassed pink kicking up to an angry red.

"Chill," Brooke says, "I'll just ask him to whip it out sometime." The skull gives way underneath the pressure with a distinct *pop.*

"Does it matter how big it is?" I ask Lilly. "I mean, do you like him or not?"

"It matters," Brooke says with conviction.

"It matters more if you like him," I say, putting a reassuring hand on Lilly's shoulder.

Lilly's face scrunches up a little bit like she might cry at the unexpected support. "Thanks, Sasha."

It's not something I'd usually say, but I've come to the realization that while I might be the alpha of our group and Brooke the firm beta, Lilly can't ever decide which one of us to please. She's a toddler getting conflicting advice from her parents, and watching her confusion is solid entertainment. I've learned that if I can veil my words in something like kindness she tends to respond better, and I could use the distraction of being a good friend right now. Isaac gave me a knowing nod in the hall this morning that sent my stomach plummeting but my pulse skyrocketing.

I checked my phone the second I got to my car yesterday. No texts had been sent in the middle of the night—to anyone. None had come in either. I'm chalking it up to some semiliterate trying to connect with Isaac for God knows what and an errant radio wave identifying it as my number.

"I definitely like Cole," Lilly says. "But I don't want to end up in a micropenis situation."

"You're not the only one who enjoys a guy with a 'boner, Sasha," Brooke adds.

I roll my eyes. "Do you have that brain exposed yet?"

"Ohhhhh yeah," she says, ignoring the tools on the tray and cracking bone away with her gloved fingers. "Nervous system, here I come."

"Also endocrine," I say.

"You need to get out more."

A sudden shriek makes everyone jump; Lilly almost topples off her stool.

"Mrs. DeBrau," Charity Newell yells from across the room. "I think my pig is totally pregnant."

"Like it could be only *kind of* pregnant," Brooke says under her breath. I think of gray shadows and twining umbilical cords, one baby born, one forever in limbo.

"No, that's not possible," I say, and Brooke makes a *duh* face because she thinks I'm talking to her.

"Not possible at all," Mrs. DeBrau echoes me. "It's a *fetal* pig, Charity, only a baby herself. However, you've done excellent work here."

She leans over Charity's tray to inspect the splayed animal, skin pinned around it like a macabre cape. "You preserved the reproductive system while dissecting. You have a deft touch." Mrs. DeBrau looks at Brooke pointedly.

"I prefer my mallet," my friend says, spinning it in her fingers.

"Mrs. DeBrau," I ask. "At what point can a fetus stop existing?"

She looks up from Charity's table, a cautious look on her face. "What do you mean, Sasha?"

This is exactly the problem. I don't know what I mean. Last night I did search after search on my laptop, ruling out the obviously wrong answers right away. Mom's stance on abortion has always been unwavering, so that's out. I have no way of knowing if a miscarriage occurred, but we both seem healthy and whole in the ultrasound.

"I mean . . ." Everyone is looking at me now, because Sasha Stone not knowing what to say is an event worth noting.

"Can there be a fetus, no miscarriage or abortion, and then . . . suddenly no fetus?"

"Sure," Mrs. DeBrau says, leaning back over Charity's

fetal pig. "That's called *resorption*. It happens alongside a miscarriage, and the mother's body reabsorbs what's left of the material. Typically she won't even know she was pregnant."

That doesn't work. Mom definitely knew. There aren't ten fingers in that ultrasound. There are twenty.

"But what about twins?" I blurt, and Mrs. DeBrau looks back at me. "What if there are twins and then . . . then there's not?"

"Aahhh." She smiles. "You're talking about vanishing twin syndrome."

I smile back. That sounds about right.

Vanishing twin syndrome: also known as fetal resorption, is a fetus in a multi-gestation pregnancy that dies in utero and is then partially or completely reabsorbed by the twin.

"'Partially or completely reabsorbed,'" I say to myself, tapping a fresh pencil against my lip.

My desk is a mess of papers and scribbled notes, half-drawn illustrations of various stages of embryo development with question marks penciled on the sides. I've been fending off texts from Heath all evening, responding with nonanswers and varying degrees of *meh* when he tried to invite himself to dinner. He's usually good about respecting my space, but when he calls I capitulate and answer.

"What?"

"Well, hello to you too," he says.

"I'm kind of busy," I tell him, my pencil sketching a version of myself in the margin, bored and on the phone.

"Do you have a minute to talk to your boyfriend about this rumor that you're pregnant?"

My pencil skids across my notes, jerking the whole paper sideways and exposing the pig-heart diagram I'm supposed to be studying. The tip of the lead shakes along with my hands, the stuttering of my heart dotting Morse code across the aorta.

"Wait, what?"

"I don't know what you said in biology today, but Charity told Cole you were asking about abortion."

"*Resorption*," I clarify. "It's when one twin absorbs another in the womb."

I expect a sigh of relief, Heath's usual noncombative tone restored so I can handle him and go back to what I was doing. Instead I get: "Why were you asking about that?"

"Why does it matter?" I shoot back. "It's not like I'm pregnant. We don't have sex."

"Just because *we* don't have sex doesn't mean *you* can't be pregnant."

Lead punches through sheets of paper down to the wood of my desk.

"Heath."

It's one word, his name. But I know how to use it. I've heard girls adopt the cajoling tone to calm down their man, an upward lilt with a flirtatious accent that changes the subject. I say his name like a brick wall. One he can run into and break his damn face on. Heath is still talking, but I'm not listening, my brain derailed by the fact that I just swore. Only in my head, but it counts.

What is wrong with me?

I can't get Isaac Harver—who is a total scumbag—out of my head. I practically stuck my tongue down his throat right in front of his parole officer for the love of God. I'm arguing with a perfectly nice, useful boyfriend over gossip. I'm using bad words and . . . my foot nudges my clarinet case, safely stowed under my desk.

As in, put away. There's a thin film of dust across the top.

I realize I haven't practiced all week.

This is not who I am. This is not me.

"This is not me," I say, interrupting Heath.

"What? Sasha? What do you mean?"

"I have to go."

I hang up, my phone dropping to the floor next to my clarinet case as my eyes devour chambers of the fetal pig heart, so similar to ours, the colors of the diagram—red,

blue, purple—vibrant against the dull grays of my ultrasound, still half curled, hiding in shame. One corner
touches my notes, the sketch of myself, bored with my
perfect boyfriend, now surrounded by a heavy script, all
caps, vicious lines meeting at sharp angles to create a
message I didn't write.

WHY THE FUCK ARE YOU TALKING TO ME?

I think of Isaac Harver and bad words, my heart racing.

This is not me.

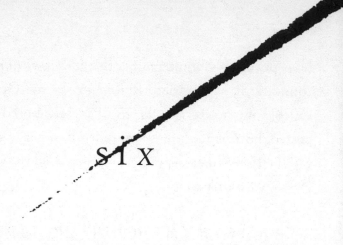

SIX

"Mystery solved," Brooke announces as she drops her stuff on our breakfast table. "Cole has a little dick."

Lilly stops peeling her banana. "You didn't seriously do it?"

"Sure did." Brooke tosses her ponytail off her shoulder as she swipes an orange off my breakfast tray. "I put in my run this morning, and he was working on sprints. I asked him to satisfy my curiosity, and while *that* may be taken care of, it's the only thing he'll ever be satisfying."

"You are unbelievable," I say, taking back my orange and tearing off some segments for her.

She shrugs. "The funny thing about dicks is that we never get to see them limp, you know? It was chilly this morning, Cole was a sweaty exhausted mess, and I'm all,

'Hey, pull down your pants,' and it's like boom—erection."

Lilly nods like this is an AP class and Brooke is spouting high wisdom.

"It doesn't matter anyway," I reassure Lilly, worried she's going to take too much direction from our less-than-modest friend. "The female G-spot is typically only three inches deep, so as long as he's past that it's a perfectly serviceable penis."

"Thank you for the medical analysis, Sasha," Brooke says, squishing a piece of orange. "When you're making out with Heath do you instruct him to create a vacuum on your areolae?"

"No," I shoot back, ignoring the blood I feel rising to my face. "And I don't think that'll be happening anytime soon, anyway."

"Oooooo . . . why's that?" Lilly leans in closer to me, and Brooke steals what's left of my orange again. This time I let her. There's something reassuring in the nearness of them, our body heat comingling with shared words, the little bit of orange skin I can see clinging to Brooke's teeth that I might tell her about. I may not like my friends all the time, but when you go to a small school you cut your losses.

And I know they feel the same way about me. So I spill.

"Heath called me last night, totally pissed. Apparently *Charity*"—I raise my eyebrows at Lilly, as if she's accountable for her cousin's actions—"told everyone I was asking about getting abortions in bio. So of course this means I'm pregnant."

"Uh, except for the whole you're-a-virgin thing," Brooke says. "When they showed us those pics of syphilis in sixth grade they might as well have signed you up for nun school."

I want to correct Brooke with the word *convent*, or inform her that I'd have to be Catholic to be a nun. Instead I shudder, remembering the picture she means in perfect detail.

"I'd have to be stupid to have sex," I say, repeating the first words out of my mouth when I walked out of that doomed health class years ago.

"Yeah," Brooke agrees. "Or normal."

"Whatever," I shoot back. "Herpes. Gonorrhea. Pregnancy." I tick off the cons with my fingers, each one a solid fact that came with its own explicit slide in sixth grade that burned into my mind, confirming that sex could only ruin my life.

"Pish," Brooke argues, raising her own fingers. "Oral. Vag—"

"Stop," I say, but she only shrugs.

"They didn't tell us the good parts, you know?"

"And no pics either," Lilly says sadly.

"Regardless," I go on, trying to get the conversation back to the fight with my boyfriend. "Heath and I don't have sex, which I pointed out to him. And then he says—and I quote—'Just because *we* don't have sex doesn't mean *you* can't be pregnant.'" I stress the pronouns exactly the way he did, so that the implications are perfectly clear.

"Wait . . . what?" asks Lilly.

Brooke smacks her on the forehead, leaving behind an orange seed. "He's saying if she's pregnant, it's not his. And that, my friend, is top-tier bullshit."

"Thank you." I smile at Brooke. She may be the most uncouth person I know, but she's loyal. And right now her back is up.

"What a penis hole," she says, drawing the attention of some nearby freshmen. "You're completely frigid, dude. And I say that with affection."

"That's lovely." I decide not to tell her about the food stuck in her teeth. Lilly does though, and Brooke scrapes it off and spends a solid forty seconds inspecting her find.

"Seriously," Lilly says, turning to me. "Sorry about Charity. She doesn't exactly live up to her name."

Brooke flicks the orange skin off her fingernail into the hair of one of the freshmen girls without her noticing.

"Not your fault, Lil. You can't pick your family."

"No, you can't," I agree, my hand slipping back into my pocket where the ultrasound lies folded, warm from my body heat.

"Hey."

Even if I didn't know Heath's voice I would sense it's him standing behind me because of my friends' reactions. Lilly's face goes into the frozen tundra mask she's perfected on underclassmen who try to correct her when she pronounces words like *flautist* and *pianist* the right way, and Brooke scowls like he's a hard grounder about to take a bad hop. Also she says, "Hey, man, you're a penis hole."

But I do know his voice, thoroughly. It's come to me through five different models of phones and over Skype, my country wireless slowing his face down so that he looks like a badly dubbed film. I've listened to his soft inflections, soldiered through puberty octave cracks, and heard the first guttural moans of satisfied desire that didn't happen in private. And it's those accumulations that erase some of my irritation, an acknowledgment that even if I'm not happy with him in *this* moment, I've got enough time invested in him to allow for an apology.

"Excuse us, girls," I say to Brooke and Lilly. My hand slides neatly into Heath's, and I lead him away from our table without looking at his face yet, a thistle buried in the olive branch. I take him to the back hall, somewhere we're not supposed to be during lunch hour. When I finally meet his eyes it's clear he knows exactly how much doo-doo he's in, that I'm willing to break rules for us to talk.

"So . . . ," he starts.

"One"—I lift a finger—"not pregnant."

His hand goes up to his scalp, disturbing the stillness of hair gelled into place this morning. "Sasha . . ."

"Two"—my middle finger pops up to join the pointer, making an audible tendon creak that we both ignore—"couldn't possibly be pregnant."

"I know that, okay? I know," he argues back, little spiked edges of irritation that would hit red on a soundboard, making my fingers want to curl back down into a fist.

"And three . . ." But I lose three as a familiar smell fills the hallway, and my ring finger can't quite make the upward journey to join the others because my hand is shaking so badly.

"Sasha?" Heath is different now, his defensiveness evaporated along with the sharpness of my voice, which is stuck in my throat, unable to burrow its way out. His hands find my shoulders, and I squirm under them, not wanting any hair product on my new shirt.

"Is it your heart? Sasha? You're pale as a sheet."

"Except her sheets ain't white, man."

Isaac's voice sends another ripple through my system, this one a warm flush that takes over the cold anger that had been directed at Heath. He's right beside us, eyeing Heath's hands on my shoulders as if he wants to strike them off. An exhale of cigarette smoke tints his words, and I know it's this scent that derailed my brain from the invective-laced diatribe that I'd been launching at my boyfriend, the smell of an unfiltered Pall Mall capturing my attention as easily as a John Williams score.

"This isn't your business, Harver," Heath says, ignoring the fact that Isaac knows what color my sheets are, in the same way I choose to dismiss the fact that I know exactly what kind of cigarettes Isaac smokes.

"Maybe not," Isaac says, eyes still on Heath's hands. "But I don't like the way you're handling the lady."

"I'm fine," I snap at him, sliding out from under my boyfriend's grip. "That's directed at you too," I say to Heath as I stalk away from both boys. Away from the concern in Heath's face and the smirk on Isaac's.

"There's nothing wrong with me," I shout back over my shoulder as I turn the corner.

"There's nothing wrong with me," I say again to myself as I find my locker, willing my traitorous heart to return to a normal rhythm and ignoring the feeling that it beat more loudly when Isaac was nearby.

I feel like my sheets are screaming their non-whiteness when I walk into my bedroom. I toss my phone and it hits the mattress one second before I do. I spent the rest of the day at school trying so hard to prove that there is, in fact, nothing wrong with me, that I'm exhausted. Usually this is my cram session, a time to crank open the cranium and insert whatever information I'll need for tomorrow's quizzes, tests, or in-depth analysis. But my eyes are slipping closed, my legs barely able to draw the twin weights of my feet up to the bed before I'm out.

Isaac Harver follows me even there, into a dream where he knows the color of my sheets because he's in my bedroom. He's leaning against the door—which is closed, something I never allow when Heath is over— and his eyes are moving over me as I pull my shirt off flagrantly, even tossing it into the air like a stripper. Which it turns out is not so smart because it hits my whirling fan blades and turns into a projectile headed straight for Isaac's face.

"Shit," he yells, diving to get out of the way and knocking into me at the same time. We land on the bed, him on top, the lace of my bra pressed against him as my heart beats wildly. I'm ready for whatever he wants to do next. Anything. I lick my lips and wait for him to come at me, but instead he does something unexpected.

"You okay?" he asks, hands on either side of my face even though I thought he'd go right for my chest.

"Yeah," I say, my voice thin and breathless as I look up at him. His thumb rubs over my check, onto my lower lip.

"Nice sheets," he says, rolling off me. "I didn't know they came in pink."

I prop up on one elbow next to him, repeating his movements, learning as we go. I trace my finger over his lips. "Your other girls don't have pink sheets?"

He grabs my hand and entwines our fingers, a knot I can't break. He rolls to his side to face me, our eyes as connected as our hands. "I don't have other girls."

My heart accelerates, breath stills in my chest, skin explodes as a million nerve endings scream to be pressed against him. It's so good it's painful and I jerk awake, fingers splayed open on the pillow where his head rested in my dream, where I see an indent on the pillow I never use, and hair that isn't mine.

I sit up fast, only to be hit by a wave of black. I'm dizzy, my heart still beating at the cage of my ribs as if it wants to get out. I collapse back onto the bed, my head landing on Isaac's pillow, a faint whiff of cigarette smoke puffing up around me.

He's been here. He's been in my bed.

I should be terrified, but instead my hands are going

up to my own face, fingers tracing my lips the same way he did, trying to recall the feeling. My heart stutters, elated, as my mind fills in the blanks. His voice. His face. The look on his face as he leaned into me and . . .

"No." I slide off the bed, too weak to stand. I reach for the desk to pull myself up but only knock off a pile of books, the ultrasound fluttering to the floor almost as an afterthought. I grab it, the comforting black and white giving me something to look at, something concrete that can't be denied.

But there's a gray area. I see it now. A smudge where my twin and I overlap, our fetal bodies entwined as my hand had been with Isaac's. I study it as my heart calms, my breath returns. My fingers are shaky, pulse still weak as I touch the point where my sister and I intersect, the adrenaline of wanting Isaac still thick in my veins.

"Oh my God," I say, the truth hitting me like a surprise stinger after you thought the song was over.

We're not facing each other in the ultrasound.

Because even then we each wanted different things.

I call Heath, the person who makes the most sense in the world. He comes over right away, like I knew he would. Mom and Dad trust me entirely, which works out great, because no one cares that I shut my bedroom door as soon as he's in the room with me.

No one but Heath, that is.

"What's going on?" he asks, clearly nervous at this sudden change.

"Why does something have to be going on?" I ask, aiming for coy but falling somewhat short of the mark. Straightforward is how I operate best, so I do what I did in the dream, taking my shirt off without a word and tossing it into the air.

It doesn't hit the fan like it did in my dream with Isaac, doesn't fly straight for Heath's head to send him crashing into me in a tangle of laughter onto the bed. Instead it lands on my desk, covering my doodles from the night before, the sketch of my own face, looking bored with the boy I'm trying to seduce right now.

Trying and failing.

"What are you doing?" Heath asks, actually back-pedaling into the closed door at the sight of me in my underwear.

"I'm . . ." I don't know what I'm doing, obviously. The girl in the dream with Isaac did, for sure. But the boy in that situation seemed to know what he was doing too. Heath just looks terrified, which I hardly think is necessary. I'm not built like Brooke or anything, but I do get checked out by everyone from the flutes to the football players.

"What's the problem?" I ask. "Don't you like what you see?"

"Sasha . . ." His eyes make the journey over my body, once, twice. He swallows hard, then crosses the distance. Not between me and him, but between him and my shirt, which he tosses at me.

"Put that on," he says. "We need to talk."

With the door open, it seems. When the sound of dinner cooking downstairs and the comforting pale pink of the hallway safely in reach, Heath sits next to me on the bed.

"I do like what I see," he says, hand encircling mine, space between everything else. Just like the wedding cake toppers. Plastic. Perfect. Placated.

"But you're going to Oberlin, and I'm—"

"Not," I finish for him. "Right, I know. I wasn't proposing to you, just be to clear."

"I know that," he says quickly, and I think I might detect the slightest trace of relief in his voice. "But . . . what if you *did* get pregnant?"

I don't remind him that I'm on the pill, a dubious gift given to me a few years ago after a horrific ovarian cyst incident. The prescription came along with an awkward conversation with Mom about how this was a medical necessity and I shouldn't regard it as permission.

"What if I didn't?" I say, hand tightening on his.

"Sasha, I just . . ." He swallows hard, Adam's apple bobbing. "I can't."

I pointedly look at his crotch, where it's very obvious that he can. That gets a smile, the even whites that his orthodontist worked so hard for making an appearance.

"I *can*," he elaborates, bumping my knee with his. "I just don't know if we should."

"Right," I say, eyes wandering to the fan above my bed.

"We've got a good thing going," he says. "I don't want to look back at my first girlfriend and think about fights and a broken heart or things we'll both regret."

It's the nice thing to say, a way to turn me down that's still slightly romantic and kind of sweet. But underneath that is the boy I actually know, and his pie chart has always been a solid color labeled "success." There's not even a sliver of something offbeat in it that could be dug up in his future political career, like a high school girlfriend who had a quiet abortion, or the same girl sharing the tale of losing her virginity to him while her trusting, working-class parents were making dinner downstairs.

No, Heath plays it safe, all the way. And I can't really blame him, because I used to be the same, until I smelled cigarette smoke on my pillow and was intrigued instead of disgusted. And to be honest, Heath has always been the same thing to me: reassurance, a boy holding a safety net that I can fall into if the wire I walk trembles, even a little. I never considered falling, because I didn't know it could be fun.

I slip my hand from his, letting go of a lot more than just him.

"Let's have dinner," I say, and we go downstairs to spaghetti night and routine, our behavior exactly what is to be expected.

As if there isn't a door to my bedroom at all.

seven

I must have scared Heath off last week. He hasn't come over since he bolted at the sight of my bra, but I'm happier with Vivaldi's company anyway, perfecting his idea of what spring would sound like. I'm considering moving on into summer when my phone goes off. I stop midmeasure, too aware that the impenetrable mantle I usually shroud myself in during practice time seems to be awfully wispy these days. I glance at the screen and know that I'm looking at Isaac's number, even if I didn't program it into my phone. My hands are stopped in place, stuck on an endless F sharp that my lungs refuse to give life to because I've been holding my breath to see if he leaves a message.

Disgusted, I pop the clarinet from my mouth and

try to wipe away the orange-tinged ring on the reed, a diluted mixture of mom's spaghetti and my spit. It's chipped anyway, the ragged end like a fingernail that hasn't been buffed. I'll probably find bits of reed in my gums again tomorrow, ground deeply in by hours of practice and then emerging toward the light for me to pluck out. I loosen the ligature and pop the reed free, hands going through the motions blind, because my eyes are on the phone.

"You're an idiot," I say to myself.

He doesn't leave a voice mail, but seconds later a text comes in, the vibration of the phone matching the one in my chest.

we need to talk

I've got a nasty response already composed, one I've used to reject everyone but Heath since eighth grade. But my hands type something else entirely.

OK when?

I study the text a second before sending it, aware of the door it will open. My thumb makes the decision for me, hitting send before I've given full thought to what might lie on the other side.

Now. Face-to-face.

I don't know what world he lives in, but I'm not a citizen of one where Sasha Stone talks face-to-face with Isaac Harver at eleven at night on a Sunday.

I'm outside

"Bull," I say under my breath, then I hear the purr of a motorcycle in the driveway. I tear my curtains out of the way to see his silhouette give me a little mock salute. How he found out where I live, I have no clue, but I need to get rid of him before Mom and Dad notice.

I pull on some flip-flops and a hoodie, poking my head into my parents' room as I head down the hall. Mom's propped in bed scowling at a romance novel and doesn't notice when I click her door shut the rest of the way. Dad is sprawled on his recliner in the living room with his earplugs so deep they'll have to be surgically removed.

The only thing standing between me and Isaac Harver having a conversation by the light of a full moon is common sense, and I pause with my hand on the doorknob. That day at the courthouse Isaac had my attention, and he knew it. My mouth was inches from his and not wanting to retreat before his probation officer interrupted. And that was in a public place. After the dream I had I'm not sure if I trust myself alone in the dark with him, but for some reason that feels like more of an incentive than a warning. My feet are cutting through the yard to the driveway before my brain sends them the signal to reconsider.

"Hey." His voice is low and conspiratorial, yet filled

with complete familiarity, as if he has every right in the world to be leaning against his motorcycle in my driveway, eyes going up and down my body. I cross my arms against my chest, half to cover the fact I'm not wearing a bra, half in fear that my furiously pounding heart is about to leap free.

"Hey," I say, when it was supposed to be, *"What do you want?"*

He watches me carefully, and I keep my distance.

"Why are you being so weird?" he asks.

"Me? I'm being weird? You show up at my house past bedtime—"

"Bedtime?" He doesn't actually laugh, but I can hear amusement in his voice.

"You think this is funny? You somehow get my number and text me out of the blue, show up at my house in the middle of the night, and imply to my boyfriend that you know what color my sheets are."

I realize too late that I've crossed the space in between us while I ranted and that Isaac is a full foot taller than me.

"One"—Isaac holds up a finger in perfect imitation of me—"you gave me your number. Two," he says loudly before I can interrupt, "eleven ain't the middle of the night. Three, I wasn't implying anything about your sheets; I know exactly what color they are. And four, I hate it when he touches you."

His voice hitches a little on that last statement, the words bouncing off a speed bump of emotion in his throat. I feel my own constricting at the idea that Isaac would have any opinion at all on Heath touching me, let alone hating it. I don't have a response for this naked feeling, this matter-of-fact statement that Isaac throws out there without any thought to his own defenses. I've had battlements built around my feelings for so long I don't know how to react to bare honesty.

"Something you ain't telling me?"

"Aren't," I correct automatically, and he flinches.

"Fuck you. Never mind. Jesus." He's turning away from me, climbing back onto his bike, and I feel panic rising, a soft crescendo starting in my belly and bursting out of my throat, my hands following my words.

"Wait. Stop." I grab him, my hand closing around his wrist, the cuff of his leather jacket rubbing against my skin. He doesn't pull away, just stares at me with a careful blankness, one I know well. It's the face of a closing door, one that will remain shut once it clicks home.

"Listen . . . Isaac." I don't let go of his arm, and I can feel his pulse jump when I say his name. "I don't know what's going on."

I haven't started a sentence with "I don't know" since kindergarten. I can barely get the words out and have to force them, a reverse of the time Heath talked me into trying calamari and I choked it down. The words are as awkward as the squid had been, rubbery and unnatural in my mouth. But I said them, and I said them to someone who may as well be a stranger.

And maybe that's what made it easier.

Or maybe it's something else—the feel of Isaac's skin against mine, the way his eyes are drinking me in, like if he looks away I might disappear. Maybe it's because he's turned his palm upward against mine and his thumb is making little circles at the base, making my blood pound through my veins more quickly until our pulses are synchronized, hearts beating in time.

"You don't know what's going on about what?" he asks, anger evaporated. "Is this about . . ." He stops, bites his bottom lip. "What's going on with your heart? I heard your—I heard *him* say something Friday."

"My heart? No. I . . . I don't know what to do," I say, and my face contorts, muscles pulling my mouth downward into a sag that feels like it will never stop, my eyes squeezing shut against the pressure of tears. I turn away in embarrassment, but Isaac's hands are on me in a second, pulling me into him, into the warm nook under his chin and against his chest. A place I somehow fit perfectly.

"You can tell me," he says, and I listen to his voice

echoing inside his chest. "If it's over, then that's it. But I'm going to make you say it."

I shudder against him, partially in fear at all his words imply, but also because I may be losing something I never knew I had. I step back from him, my hands sliding down his arms. Our fingers intertwine automatically, out of habit, and it feels as natural as holding a clarinet. And that's how I know we've done this before, stood here staring at each other in the dark of night. I've touched him and been touched, and as I feel our blood leaping toward each other through the pulse of our hands, I know we both want whatever this is to continue.

"You're right," I say. "We do need to talk." I glance back at my house, which is lit up against the night, warm and welcoming. I don't want to go inside.

"Can we go somewhere?"

He pretends shock. "In the middle of the night?"

I take a smack at him, but he evades it easily, like a dance we've performed before. And I know the next step is for me to swing up behind him onto the bike, the warmth of his back against my chest, the cold fingers of the wind in my hair as he heads for the old trestle bridge on the county line that trains stopped crossing twenty years ago. It's a skeleton in the woods, one whose bones go deep into the ground, resolutely doing its job even though the heaviest weight it's held in two decades is the aftermath of a kegger.

There's no one there now though. We have the whole bridge to ourselves as Isaac eases the bike over the boards of the old footpath, their unevenness sending small shivers up our bodies, mine shaking more than his as my fear of heights settles in. We're three hundred feet in the air, the river below and the only thing separating us from it is a safety barrier built as an excuse for jobs during the Depression.

Isaac swings off the bike as calmly as if we were in a parking lot, taking my hand to help me. He doesn't let go, leading me to the edge where he sits, legs dangling into empty space and elbows resting on the bottom rung of the wooden fence that started deteriorating the second the tree was cut down almost a century ago. I sit down beside him because I know he thinks I won't.

"Sasha Stone." He shakes his head, as if my name is amusing to him somehow, while lighting a fresh cigarette.

My feet are dangling over rushing water, I'm sitting next to Isaac Harver above a three-hundred-foot drop and getting lung cancer from secondhand smoke. Not one of my better days. Yet, I feel awesome.

"Yeah, I hate it when he touches you," Isaac repeats what he said in my driveway, as if our conversation wasn't broken by a midnight ride to a broken bridge. And I remember why I'm here. And want to be here. At least, part of me does.

"So what's up, lady?" he asks, smoke that smells just like my bedroom pillow exhaling with the words.

He might be able to say what he's feeling as easily as he smokes, but it's something I've got to warm up to. So I stall.

"If I'm Lady, what's that make you? The Tramp?" I ask.

"Definitely." He says it with total assurance, and any barriers I had inside of me come down with his conviction.

"You know what color my sheets are," I say.

"Yep."

"And I gave you my number."

"Uh-huh."

He offers his half-smoked cigarette to me, the tip bobbing in between us as I shove it back toward him.

"What? You don't want to smoke with me?"

"No." It's an easy answer, one trained into me long ago.

"Why not?"

"Because it's bad," I say automatically, the abject truth so obvious I don't understand why he starts laughing.

"It's bad," he repeats, taking a long draw, then flicking

what's left into the river.

"Littering is bad too," I tell him, but there's not a lot of bite in my words because his hands are on my face, framing my cheekbones and trailing a line down toward my lips.

"I must be a pretty bad guy then," he says quietly. And for whatever reason I can't agree with that. Maybe it's because his hands are callused but his touch soft, or that his eyes are a cold shade of blue but somehow look more inviting than my own house.

"You're not," I say.

"And you don't know what to make of that, do you?"

I don't, but admitting that isn't easy either. I pull back from his touch, suddenly wishing I had taken the offer of a cigarette just so I had something to do with my hands as I explain to him about the woman I'm supposed to become, an older version of Sasha Stone who has everything she deserves for doing all the good things and none of the bad. The girl who gets what she wants because she always does the right thing.

"And that stuff matters," I say. "I've been following my class rank since seventh grade, it's that important to me."

"Oh yeah? And what are you?"

"I'm number one," I tell him, my chin lifting up as I wait for him to tease me about it.

"Number one, huh?" He doesn't disappoint, raising his middle finger. "So what?"

"Being valedictorian will help me get into a good school," I say, and he rolls his eyes.

So I tell him about college and how those of us who go pick our universities, most of them yoked to our careers. We add them to the timeline as we fulfill our destinies within the machine of progress. Class rings become graduation caps, college degrees swapped out for doctor whites or, in my case, a sensible black pantsuit that will set off my clarinet nicely on the stage.

Except lately I've been thinking that pantsuits are a little too sensible, and maybe I want to wear a pencil skirt that makes Isaac Harver look at me.

"And that's a problem," I tell him. "Because it's not me."

Isaac makes a noise in his throat like maybe he understands, but then I realize he was just clearing it because the next thing he does is spit into the river.

"That's disgusting," I tell him.

"So all this time you been telling yourself you get a reward for being good. Know who else thinks like that?"

"Who?"

"A dog," he says, looking at me hard. "A dog that's been trained to act a certain way because someone told him so. Thing is, you can train a dog right, but you can also train it wrong, know what I'm saying?"

"You mean like dogs in a fighting ring?" I ask.

"What? No. I mean . . ." He trails off, eyes on the river and the rippling line of light the moon casts there. "More like, okay, so you teach a dog not to shit in the house by rewarding it when it goes outside, right? But you could switch it up, train a dog the wrong way by giving it a treat whenever it pisses in the kitchen."

"Why would anyone ever do that?"

"I'm not saying they *would*, I'm saying they *could*," Isaac goes on. "The dog knows the difference between good and bad only because of who trained it, and the trainer decided for the dog what was right and what was wrong."

"So you think I'm just a trained dog?"

"I think you jump through the hoops real nice," Isaac says, and it's so close to how I feel about school that a shiver runs through me.

"And maybe I don't like seeing a girl who's smart enough to make up her own mind swallow what everyone tells her hook, line, and sinker."

"You're mixing the metaphor," I tell him. "I went from being a dog to a fish."

"Fuck metaphors," he says, and lights another cigarette.

"And I don't do what everyone tells me," I argue. "Dad

wanted me to be an accountant, and I'm going to major in music." I don't add *so there*, but it's all over my voice.

"I didn't say you do what everyone tells you," he clarifies, and somehow I feel like my tone didn't quite get through to him because he definitely thinks he won that one.

"You always do what good people are supposed to do," he goes on. "But I don't think you always want to. There's a little bit of bad in you, Sasha Stone. And I think it needs to get out more."

This time I take the cigarette when he offers it to me. I have no idea what I'm doing, how to hold it, how much to breathe in, whether to leave the smoke in my mouth, my throat, or my lungs. I end up coughing it all back out in a cloud, and dropping the cigarette as I hack. The ember falls between my feet, its light disappearing long before the river extinguishes it.

"You'll get better at it," Isaac assures me. "If you want to."

I think about the future Sasha Stone in her sensible clothing, her current boyfriend refusing to take her virginity. Pins and needles have taken over my feet, and I sag against Isaac, suddenly tired.

"I want to," I say, staring down at the black abyss between my feet. "If you'll be my Virgil."

"I'm definitely not one of those," Isaac says, and I smack him again. This time he catches my hand and keeps it.

"Vir-*gil*," I clarify. "He was Dante's guide to the underworld in *The Divine Comedy*. Have you ever read it?"

"Nope."

"Why not?"

"Because it's bad," Isaac says, in yet another dead-on impersonation of me.

I want to hit him, but instead I start laughing, the cold night air invigorating. "You read *The Inferno* and I'll smoke a whole cigarette. How's that?"

"Deal," Isaac says, pulling me closer against him as a gust comes up off the river.

We share heat for a moment, my forehead resting against his tattoo, his pulse beating against my eyelid.

"I had a dream about you," I say.

"Oh yeah?"

I tell him about taking my shirt off and how it hit the fan, and we ended up on the bed. I don't explain that I tried to reenact it later with Heath and achieved different results.

Isaac pulls away from me, eyebrows drawn together. "See this is where you start to worry me, lady. 'Cause I had that dream too. But I was actually there and you sure as hell weren't asleep."

I sigh and drop my head into his chest.

"That's what I was afraid of," I say. "Take me home. There's something I need to show you."

eight

Having Isaac Harver in my bedroom should be awkward, but instead it feels totally comfortable. And so
does he. He takes off his jacket and puts it across the
back of my desk chair, turning it around backward and
resting his chin against the top.

I'm pressed against the far wall, arms back to being
crossed over my chest. We snuck past Dad, asleep on
the recliner, Isaac picking his way up the staircase like
he knew exactly which steps creak, and closing my door
with the only motion that ever works without squeaking—a swift push until it rests in the frame, followed
by a soft pressure as the latch clicks.

"All right. What's up?" he asks.

As if I could answer with one sentence, a satisfactory

explanation that sets my world right. I exhale quickly, aware that I'm going to have to approach this the same way he did the bedroom door, mercilessly fast with a tender coda that doubles as an apology.

I cross the room, reaching past him to unearth the ultrasound on my desk and trying to appear unaware of our mingling body heat as I do. His eyes follow my motion and he goes stiff as a bass drum player's spine when he sees what's in my hand.

"That's not . . . yours, is it?"

"In a sense," I tell him as I sit on the bed, leaning forward enough that I know my tank is gaping slightly. "That's me," I say, choosing one of the fetuses.

"Okay," Isaac says, watching me closely for whatever cue I might give on how he's supposed to react.

"So who's this?" I ask him, sliding my finger to the other one like a teacher prompting a student who might be a little slow on the uptake.

He shrugs. "Don't know. Sister. Brother. Something."

The animal magnetism that I can't quite corral when we're near each other isn't enough to override my irritation. "Obviously," I shoot back. "Except I don't have any siblings."

"Okaaaay . . . ," he says, dragging out the last syllable so I know I'm going to have to close the logic loop for him.

"Here's what I know—" My hand instinctively goes up to tick off facts, but Isaac's fingers close over mine before I can start.

"We're not in school. Just talk to me."

I've got a sharp answer, but it folds under the pressure of his hand on mine, where I let it stay. "I had a sister," I say, all the edge out of my voice; the low notes of a secret slipping out throb in my chest. "She was never born, and she never died."

"Okay," Isaac says again, but there's no mocking in it, or disbelief. He accepts the irrational the moment I say it. My lips are dry, so I lick them, the cracked surface of my lower callus rubbing against my tongue. I touch it quickly with the tip, a constant in my supposedly ordered life that reassures me before I tear what's left of normality out of my grasp.

"I absorbed her in the womb. It occurs in up to thirty percent of multi-fetal pregnancies, typically because the absorbed twin had chromosomal abnormalities," I tell him, the precise language of the hundreds of web articles I've read in the past week stripping the fact of any emotion.

"There was something wrong with her, huh?"

"Probably," I agree, watching as his thumb starts to rub hypnotically across mine, making the trip from first knuckle to second at a slow, steady pace.

"Not to go all court-appointed therapist or whatever, but . . . how does that make you feel?"

"It's not what I feel that's the problem," I tell him. "It's what *she* feels."

"Yeah?"

"Yeah," I echo. "See, my body was the stronger, but her heart stayed true. She's been quiet all this time, growing with me, staying in step. Until . . ." I finally look away from our entwined hands, eyes locking on the ultrasound so that I can reassure myself of the truth that I came to earlier.

"Until she fell in love with you."

Isaac isn't like me and Heath—practiced looks with even the most miniscule muscles kept under control—or even Brooke with every expression so exaggerated I'm not able to judge what's honest and what's for flair. On him everything flickers, from the vibrant light of his eyes when I say *love* to the five o'clock shadow undulating as his temper flares.

"Chromosomal abnormality, huh?" he says, flinging my hand away from his. "Must be, for her to fall for a guy like me."

"Shh," I shush him, ignoring the drop of my heart as he pulls his jacket on. "Wait—are you leaving?"

"Why the fuck would I stay?"

"Because I just told you the biggest secret of my life,"

I say. "Maybe the only one I've ever had."

"Right, the one about how your evil twin is making you wet for the bad boy."

"Don't you ever speak to me like that," I say, righteous indignation vibrating my vocal cords and stopping him in his tracks as he heads for the window.

"Jesus, really? I've heard worse out of you when we're—"

"Shut your mouth! Shut your filthy mouth," I yell, crossing the distance between us and covering his lips with my hand. He steps back against the wall, grabs my wrist, and pulls it away from his face, all the while hissing at me.

"Sshhh . . . Christ! Okay, all right already." His eyes shoot to my door, which remains closed, the silence that fills the rest of the house in stark contrast to my room, which feels like the inside of a timpani, noises rolling off tight surfaces to bounce back from the next.

"Could you not get me arrested, maybe?" Isaac says, but I'm not really hearing, the continued roar in my ears feels like the pulse of something new and different, a creature I've just become aware of that can exist only here, between the two of us.

We're pressed against each other, anger faded, but blood still up, our potential energy about to unload on each other in a frenzy of action that must be spent in one way or another. I move away quickly, until the back of my knees hit my bed and I crumble onto it, all fight gone.

I'm about to cry, tear ducts that haven't been used in years perking painfully at the very thought. I cover my face with my hands so Isaac won't see it happening, all my control slipping out from under my eyelids in a river of salt. I want him to go, want the smell of cigarettes out of my house and the feel of rough hands off my face. I open my mouth to say so and instead I ask: "Do you believe me?"

"Yeah. I mean, you're pretty smart, right? Sasha Stone. She's number one. If you say that's the deal, then that's the deal."

Whatever resolve I have breaks completely, a sob shaking my body as someone tells me I'm right, that I'm not crazy, that all this darkness inside me isn't my fault.

"Sasha . . ." My name has never sounded so much like music, every step he takes toward the bed a note leading me closer to a measure that can't be played.

"You need to go," I say, dropping my hands to meet his gaze.

He holds mine for a second before shaking his head. "You're—"

"I know, I know," I interrupt, scrubbing away the tears as they fall. "I'm a mess."

"I was going to say *addictive*," he tells me, before throwing open my window like he's done it a thousand times before. He's got one leg out, one in, before he turns back to me. "And that means you're not the only one that's got something wrong with them."

And then he's gone, the black emptiness of my window staring at me as if I'd done something I shouldn't.

nine

I can't sleep after that.

The truth of what's happening to me is like a thick fluid in my chest, a pressure no amount of coughing could dislodge. But I said it all to Isaac, the one person in my life who doesn't belong, the puzzle piece that turns my perfect square into an unnamed shape. And he believed me—granted, he got totally pissed off at the implications—but he believed me, which was more than I bargained for.

Part of me thought he'd tell me I was crazy, and make an invective-laced escape before my insanity spread to him. In a way, I'd counted on that being our end, an easy way out for both of us. Isaac had surprised me by rolling with the punches, accepting everything I said as truth—something Heath couldn't do even when my words were much more believable.

I hop online, nerves telling me there's no sense lying in bed. I pull up my assignment for English, maximizing the word processor window to glance over where I'd left off on my paper about a Faulkner short story.

Much in this story depends upon the classic and stereotypical gender roles that both men and women succumb to. For instance, on the surface, it seems that the majority of the men's primary focus is on defending women.

It's a decent start, but I have no idea why I apparently hit return a thousand times before typing the next sentence. There's a huge block of blank space, and I can just see the top of the next line of text peeking at me from the edge of the paper. I scroll down.

And nearly vomit.

It's only one line, but even her font is aggressive to me, to be sure this is a message I can't ignore.

WE NEED TO TALK

If I saw that written on the top of a test I'd feel my heart plunging along with my GPA. It's a damning sentence, one that invites the reader to freely interpret until the conversation is rejoined. It sends alarm notes through my entire system, like the marching band just matched the natural frequency of the football stadium and the whole thing collapsed in a pile of concrete dust and broken rebar, human limbs sticking out at odd angles.

So talk

I type, having to delete and fix those two simple words three times because of my shaking hands.

I sit there stupidly for a full minute, staring at the blinking cursor, but nothing happens. Which is not all that surprising, since this isn't exactly a text message I'm sending here. Plus, the person I'm expecting to answer me *is me* so . . .

I rest my hands on the keyboard and exhale, doing my best to empty my mind the way Lilly always says to when she pulls out the Ouija board at sleepovers. I'm as blank as can be, focusing on the beating of my—or her—heart, willing the twin inside of me to answer, when Mom opens my bedroom door.

I make an inarticulate shrieking noise that would get me expelled from any and all music programs, and fly about two feet up in the air, banging my knees on my desk.

"Jesus, Mom!"

"Honey, language," she says, brow furrowing.

"Sorry," I say, my hands rubbing my bruised knees.

"No, I'm sorry. I didn't mean to scare you, but I saw your light . . ." Her eyes trail to my laptop, like she expects to see something as equally appalling as my taking the Lord's name in vain. "Are you doing homework? At this hour?"

"I couldn't sleep," I tell her.

"Honey, it's . . ." She looks at her wrist like everyone her age who used to wear a watch, then squints at my bedside clock. "It's four in the morning. You need to go to bed."

"You're right, I should," I agree, quickly minimizing my Faulkner paper before she sees I'm using it to communicate with . . . myself.

My laptop goes to sleep before I do, the dark screen staring vacantly back at me.

I wake up with a scratchy throat and swollen feet. I know exactly what's going on with my throat; the smell of cigarettes is still in my hair, something I remedy immediately, washing away Isaac and moonlight and words I should've left unsaid with a thorough scrubbing of raspberry shower gel. How the heck one cigarette made my feet swell I don't know, but I wouldn't be surprised if

I'm allergic to tobacco.

"Virgil my ass," I say to the showerhead, then clap my hand over my mouth.

"Get it together, Stone," I say once I'm out, hair up in a towel and fingernail file rubbing off the tips of my nails, the pads of my fingers, anything that might've touched that cigarette—and Isaac.

My twin might have my heart, but that's it and that's all. And it's not like it's ever been a huge part of my life. The rest of my body belongs to me, and the ratio is not in her favor.

I make hasty apologies to Mom as I brush past her in the kitchen, my laptop bouncing against my shoulder blades inside of my backpack, each thump reminding me of how warm it felt this morning when I picked it up. Warm from use.

I cut band for the first time in my life, utilizing a shaky lower lip and the word *cramps* to break down any barricades Mr. Hunter might have thrown up against me, leaving before I even took my clarinet out of the case.

The library is busy, students with first-period study hall and second-period English typing as fast as hunt and peck will allow. I shake my head as I brush past them to a corner where my only company is a ficus plant. I settle into a study carrel as the Faulkner paper fills the screen. Except my sister has erased everything I had written, her words ballooning to fill pages now that she can be heard.

First things first, let's clear the air, get this off my/our chest—no pun intended. YOU KILLED ME. Killed me dead [almost, not quite, better luck next time]. Those once tiny toes you buff and scrape dead skin cells off of now are murder weapons, sis. Not like you meant it, but damage was done BUT I'M NOT ~done~. The cord, the cord, the cord. You kicked it, I died. S—l—o—w—l—y while you sucked your thumb. Yeah, really. Just one of the twenty /ten fingers / ten toes / but I didn't get / any of those/. I was starving but you did the eating—no mouth, no teeth, no, no— you gorged your(cell)f—ha, ha, get it?—on mine. But not this heart, my heart, our heart—yours was a pussy little thing, I'll tell you—MINE WAS STRONGER.

I know she's right, even as I feel a habitual defense rising in my throat. I'm not accustomed to being accused of things; being wrong is not my forte. Even so, I can't argue with what she's saying. For years I've felt spikes of anger, the hot-blooded rush of a temper I'm not supposed to have, curdling my words so that I can almost feel a permanent filter on the roof of my mouth, a physical thing required to keep myself in check.

But it's not me, and never has been. It's her, revolting against a lifetime of working for my body, feeding my needs, pumping my blood, with no chance of escape and no release of duties. Even as I read I feel a calm spread over me, an assurance that these darker moments, these breaches of who Sasha Stone should be, are not my fault.

I was okay with it, for a while, living vicariously through you . . . but here's the thing. YOU'RE NOT VICARIOUS. I could shut off the blood supply—you might not notice. You're a cold, cold thing, Sasha Stone. Set the metronome by her. Practice practice practice makes perfect and THAT'S WHAT YOU ARE, RIGHT? Except, except not quite. Other girls they say maybe their pulse skips / heart misses a beat. Not yours though, not yours IT'S NOT YOURS. He[ath] is not what I want I will not have him.

Here too lies an explanation for why my perfect boyfriend with symmetrical hair and a wardrobe of nonaggressive colors does nothing for me. He wouldn't. How could he stir the love of this passionate girl, whose emotions are dark slashes on paper? There's a delicious thrill in seeing her words, the pent-up violence that I incapacitated long ago with a simple swing of my foot. My twin in the flesh would be intimidating; I can see that. But it says something that I undid her, in the beginning.

So, let's fix this. Fix it. How do we (fix it?) You work hard, I play hard. Equation solved. X+ y = sasha (who am I?) stone. Two parts of one w(hole). You've had your time, now it's mine. So is (I)saac That's-My-Type Harver. But it's—what do they say?—"complicated." No shit to that. This won't be easy, sis. But it will be F-U-N.

Get some sleep. You've got a GPA to maintain. Night-night.

I've kept my cool through most of her ranting, even though my fingers itch to correct the punctuation that I'm sure she considers artsy, instead of just plain incorrect. I imagine her bashing my laptop keys, all emotion and no thought, an indescribable flow of feelings that Strunk and White have no bearing on. Illiterate or not, my twin has me flustered, and it's one of her last statements that sticks with me as I head to second period, plastering a self-assured smile on my face for everyone's benefit.

This won't be easy, sis. But it will be F-U-N.

That line has me scared, because I'm not familiar with either one of those things.

Friday at lunch I kind of bite Heath's head off, and it's not because I'm starving. I've spent most of the week hoping that my body doesn't either collapse or run off to be slutty with random boys. It takes constant vigilance and I'm exhausted.

"What the hell is going on with you lately?" Heath asks me, after I tell him for the third time that he's chewing too loudly.

I sigh and stab my salad like it's the one irritating me. "I really don't want to fight," I tell him. And it's the truth. I really don't. It'd be much easier if we could just move forward.

"Too bad," he shoots back, in an unexpected display of spine. Brooke raises her eyebrows at me from the next table over, and I know if I give her the sign she'll cross the distance and remove whatever discs have started to re-form back there. I roll my eyes to let her know I've got it.

"Why do you insist there's something going on with me?"

"C'mon, Sash, really? You collapsed in the hallway last week, let a complete stoner sniff around you, started talking about abortions in class, you took off your clothes in front of me with your parents right down-stairs, for the love of God—"

I haven't even finished the first eye roll, so I just let it become more expansive.

"—and you skipped band on Monday. Now tell me, when has that ever happened?"

"Heath, I'm under a lot of pressure right now."

Which is true. But he knows me, knows that I love exactly that. So the excuse won't fly far. "And . . . ," I add, before he can mount an argument, "I've been think-ing maybe we could use some time apart."

His face falls like the puppy that gets left behind at the pound.

It's an old trick I've used on myself a few times. If I can't decide between two things, I imagine depriving myself of one—and let my stomach tell me what the answer is. Heath has been irritated with me, yeah. But he'd rather be angry at his girlfriend than not have one. Now he's the one who's gone pale, the one who looks like he's about to go to the floor, right down there where his belly just bottomed out. I twirl a bit of carrot in the bottom of my salad bowl, letting him process the fact that it's more interesting than his emotional distress right now.

"It doesn't have to be like that," he says, his voice dropped yet another octave in an attempt to secure a cone of silence around what he's realizing might be a breakup conversation.

"No," I agree, with a nonchalant shrug, "it doesn't have to be like anything. Do you want to be with me or not? Make a list, pros and cons, whatever you feel is appropriate. Then get back to me."

I get up to toss my trash as the bell rings, feeling lighter than I have in years in comparison to the black hole opening up behind me. What used to be—and maybe still is—someone I'm supposed to care about.

"Dude, that was totally badass," Brooke says from the backseat of my car.

"I know," I say, still flying a little from the high of quasi-dumping Heath. The plodding nature of our relationship, like a calendar planner that goes five years into the future, had always felt like safety. With safety comes comfort, but also mind-numbing consistency. I feel the newness of my life right now, down to a tingling in my fingertips as I drive. My sister said it wouldn't be easy, but that had been.

"Fun, too," I say aloud.

"That's a bit much," Lilly says, glancing up from her phone as she sits in the passenger seat. "You don't have to be mean about it."

"I'm not trying to be mean," I shoot back.

"Yeah, it comes natural," Brooke agrees.

"Not quite what I was saying." I give her a dark look in the rearview mirror as I pull in to Lilly's driveway. "Make it quick," I tell her as she hops out to grab her spats. "Even I won't be able to talk Hunter out of busting our butts if we miss pregame."

Lilly doesn't have to pretend to shiver. Punishment in band means lining the practice field before early rehearsal, a cruel job involving flashlights and heavy layers in the dark morning hours of the late-autumn Midwest.

"So?" Brooke prompts me once Lilly disappears inside her house.

"So what?"

"Don't give me the doe eyes, Stone. You suddenly ditch the one guy you've let up your shirt and don't think I'm going to ask you about it? Spill, and don't try to tell me you're just on the rag, because you and I have been synced since sixth grade and I'm sporting whities tonight."

"TMI."

I turn in my seat, but Brooke just stares back at me. She once stared down a tuba player for a straight hour on a long bus ride, so I might have to concede this one.

"Fine," I give. "What do you want to know?"

"What's the deal with you and Harver?"

"No deal," I half lie. As far as I know there is nothing going on between Isaac and me. That's all my sister.

"I call bullshit. I'm not saying you guys have, like, long philosophical conversations about nature versus nurture. You probably don't even talk, but there might as well be a highway of fire drawn between the two of you for all the hot looks that go back and forth."

"Nice. So you think Isaac and I are friends with benefits?"

"Friends? Don't know. Benefits . . . well, I'm just going to say that your complexion has never been better. Like, you know, blood flow has increased to certain parts of the body. Maybe you grew a heart."

"Maybe I did," I snipe back, alarmed at how close she is to the truth.

"Whatever. I was just curious."

"Curious about what?" I drop my voice as I see Lilly shut the front door behind her, waving her spats triumphantly.

"If Sasha Stone found out how good it feels to be bad," Brooke says, and tips me a wink.

The truth is most of me doesn't know how it feels to be bad. My sister feels so vibrant inside my body now that I'm aware of her; it's like everything else about me—skin, hair, teeth, arms, legs, toes, and eyes—are merely part of the vehicle that was made for her, just waiting patiently for the takeover when they got to live too. I'll fight it as long as I can, my mind the last holdout once everything else has abandoned itself to this new experience.

I ignore my phone during the football game, squeezing out the fight song like it's the best sixty-four measures that ever existed and avoiding eye contact with the brass section. They don't even make it into my peripheral.

I drop off the girls, ignoring a weighted suggestion from Lilly that I check my texts and a knowing nod from Brooke when she gets out, shutting the passenger door with her butt and then smearing her face all over the window as I try to back out of her driveway. I laugh, my mouth making the right shape and my throat producing the sound it's supposed to, but the truth is I can't wait to get home.

I can't wait to stop being myself.

Hands that don't fumble or hesitate, no waiting for permission or asking in the first place. Tree bark scraping across my skin as I slide down to the ground, knees a weak mess of desire. But I don't feel the pain, don't feel the hard ground underneath me or the pressure on top now. I can't feel these things, because it's not me. Not my body curled in ecstasy, toes pointed at the moon. Not my nails slicing red ribbons down his back. Not my blood rising to the surface of my neck, something I'll have to hide later, when I am myself again.

There are no words, only sounds, as if my clarinet were jammed down her throat, every breath passing unintelligible sounds that compose a song of victory. She is a feral thing, my sister, long denied and now unleashed. She takes what she wants, scratching, pawing, tearing at him. She'll have bruises, but so will he.

The three of us will study them later, and remember.

I wake sore, lips swollen as if I'd played for hours. My fingers stray to my face, brushing aside hair somehow laced with dead leaves. The rising sun catches a note taped on the footboard, lined paper bearing a message meant only for me.

Told ya it'd be fun

And underneath me, a smear of blood on my sheets.

ten

I. Things I Know

    A. This has gone too far.

        1. My sister had sex with Isaac.

        2. My sister lost my virginity.

        3. I can't control myself.

II. Things I Don't Know

    A. How to stop

    B. If I want to

My mom is always begging me to talk to her more, and that could be kind of a problem. If I open my mouth, all kinds of things are going to come out: accusations, admissions, confessions. I can tell her about my sister, her heart pumping away inside of me, and I imagine my mother's will respond, picking up a rhythm it believed it lost years ago. Now that I know about my twin, I wonder how I could have discovered her only recently, never spotting her in the perpetual dark circles under Mom's eyes, whoever the woman is on the other end of Dad's mysterious calls, the long silences between my parents that stretched out longer over the years.

She's there between them, a phantom that is not named or talked about, but around and through, their words tearing holes in what's left of her, a brutality of neglect. I see her in the sidelong glances from Isaac in the halls, hear her in the loud curses tossed by the people who would've been her friends, feel her in the lingering soreness between my thighs. I even taste her in the food that didn't decorate the wall behind my head in the dining room, mashed potatoes not thrown in a fit that never happened.

I chew slowly, as if being hyperaware of my actions will lead me to some form of control over hers. My food is ground to a pulp, saliva running down my throat before I catch Mom looking at me over the rim of her glass, water paused at a perpetual angle. We stare at each other for a moment, Dad's steak knife grating against his plate while the glass magnifies her lips, drawing out the cracks that years ago she would have balmed away before dinner.

"Mom?"

"Sasha?"

We talk at the same time, a small question in the upended lilt of our voices. We don't speak the next part, *Are you all right?* Because it seems that she knows I'm not, perhaps has known for a while. And maybe I knew *she* wasn't either.

"Help me with these?" She nods toward the plates, and I follow her to the kitchen with mine in hand, trying not to stare at the mess of bone and gristle that remains. The door swings shut behind us, and Mom leans against the counter, dishes forgotten in the sink.

"What's going on with you lately?"

I scrape what's left of my dinner into the garbage disposal, listen to the grind of flesh and bone being pulped and forgotten.

"What do you mean?"

I ask not in denial but out of true wonder. How do I seem to them, this new daughter erupting forth from the existing one?

"You've been . . . different."

She is careful with me, hesitant. I think of the wall behind my dinner seat, a life's worth of arguments accumulating in a point of impact that is boring down into plaster. How many times have I stormed away, leaving behind a mother who wonders . . . what if the other one had lived?

I think there'd probably be a hole in the wall, that's what.

But Mom doesn't know that. She probably pictures someone like Lilly in my place, a nice girl with my face who is malleable, picking up suggested hobbies that we can practice together, long ponytails overlapping each other's shoulders as we sit side by side knitting, scrap-booking, journaling.

"I'm fine, really," I say, any thought of coming clean chased away by the image of this kinder, nicer child that she never would have had.

"That's my point," Mom says. "When I said you've been different, it's not a bad thing."

"Then what is it?" I realize my shoulders are tense, pulled back straight and tight as if I were at attention on the field, waiting for the whistle to release me.

"I think you might be happy."

I've barely talked to anyone in the past few days. Heath's texts line my phone like bubble wrap that I've got to dig past to find anything else. They sit, unanswered. Brooke has never required anything other than an audience, and to watch while I pick splinters from my gums. Lilly is the one who notices my silence. I see her mentally cataloging it, along with every time Isaac and

I make eye contact, which always sets ablaze a stolen memory of flesh on flesh, the ground against my bare shoulder blades.

My sister isn't talking to me either. In the week since my bloody sheets I've checked my phone more than usual, sliding past accumulated texts from Heath to see if any from Isaac have come in, but none have. I feign indifference, casually tossing my phone onto my bed as if there were someone watching me, that they might know how little I care. But when I went to finish the abandoned Faulkner paper, my fingers typed something else, a note for my twin, letting her know the consequences of her actions.

Hope you're happy. He's not talking to us and my sheets are stained. There's a word for boys like him, and that's trouble. *You want to live, I know, but at what expense to me?*

The paper flowed more easily after that, the words that had been blocking my brain now set aside in a document I refuse to save or name, only minimizing it as I wait for an answer. But there was no response from her that night, or any thereafter. Even the red C+ on my paper, written hesitantly as if the teacher couldn't quite believe it herself, doesn't penetrate my thoughts. It takes Brooke's voice, every word punctuated with a staccato, to do that.

"Shit a brick, Stone," she says, pulling the paper off my desk before I can hide it in my backpack. "Did you have an aneurysm or something?"

"No, but my parents will," I whisper. "Could you not—"

"Not what?" Lilly asks, leaning forward in her seat to rest her chin on Brooke's shoulder. "Oh my God . . ." She fades out, her hand covering her mouth when she sees my grade.

I swipe it out of Brooke's hands and crumple it, my face matching the bleeding red of the pen. "It's nothing. Forget it."

"Sasha," Lilly says, eyebrows drawn together like an art project titled *Concern*. "If you need to talk, or something."

"Seriously," Brooke adds. "I mean, you're like the Hester Prynne of the group, so you can't tell us there's nothing going on."

"Yeah," Lilly agrees automatically. "Wait, what? Hester who?"

"Cute," I say to Brooke. "Shame you don't apply your cleverness elsewhere."

"Yeah, that one was pretty good, I gotta say," Brooke goes on. "See," she explains to Lilly, "Sasha's like the chick from Hawthorne—only letter you're ever going to see on her stuff is a big red A."

"Ooooohhh," Lilly says, but I'm not sure she actually read *The Scarlet Letter*, so even the explanation of the joke is probably lost on her.

Brooke's mouth is suddenly a thin line, cheeks puffed as she tries to suppress whatever drop of comic genius is currently brewing. It's a Friday, the last few minutes of class dwindling to nothing while everyone huddles in groups.

"Just say it before you stroke out," I tell her.

"Err . . ." She glances around and has the dignity to lower her voice. "I was gonna say that you always got As . . . until you started getting some D."

Brooke regrets it the second she sees that it's true. I can tell when our eyes meet that whatever semblance of honesty exists in me flashed for a moment, and she caught it. Lilly only gapes, mouth open in what has become her signature expression.

"Sorry," Brooke says quickly. "I didn't mean . . . it was just too funny to not say it."

"Yep. Pretty goddamn funny."

I hear Lilly's gasp before the door slams shut behind me, my shoes smearing the tears that fall so that anyone who sees could follow them like bread crumbs, a trail of confusion that leads to the bathroom, where I curl protectively in a stall, waiting for the day to be over.

"Sasha?"

It's the last voice I expect to hear bouncing around the girls' bathroom, echoing with a vibration much lower than what these walls are used to.

"Heath?"

I'm so surprised I lower myself to speaking to him, even pushing open the stall door. We're alone, the long mirrors on the far walls reflecting back an endless line of Sashas and Heaths, none of them knowing what to say. We look at each other for a second, him breaking away first to inspect the tampon dispenser like it might have a suggestion.

"You shouldn't be in here," I tell him. "You'll get in trouble."

"I put a sign on the door," he says. "'Caution. Wet Floor.' You know, *Cuidado piso mojado.*" He cracks an old joke, bending his body into a ridiculous position.

"Thanks, Captain Accident," I say, a small smile tugging on my lips at the name we gave the anonymous silhouette of a man who always seems to be falling on floors, jamming his hand into tight spaces, and dropping hair dryers into bathtubs.

But it's no accident that Heath has followed me here, and I know it. I'm trapped, the stall door against my back, myriad copies of myself staring me down. Heath leans against one of the sinks, the tail of his shirt dipping into more STDs than he'll have a chance of catching in the next twenty years.

"You didn't answer my texts," he says. It's not sad or accusing. It's a statement of fact; typical Heath. I don't tell him that I never read them in the first place.

"I'm sorry," I say. And I kind of am. Maybe. He might be boring, but that doesn't mean my salacious sister gets to skewer him for entertainment. "I've got a lot going on."

He holds my gaze for a minute, and I wonder if he's going to call me out on the fact that I've always had a lot going on. Instead he studies the puffed skin around my eyes, the dark circles underneath.

"I'm worried about you," he says.

"I'm fine." These words are stockpiled for me within easy reach. Always locked and loaded, both a weapon and a defense. But Heath has heard them too many times and familiarity reduces their effectiveness.

"You're not fine," he shoots back. The endless line of Heaths on both sides of the bathroom are an army now, one I know I can't hold off for long. The tail of his shirt is wet, hanging against his jeans to spread a dark oval there. "Something's . . . off, Sasha," he says. "Something is wrong."

How can someone who knows me so well not realize?

Sasha Stone is not off.

Sasha Stone is not wrong.

But Sasha Stone is closing the distance between us,

watching as thousands of Sashas and thousands of Heaths find some comfort in the nooks of each other. And while these places are not a perfect fit, they are at least familiar.

He smells like Tide, because heaven forbid his mom ever buy generic. I'm simultaneously repulsed and attracted to his cleanliness, the fact that he's not Isaac both a magnet and a mark against him.

Newton says that for every action there is an equal and opposite reaction, but lately everything that happens inside of me ripples out in twos, my love and hate doled out equally between Isaac and Heath, satisfying no one.

"We okay?" Heath says into my ear, his breath moving a lock of my hair.

It's so normal, so deeply programmed into who I am that I lean forward just enough that his lips are against the soft skin of my neck. "Yeah," I say. "We're good."

And that's the thing. We are. Heath and I are good. Good the way sugar cookies with no sprinkles and white cotton undies and organic deodorant are good.

We're good.

I'm good.

Sasha Stone is good.

I repeat this as I walk into the hallway, my hand in his, my heart a dead thing in my chest.

eleven

What. The. Fuck. Wait, I K(no)w this one. DON'T tell me. He's so n-ice. So goÒd. What if he K(new)? I said out with the old—you remember the IN part. These boys . . . your FEELings. Equal and opposite erection. HA. What Would Jesus Do? What Will Mom Say? Will Dad Even Notice?

I owe you something but not everything. The one for you is not the one for me.

Love y(our) choice of w(or)ds. The 1 4 you is not the 1 4 me. Paradigm shift, sister—Now 1 + 1 = 4— Math is hard. You + Heath = Good, Me + Isaac = Bad, You - Me = ?

I look at my sister's response on Saturday night and sigh. I'm going to have to make some hard and fast rules about punctuation if we're going to continue to communicate like this. I can feel my GPA slipping as I read her embarrassingly inaccurate blocks of text. I minimize the doc and scroll down on the browser to discover that my crack about the GPA isn't just a turn of phrase.

The Faulkner paper I turned in and subsequently crumpled before dissolving into a hot mess and hiding in the bathroom did not do me any favors. Neither did the take-home government test where I answered the essay section with a series of exclamation points and unhappy faces—or, somebody did. If my sister insists on sharing this body she's going to have to agree that it's going to Oberlin next fall, or else.

My phone vibrates on the laptop, mercifully sliding across the touchpad and relegating my grades to a folder labeled *To Improve*, alongside an app I'd downloaded to brush up on my Italian and an online course covering the musical history of the baroque period. It's a text from Lilly, whose been monitoring my relationship status like she's a cardiologist and it's got a pacemaker.

So you and Heath are back together?

Don't know that we were ever apart.

What does that mean?

And while I acknowledge the inherent bitchiness in

my statement, it's also technically true. I didn't break up with Heath, I simply told him he could choose to not have me for a girlfriend and then never read the texts that may have held his decision.

And then I had sex with someone else.

"Shut up," I say. Unfortunately my fingers are working in tandem with my mouth and I end up texting exactly that to Lilly, who for once didn't deserve it.

WTF?

Sorry. Not for you.

She texts me back but I ignore it, the low purr of a motorcycle pulling into the driveway drowning out the vibration of my phone. It's one in the morning, and I should be asleep, reading, studying, *improving*—doing anything other than what I'm doing, which is pulling on a pair of shoes and a jacket and sneaking downstairs to talk to the boy who I lost my virginity to last week and haven't spoken to since.

I put on my pissed face as I walk out the door, considering if I've got it in me to slap him. Even if I do, most of the anger that's fueling me has morphed from steam in my head to bubbles of anticipation in my stomach. I don't know whether I'm going to hug him or hit him until I see him leaning against his bike, the bobbing ember of a cigarette in his hand.

And it's a hug. A full-out, body-to-body, squeeze-me-please hug. One that goes from soft squishy to hard angles in a second, our mouths finding each other and his cigarette dropping to the ground. A tendril of smoke finds its way to my nose as my heel crushes it out, and I pull away.

"Hi," we both say at the same time, breathless. I swear he's blushing.

"So, uh . . ." His eyes go to the crushed cigarette. "I thought you were mad at me."

"I was mad," I tell him. The words sound funny coming out in the shape of a smile, the dichotomy of my sister and I fighting for control. "I still am."

"You don't look mad," he says, thumb tracing my lips, which are stuck in a grin I can't wipe off until I summon the image of my bloodstained sheet.

"Looks can be deceiving," I say, taking his hand away from my face but leaving our fingers intertwined. A little for me, a little for her. $1 + 1 = 2$, sister.

"Why didn't you call me? Text? Something?"

He looks away from me again, like the broken cigarette might be able to offer up some sentence structure that's escaping him. I squeeze his hand, aware that I'm going to have to wash mine later in order to get the lingering nicotine smell off.

"Thought you might be pissed. I mean, I've never—"

Twisted bodies under moonlight, capable hands, my breath caught in my throat. "Yes, you have. You're no Virgil, remember?"

"But you *were*," he snaps. "I didn't know how you'd feel about it. Or . . . her, or whatever." Isaac's other hand goes to my chest, finger drawing a small circle. Her heart leaps to meet his touch.

But it's my skin that gets goose bumps.

"What I'm trying to say is, I've never . . ." He actually blushes, and I finally get it.

"Deflowered anyone?"

"Um, is that like popping a cherry?"

"That's a slightly more violent metaphor for the same action, but yes," I say.

"You and me and metaphors." Isaac shakes his head. "I was afraid you'd be mad, is all."

"Isn't that what you wanted though?" I ask. "Help Sasha Stone do something she's not supposed to do? Bring out the wild in me? Teach the dog some new tricks?"

"You're no dog," he says, hand trailing up my neck. "You're a girl. A good one. And I . . ." His thumb brushes my cheek, and I watch his pulse leap in the hollow of his throat, naked and vulnerable.

"I've never said this to anyone before . . ." He stops, swallowing so hard I don't know if this is a pronunciation issue or what.

"I like you," he says, and I burst out laughing.

He smiles along with me, unsure. "What?"

"You," I say.

He shrugs. "I don't like many people."

"Me neither," I tell him.

"I don't want to mess this up," he goes on. "And I feel like in a world where Isaac Harver gets to talk to Sasha Stone about metaphors in the middle of the night, I'm the one that's going to ruin it."

I don't know what to say, because whatever *it* is will only have the lifespan of a gust of wind in my hair, or however long it takes to get the smell of cigarettes off my fingertips. But I don't want to tell him that right now, because then I'm the one to ruin it.

"So how's this gonna work?" he asks, reclaiming the small amount of distance I'd put between us with my laughter. He laces his hands behind my back, resting them on the base of my buzzing spine.

"I don't know." I'm honest for once, the well of confusion that has become my middle overflowing up through my throat. I can't tell him I'm of two minds on the subject, because I'm not. My mind knows exactly what it wants. A high GPA. Oberlin. The future I've been guaranteeing myself since the first day of kindergarten. It's the rest of me that's in revolt, any ideas I had about my sister only having my heart obliterated in one night under the trees. I shiver at the memory, in a good way.

"I think her needs are very basic."

"Roger," he says, pulling me in even tighter.

I can smell smoke on him, emanating from the folds of his clothes. It should be a huge turnoff, but it's not. Neither is the sickly sweet tinge of alcohol that I can smell on his breath. Quite the opposite.

"And what about you?" he asks. "You got needs?"

"No," I say, pulling him toward the trees where the shadows are complete. "This is for her."

There's the slightest resistance, a moment where our arms are taut and he hasn't quite followed me yet. Isaac now the dog, one on a leash, that might put down his head and disobey. But my shoulder dips when I turn back, one eyebrow raised, and my jacket slides down so that the thin tank I'm wearing is bright in the moonlight, the rise and fall of my heart underneath it calling to him.

"Jesus, lady," he says. "And I bet people think *I'm* a bad influence on *you*."

"Now what?"

I still don't have words. The time when I'm me but not myself hasn't faded away completely, and won't until the pleased flush that covers my whole body is safely hidden by my jacket, zipped tightly, sleeves punched down into curled fists. The warm buzz of anticipation is gone, leaving behind the coldness of regret, my mind taking over now that the polluted blood of my sister's heart is satiated.

"Now you go home," I say.

I hear him moving, the rustling of leaves and the quick snick of his belt going back together. I tell myself I won't, but I sneak a glance over my shoulder when he's bending down for his shirt, the moonlight turning him into a landscape I want to explore again, all lean muscle and flickering dips. I can't help but wonder what it looks like when I can't see it, while he's—

"That's fucked-up," he says.

"What, you want to cuddle?" I snap, and the tiniest twitch in his jaw makes me think maybe he does. I'm left feeling like Lilly, all wait— What?

But the look is gone once his T-shirt is back on, like an eraser passed over his face. "Nope," he says, and smacks my ass as he walks past me. I follow for once, the air behind him smelling like smoke and beer and sex. My sister's heart speeds up in reaction, urging me on.

"Wait," I call after him, actually jogging to keep up. Pathetic.

He turns when he gets to his bike, rummaging through his pockets for a fresh cigarette. "What?"

"I'm sorry," I say, the words coming out more easily than I ever expected they could. So I must actually be, somewhere inside. "It's just . . . I don't really know how to do this."

He flicks the lighter, his face lit up magnificently for a second. "Lucky for you, I've got practice. You want to be bad, Sasha Stone. I get it."

I don't bother to correct him that it's not me who wants to be bad, but my sister. Whatever flicker of affection I thought I saw under the trees is gone; the face behind the bobbing ember of his cigarette is stone cold.

"I'll teach you," he says.

"Sasha?"

The soft scent of sex is still on me, mixing with the acrid cigarette smoke to make a contradictory fume that clouds my mind. I'm not fully myself, can't be when I smell like this. The conviction is so deep that I almost don't respond to my mother calling my own name.

"Sasha?" she says again. It's hesitant, rising up from the darkness of the dining room just as my hand pauses on the bathroom door. I need to wash. Need to get clean and go to bed. What I don't need is to try and explain myself to her.

"What?" I copy Isaac's voice, a question spoken in a voice that doesn't invite an answer.

"Don't *what* me, young lady," she responds in kind, the tentative thread snipped in half by parental control masquerading as concern. "What were you doing?"

My eyes are adjusting to the dark and I can just make her out, sitting at the dining room table. She's in her usual chair, facing the window. Which means her question is mostly rhetorical.

"I guess I was being bad, Mom."

There's a sharp intake of breath that must come from somewhere behind her forehead because it pulls her eyebrows inward. "What's gotten into you, Sasha?"

I almost say *Isaac Harver's dick*, but then cut it off with a laugh at the literal answer my sister would want me to toss out. At the fact that I'm getting in trouble for something that's not my fault.

"You said yourself that I seemed happy," I tell her.

"But why are you?"

It's a good question. How can I be happy when the clasp on my clarinet case actually creaks from lack of use? How can I be happy when I flubbed a basic scale this week in band, my fingers correcting automatically, but not before Charity's eyes made a quick dash in my direction, noting the mistake? How can I be happy when my boyfriend and my lover are two different people?

"Because I'm two different people," I say, answering myself aloud, feeling the jigsaw of my new life click together. I'm a puzzle, definitely. But not the kind that lies flat on the table waiting for someone to piece it together. My broken bits have flurried through the air of their own volition, creating in three dimensions.

And I don't need finishing.

"Sasha, are you drunk?" Mom asks in disbelief. She gets up, crossing over to me in the dark, her own breath laced with wine from dinner—I take a deeper whiff—and perhaps some after too. I'm not drunk. I just did a lot of intimate things with someone who was, and now we both smell like each other, entangled, inseparable. Like me and my twin.

"What is my sister's name?" I ask her.

She stops, sagging against the wall for support, her hip pressing into the plaster where my anger used to go until it found the path to my mouth. "What?"

"Her name." I advance on Mom, my words tight and precise in a way that won't allow for denial or explanation. All I'm after right now is a fact.

"Shanna," Mom says, her hand going to her throat as she does, as if the name needs the extra help to be pushed out into the air between us. "Her name was Shanna."

"Shanna," I say, and my heart explodes into a stuttering beat at the name, black eruptions fill my already dark vision. I sink to the floor beside Mom, a miasma of smoke and sex rising up from my clothes.

"She's here, Mom," I say, my hand going to my chest. "She's here and there are things that she wants."

"Don't say things like that," Mom says, but she's two people right now as well. The woman who only finds hope in the pages of romance novels, and the one who is staring at me through tears lit from behind by joy. The woman who keeps one hand to her own throat as if to deflect a death blow, and the other reaching toward me, clasping her fingers with mine as the pulse beats through us all.

"You need to explain," she says.

twelve

There is a fight.

For once I'm not participating. I sit in my chair, staring at the empty one across from me where my sister was always supposed to be, Mom and Dad throwing words at each other so quickly, they're like a physical bond between them. The only one left standing.

Dad clearly thought I'd finally ratted him out about his affair when he got home from golfing to find no dinner, his wife and daughter stern-mouthed and stiff-spined at the table. I think that conversation might have actually gone better than what Mom served up, a calm repetition of what I'd told her the night before.

"Jesus Christ. Just . . . Jesus Christ," Dad is saying. I almost don't recognize him without his earplugs in, his forehead touching the table where his dinner usually is.

"Honey, I just think we should listen and consider. Sasha says—"

"That our dead daughter is living inside our other daughter," Dad finishes for her, finally lifting his head. "That's what she says."

Mom looks at the table, the high polish that she gives it every week providing her own twin. "Is it entirely unbelievable?"

"Yes," Dad says, raising his arms like he's the band director about to take us into forty-six measures of whole rests. Nothing there. Should be obvious.

I get up, my chair smacking the wall behind me. I can hear bits of plaster filtering down behind the wallpaper, see small grains of it slip out from under the baseboard.

"You're going to tear this house apart," Dad yells at me, and I'd almost award him some points for a great metaphor if I thought he did it on purpose.

"Back off," Mom snaps at him, and he does, jaw coming together with an audible click. I don't think she's told him to do anything in the last ten years or so, but he must have been well trained once because the skills are still there.

"Honey, do you need anything? What's wrong? Can I get you something to eat?" Mom's hands are on my shoulders, running down my arms. Her skin trying to give heat to a baby who died inside her and her words trying to feed a child who hasn't eaten in eighteen years.

I am suddenly very important.

"Sure," I say. "Leftovers are fine."

I sit down in the perpetually empty chair as Mom leaves the room, unspoken words trailing behind her and promising a fight upon her return. The house looks different from here, like I've found a new world in our own dining room. Dad watches me as I settle into the cushion, which is stiff and like new.

"Sasha, I don't know what's going on," he says. "But it's not what you think it is."

I nod to let him know I'm listening, but I definitely don't agree. From the kitchen I hear the clink of plates, the patient hum of the microwave that was a wedding present they haven't given up on yet.

"If you need some help, any kind of help . . ." He trails off, obviously hoping I'll finish his sentence with the words he doesn't want to say.

I don't know when Dad and I stopped communicating. The awkwardness between us is a slow growth, one no one noticed until it was too late, metastasized. He's trying, I know, and I should be meeting him halfway. But it's been so long since there was anything more between us than lame jokes he throws at me to tease; the only interaction we're familiar with when it comes to each other is irritation. But there's nothing funny about his daughter possibly being insane, no tidy column for the deceased twin to be crammed into.

"I don't need help," I tell him. "There's nothing wrong with me."

Mom puts a plate in front of me, her lips twisting a little when she sees where I'm sitting. Steam rises up from my plate, heat escaping with little pops from a pork chop that I ignored at dinner last night.

"Sasha," Mom says quietly. "Maybe it will be easier for us to understand if you can tell us more about why you think that Shanna—"

Dad slaps the table so hard, the chandelier shakes, tiny music drifting down among us. "Don't encourage her," he yells. "We only have one child and I'll be damned if I'll watch her go crazy and let you help her."

"You never mourned her!" Mom shrieks, anything she was holding in check flowing out on the last word, a crescendo that feels like it will break the window.

"She never existed!" Dad roars back, with a volume I didn't know he had the capacity for. If I combined all the words he's spoken to me over the years they would not equal those three, words borrowed from a fight they should've had years ago.

I look down at my plate, the corn safely tucked to one side, what's left of the pork chop mangled but not touching anything else. I've even taken my knife and scooted the breading crumbs away from the pooling butter from the corn. I didn't know I was so much like Dad until now, so compartmentalized and factual. His food never touches, either.

They're still yelling at each other when I throw my plate. All of it's touching now, smeared on the wall and dripping down to mingle with the plaster dust.

They look at me, mouths both agape at this new person. I might be nasty once in a while, push back from the table too fast and leave the room in a huff. But Sasha Stone is a good girl. Sasha Stone does not throw her dinner across the room and watch it puddle on the floor with something like satisfaction brewing in her gut.

That's someone else entirely. And they don't know how to handle her.

"Sasha . . ." Dad's eyes are still on the floor, not able to meet mine. He says, "Go to your room" at the same time Mom says, "Clean up that mess," and they look at each other, unsure how to coparent when the child isn't a perfect ten.

So I don't do either. I walk out the front door and get in my car, wondering where I should go and who I should see. My hands find my phone, and my sister decides without asking.

There's a subtle shift Monday morning after the revelation. Mom and Dad are being very careful with me, and each other. Whatever fragile peace they found between the two of them after I left seems to be based on pretending nothing happened. Dad grabs toast and leaves as if work might evaporate if he doesn't get there on time. I seriously doubt anything so substantial as a tax firm could cease to exist, but if you asked me that about a twin six months ago I would've said the same.

Now I know better.

I feel her inside me, beating more quickly when I picture Isaac's face, responding whenever I say her name mentally. I only thought of her as *sister* until yesterday. Mom had said her name hesitantly, like a bad word you whisper because you don't actually know what it means yet.

Like fuck. Except you K(now) what that means.

That's waiting for me on the Notes app on my phone when I get to first period. I roll my eyes at the parenthetical, but the tingle that I feel all over my body is testament to the truth of Shanna's statement. When I passed Isaac in the hallway my fingers instinctively clenched Heath's, earning me a subtle pressure in response that barely registered against the tumult Isaac's wink sent through me.

Her heart reacted, certainly, but I can't ignore the fact that since I've given her some free rein with my body it's starting to get some ideas of its own, too.

I ignore the blush spreading in my cheeks at the thought of Isaac, the pins and needles rushing through my spine as I remember his naked back in the moonlight, and tell my hands it's time to prioritize.

Mr. Hunter's handwriting is sketchy at best, and when there's a challenge he deteriorates into a first grader with a caffeine buzz. He's written that word—*CHALLENGE*—across the white board in red Expo marker, but he was overly excited and made the first letters too large, so the last few are squeezed in like a bowel obstruction. Somebody thought they'd be clever and added a tiny *R* in the corner, complete with an explosion. Insensitive or not, it's accurate.

Because somebody is going down.

When there's a chair challenge, the second- or third- or fourth-chair instrument makes a play for the seat ahead of them. It either ends with someone firmly entrenched in their proper place and an expanding sense of superiority to their immediate right, or a palpable air of embarrassment while the challenged shifts to the left, taking their case, music, and a tucked tail with them. It's a weird moment, complete with mumbled *excuse me*s and other pretenses at politeness as the demoted and the promoted switch places, one barely keeping a lid on a victorious smile while the other is probably considering ending somebody's marching-band career with a solid whack to the back of the knee.

Not that I've ever been in that position. I've never lost a challenge.

I head back to the cages and spot Charity Newell huddled in a corner with her friends, practicing deep-breathing exercises like there's a baby on the way. I've still got moonlight and back muscles on my mind, so I haven't put it all together until I spot Lilly stand-ing with the Charity supporters. Our eyes meet and she makes an *oh shit* face like I just caught her on a couch with Isaac.

I mean Heath.

"Nice," I say, loudly enough for her to hear. I don't need Shanna's foul mouth to shred people; kind words said nastily are sufficiently sharp.

Lilly immediately ducks her head and comes to me as if I called her to heel, but Charity says her name in a way that sounds like she's half drowned already and needs all the buoying she can get. Lilly stands in between us, a piece of unthinking metal stuck between polar oppo-sites, her eyes loose, swiveling marbles.

"I'm telling you, his dick is the width of my gear shift, and I've had my hands on both enough to kn—"

Brooke drops the penis lecture she's delivering to some poor freshman when she sees us, putting together what's going on much more quickly than I did.

I'm slipping.

I swing my cage door shut at the thought, pinching my index finger hard enough to pop a blood vessel. "Dammit," I yell, going down on one knee to assess the damage, clarinet case clattering to the floor.

"Not bad," Brooke says, hovering over me. "You've got the tone right, but when it's pain a nice solid one syllable is the way to go for a swear. Much more satisfying."

I cradle my hand to my chest, letting the pain sweep up my arm so I can pretend that's why there are tears in my eyes. Not because I know I'm about to lose first chair, and definitely not because Lilly left with Charity's entourage. I'm not even going to acknowledge the possibility that tears are pooling because Brooke is still here, offering a hand to help me up, keeping up a steady stream of useful swears for any situation. I'll pretend the pain is what's making me cry.

That way she can too.

thirteen

WTF sis? I'm the one who loses things. Your virginity. Your min(e)d.

It's not funny anymore.

(I never was) Kidding.

I close out the Notes on my phone as I walk in the front door. My whole day at school was spent either pretending not to cry or pretending I didn't want to kill Charity Newell, and do serious structural damage to Lilly as well. Heath did his best to comfort me, which means that he kept rubbing my shoulders in a platonic way that only made me want to drive a pencil in between his ribs just to get some kind of passionate response out of him. Brooke would usually offer to mortally embarrass whoever the problem was, but since Lilly factors into that equation, she was oddly silent about balancing it. Judging by the exchanges with Shanna on my phone, she's completely unapologetic about her part in making me lose first chair.

The only good thing about my day was when a text came in from Isaac that read, *Found a better chair*, and had a pic of something designed so that the user could get into all sorts of weird sex positions. I wasn't even really sure if you were supposed to sit in it or what, but I was smiling when I deleted the text.

Mom is coming down the stairs as I close the door behind me. "Sasha?" she asks.

Usually the question in her voice would mean she's asking who just came home, and technically I suppose it still does. But we both know there's more to it.

"It's me," I tell her, silencing my phone in case Isaac tries to cheer me up with anything explicit.

"Okay," she says, but the smile on her face stretches a little too tightly, and I can't help but wonder if she's disappointed. "We need to talk," she says.

I follow her into the living room, ignoring the buzz of my phone in my jeans even though I'm highly curious about whatever perverted furniture Isaac may have found.

"Your dad," she begins, and I'm already rolling my eyes in reflex. Years ago we silently agreed to ban each other in some way, a revolt of one of the five senses; his ears don't work when I'm around, and my eyes roll at the mention of him.

"Your father is worried about you," she goes on.

"A nicer way of saying he doesn't believe me."

"It's a lot to take in," she says. "You have to understand how Shanna's—"

She hesitates, as if saying *death* might stop the heart patiently beating inside of me. I stare at her, whatever chamber of Shanna's heart that has *mother* written on it hardening as we wait to see how she'll finish. Mom goes on, skipping the word entirely, leaving a blank space in her sentence like the one that sits across from me at the dinner table every night.

"—affected us. We'd already bought two cribs . . ."

Mom fades out again, her face collapsing inward like there's a vacuum in her throat. At the rate she's producing words it's a distinct possibility. I watch, wondering where the other crib ended up. Later, on my phone I'll find:

on the o( )ɓ (ur) (ri)

"Your father," she says, and I'm starting to think we're just going to keep identifying family members all afternoon, which honestly might have avoided a lot of confusion if it had happened sooner. My phone buzzes in my pocket again, and Mom's eyes cut to it.

"Could you turn that off so we can have a conversation without interruption?"

She's barely finished a sentence yet and my phone isn't the reason, but I slip my hand into my pocket anyway. "Dad's worried about me," I prompt her.

"Yes." She nods. "He's afraid that the issue isn't with your heart so much as your mind."

More like the problem is with my mind being sharp enough to know he's been stepping out on Mom for the last two years, and *his* heart not catching on to the whole monogamy thing. Or maybe his heart doesn't factor into it at all and it's just his . . . ew.

"And what do you think?" I ask, rerouting my mind away from that particular thought. Getting Mr. There's a Sense of Calm to Be Found in Numbers on board with my twin sister living inside me was always a long shot, but with Mom I wonder if I'll see that light of hope that flashed so brightly when she first thought *maybe* . . .

"Well, I know that you've been under a lot of pressure lately."

She says it delicately, as if maintaining a polite tone while inferring insanity will soften the blow. It's the inverse of my approach of saying nice things in a horrible way, so I give her the benefit of the doubt and let it settle in my ears, slipping into my possibly unstable mind to be absorbed by the bloodstream, the course of my veins carrying it to my heart.

Which revolts.

It stutters at first, fluttering like eyelashes in a sharp wind, then drops the beat completely, leaving my body empty, waiting for something that doesn't come. I'm still, not breathing, hoping it will pick back up. When it doesn't, my hands go to my unmoving chest, no rise and fall of breath, no deep thrum of a pulse.

"Sasha?" Mom's hands join mine, our fingers interlaced over my sternum. "Sasha?" This time the concern has elevated to worry, and the last reiteration of my name comes at a full-blown panic, but I hear only the first syllable as darkness fills my vision. It's not a fade to black, but an explosion of dark pinwheels that burst across my mother's face. My whole body is liquid and it's so soothing, I give in to it. I slide from the couch to the floor, pooling into the form of a bass clef before Mom smacks me across the face.

I pull in a breath reflexively, lungs telling heart the point has been made. It picks back up, the steady beat in my chest Shanna's silent agreement.

"I'm sorry I hit you," Mom says, hands on both sides of my face, the hardwood floor pressing my bra clasp deep into my back. I take another gasp of air, this one so deep I hear vertebrae popping. "I didn't know what else to do."

"I'm okay," I tell Mom. "I'm okay now."

"What happened?"

"I don't know," I answer honestly. "I've blacked out a few times lately. I don't think Shanna—"

"Please don't." Mom raises a hand to stop my words. "Let me talk to your father," she says as she helps me from the floor, a protective hand on my elbow. "I don't want him upsetting you, or honestly you upsetting him either. Bringing up . . ."

"Shanna," I supply, and her hand tightens on my arm.

"Bringing up your sister isn't going to be easy."

"Being her isn't easy."

fourteen

I disentangle myself from Mom with a little difficulty, making an excuse about homework so I can go upstairs and check my texts. There's a string of apologies from Lilly, more mundane kindness from Heath, and a few pile-of-poop emojis from Brooke.

And one from Isaac.

Want to see something?

I definitely do. Preferably not my parents' faces. I text him in the affirmative.

Cool. Come out to the glif.

It takes me a second to figure out what he's saying, since spelling is part of our communication barrier. The petroglyph is one of our little town's dubious claims to fame, a wall of granite out by one of the streams that an ancient tribe of forever ago carved pictures on. There's definitely a fish, a couple of concentric circles, and if you look hard you can make out little stick men. The historical society ran a fund-raiser when I was a kid to get a shelter of sorts built over it, and occasionally some stuffy types wander out there to do charcoal rubbings. But in general the glyph is relegated to school field trips, the painstaking effort of someone from thousands of years ago explained to little kids who try to spit in the dead center of the circles.

I head out to the glyph, leaving Mom and Dad behind me, Shanna tucked safely inside, ready to see Isaac. I can feel her quivering, her anticipation sending electric shocks into my fingers and toes. The parking lot is empty in the dying fall light, except for Isaac's bike, which I park next to. Apparently we've got the glyph and the surrounding woods to ourselves, which can only bode well. I smile as I take the path down to the stream, ready for whatever he has in mind.

Which, it turns out, is a picnic.

"Hey, what's . . ." I fade out, taking in the improbable image of Isaac Harver setting out food on a blanket. "Food" might be stretching it, since it looks like we'll be dining on gas station subs and Pringles, plus a couple of cans of the cheapest beer in the world. But it's nice. A weird kind of nice that makes my heart—her heart—stutter as we come closer.

"This is different," I say, coming up behind him.

"Thought I'd try it." He smiles at me and pops his can of beer. I sit down next to him, and he opens the other one before handing it to me. All the medical and social reasons not to drink beer leave my mind the second I drink it, leaving me with the most obvious drawback. It tastes awful.

"Cheap stuff, sorry," Isaac says when he sees my face. "I had to choose between cheap beer and cheap wine, so I thought we'd go with the one that'll make you piss before the one that makes you puke."

"That's lovely," I tell him. It was supposed to be sarcastic, but it doesn't come out that way, because the image of him standing in the gas station and trying to decide which crappy drink will cause me the least damage is oddly endearing.

"Do you have a fake ID or something?" I ask him, tearing the plastic wrap off my ham and cheese sub.

"Nope, my cousin was working."

"Hmmm," I say around a mouthful of food.

"So I don't know, I thought . . ." He takes his own swig of beer, then another before finishing his sentence. "I know you had a bad day with the band thing, or whatever. And I thought, maybe this would help."

It does help; I don't even want to admit how much.

Brooke encouraged me to fight for my spot back, Lilly laid low, and Heath . . . I can't really remember what he did, other than say things that sounded like there was a teleprompter over my left shoulder. Isaac did something real, broke whatever this twisted routine between us is and took me on something resembling a date.

And I like it.

"I did have a bad day," I tell him, popping open the Pringles can. "The weekend was, amazingly, even worse."

He takes half the sleeve of chips from me. "Why's that?"

"I told my mom about Shanna. I think she kind of . . . saw us."

Isaac stops midchew. "You shitting me? What'd she say?"

"About you? Not much." I shrug. "After I told her about Shanna, that kind of took precedence."

"How'd that go?"

"Like a bull in a china shop," I tell him, tossing back another swallow of beer.

"Whatever it don't break, it shits on," he says, somehow sounding wise.

I laugh. "That pretty much sums up my dad's reaction."

I tell him about throwing my dinner, how my parents were fighting when I left. "And my dad's having an affair," I add, which wasn't supposed to come out. The beer might be cheap, but I've never been a drinker.

"Sucks," Isaac says.

"Yeah," I agree, finishing the last warm drops in the can. "He sucks."

"My dad would never do that."

"Why? Because your mom would kill him?"

"Uh, no, because he's a good guy," Isaac says, tossing his beer can into the plastic sack. "That so hard to believe?"

"No," I say carefully, watching him as the shadows of the trees around us lengthen. I have never met his parents and don't intend to because I can't imagine a future for us. One where we have to get into an argument when we move in together because my antique bed won't fit through the door of his trailer.

"My parents like each other," Isaac goes on. "So much that I've gotta be careful not coming home unexpected, you know?"

"Nice, that's . . . great," I say, trying to summon enthusiasm for his sexually active parents. If I can get them out of the picture though, I mean, we do have a blanket. "So, your text said you had something you wanted to show me?"

I say it just right, so that he knows what I mean. He smiles and picks up the rest of the trash first. "Littering is bad, remember?"

I smile and lay my head back to see the first of the stars coming out, pinpricks of light. My head swims a little, and I know it's going to be very easy to let Shanna have her way this evening. When Isaac comes to me I'm surprised when he pulls me up instead of joining me on the blanket. He leads me down the glyph, where the shadows have already fallen.

"All right, so. Before I show you this . . ." Isaac takes a deep breath. "What you said before about your dad having an affair, how do you feel about it?"

"I don't know," I tell him. "Bad, I guess." And I think I did at first, before I realized I could use it to my advantage.

"Bad," Isaac latches on to that. "So, I'm kind of feeling the same way."

"Why?"

"Really? Sasha, I walk past you in the hall every day with *him*, and it's like, yeah, I'm banging the valedictorian and her dick boyfriend doesn't know it. And I should feel good, like he's the system and I'm fucking his girl, so, whatever. But really I just feel like shit. Like you'll hold his hand and let people see it, but me, I'm the guy you screw in the dark and don't tell anyone about."

I shake my head. "It's not like that. What am I supposed to do, Isaac? Tell everyone about how Shanna needs you? They won't understand."

"*I* don't understand," he yells, his voice bouncing back at us from the glyph wall.

I don't like being yelled at. Sasha Stone does not stand in mud and get yelled at by Isaac Harver. "You said that if I told you that was the deal, then that was the deal. That I'm smart, and if I say Shanna is real, then she is."

"What about this?" Isaac asks, his voice softer now, his body coming closer to mine, his hands capturing my fingers so that I don't know where my sister ends and I begin. "You're saying this isn't real? Because this is you here, right now, with me."

"I don't know," I say, those words always bubbling to the surface when he's around, my voice losing conviction in his presence.

"Know what I think?" Isaac goes on, his hands now crushing mine. "I think you want me to be stupid, do whatever you say and believe whatever you want. Me for the night, him during the day."

"Isaac . . ."

"What about what I want?" he says, letting me go and fumbling in his pocket for a lighter. "Maybe I'm the kind of guy that doesn't like cheating. Maybe I'm a better person than you thought. Maybe I'd like to hold your hand in the hallway and have people see us together. Maybe *I* want to try being *good*."

"That's just . . ." I don't get to finish my sentence, because he flicks his lighter and I see what he wanted to show me.

ISAAC & SASHA is scored into the rock, right under the fish glyph. I wipe my hand over it, once, twice, frantically. But it's no use. He used a knife, scratching deep into the rock and leaving something permanent and profane alongside the ancient and sacred.

"What did you do?" I seethe, cupping handfuls of water and tossing them over the letters. It only makes the rock around them darker, throwing our names into bright relief.

"I put it out there," he says calmly.

My fingers trace our names, running over the fin of the fish left behind by another hand from another time. "This is bad, Isaac."

"I guess that's just what I am," he says, and turns to leave.

I spend a few more moments trying to undo what he's done, but it's no use. As the moon comes out and I hear him start his bike and drive off, I'm left staring at the new carving. A boy and a girl, etched in stone, together forever.

It would be so sweet if he had gotten her name right.

fifteen

When I get home I collapse onto my bed and stare at the clarinet case jammed under my desk. Last Christmas Mom and Dad sprung for a second one so that I could have one at school and one at home. It was the most exciting thing to happen to me since they redesigned *The Phantom of the Opera* stage, but now it's resting beside a lone sock I can't find the mate for and a pamphlet from a second-rate music school I wouldn't go to even if they offered me a lifetime supply of reeds.

I roll onto my back and check my phone again, spotting the message from Shanna in the Notes app about the crib that ended up on the curb. I'm about to answer her when the phone vibrates in my hand and Brooke's face—with a hot dog jammed in her mouth and the most innocent expression in the world—fills the screen.

"Hey," I answer.

"Yeah, hey," she says. "So listen, you've really got to answer Lilly's texts because she keeps texting me asking why you won't text her back. And I told her it's not like I know because you're not responding to mine either."

"You sent me poop," I tell her.

"I sent you a visual representation of my solidarity with you on a crappy day."

"Only you would interpret it that way."

"That's because I speak the language. I'm good at talking shit," she says, purposefully leaving a pause so I can laugh. I don't.

"Seriously, Lilly cried her body weight in tears already. She's been punished."

"Mmmm . . ." is all I can give on that one, because I'm not so sure. "I've got to go," I tell Brooke, gaze landing once again on the case under my desk. "I need to practice."

"Atta girl," Brooke says. "Reclaim that throne."

"I will," I say.

Because that's what Sasha Stone would do. Reclaim what's hers, planting a flag so deep it grows roots that grip and twine, becoming one with whatever I choose to align myself with until extraction would only kill us both. That's who I am, and Charity Newell needs to be reminded of that.

Maybe I do, too. Especially after Isaac Harver carved my name next to his in stone.

I snap together my clarinet, wetting a fresh reed and taking a pic of myself with it resting alluringly on my tongue, elbows pushing together my cleavage just enough to make it obvious it's on purpose, and send it to Heath. It's not exactly an apology, but there's enough mixed imagery there to distract him for a while so I can practice in peace.

The music does what it does best, swelling the air around me into a protective bubble, floating though my brain and soothing all the jagged edges that have hooved up lately. I remember this, and miss it. The placidity of Heath and me, the predictableness of Lilly, the assurance that Brooke will offend me at least once a day; all of it is wound up with music, our lives dictated by notes we know by heart, our feet in step.

It has a beauty, this pattern. I lived it so long that the monotony was all I felt, ignoring the stability of the structure underneath. My fingers need little reminder once the stiffness has worked its way out after the first two hours. I'll hurt tomorrow, and deservedly. My wrists will creak and joints will snap; my fingers will curl into themselves, resting in a loose fist because they've wrapped around a clarinet for so long they don't know how else to be.

Except I like the way Isaac feels in my hand. Suddenly my fingers slip and put a sharp where no sharp should be, the safety of my old life whisked away with one irreverent thought.

"Stop it," I say, teeth clenched onto the reed even though I know I'll be picking more splinters out of my gums tomorrow.

But there's a compulsion in me, buried deep. I check my phone again, not even kidding myself that I'm hoping Isaac has texted me. Instead I've got a notification on my Notes app.

Spl-in-ters are bones. I will rise er{up}tion. One day you h{ate} me.

Now you're not making any sense.

I write back blindly with one hand, the other still on the clarinet as my eyes follow music notes, my mind turning it into music in my head, a Schumann piece that everyone should know and nobody plays anymore. I've almost reclaimed serenity when my phone lights up with a text from Lilly that I'm going to ignore. But there's a response from Shanna in Notes.

Heath's is not the only bone m[Ne y(our) mouth.
Mine you pull white from pink extr/a-action. I am
dEEP. Your teeth have roots in my skeleton. Wlill
find my way to)o(ur surface), I am her-e.

I toss the phone away from me, but I can't get Shanna's words out of my head as easily. Schumann has lost
his grace, my fingers are suddenly quite dumb, and my
teeth crack down on the reed in frustration, sending
fragments across my tongue. I pick away the tiny white
pieces, triggering a gag reflex as I go after the farthest
ones.

My phone vibrates against the floor, and I can see
Brooke's face from across the room. I wipe my hands
on my jeans, wondering what she would say if I told her
that it hasn't been bits of reed she's watched me tweeze
from my gums, but the soft fetal bones of my twin sister, forcing their way to the light.

The truth is she would probably think it was awesome.

I grab the phone, answering just in time. "What's
up?"

"Wanna three-way later with me and Lilly? Skype,
that is. I know you're not into chicks. Or displays of
affection."

I thumb across my screen, erasing the note from

Shanna. "Yeah, that's fine."

"Wow, that was simple."

"Sasha?" Mom's voice sails up the stairs.

"Gotta go," I tell Brooke.

I flex my hands as I go downstairs, easing out the kinks that I should have never allowed to settle, weeks without practice ending in my first chair loss. Dad looks up from the table, an attempted smile aborted into a mild grimace when he realizes he can't quite force it.

"Well, look who it is," he says, which is a stupid thing to say under any circumstance and particularly confusing in ours.

"Seriously?" I sit in my usual chair, making sure that the back hits the wall so I can see him wince. Instead he reaches out, his hand resting on my wrist. We haven't touched since I got boobs and it made things weird, so I forget to roll my eyes.

"Sasha, honey," he says, his voice low like when he used to read to me at bedtime. My heart stutters again, as if Shanna had been listening then too, examining the letters that turned into words that he helped me learn.

"What?" I say it with no edge, an honest exclamation of curiosity, just as Mom's hip hits the swinging door from the kitchen and she brings in dinner.

"Chicken," she announces, setting a platter on the

table that has more food in it than we could eat in the next three days.

"Mom, I've still only got one stomach," I tell her.

"I know that," she says, with forced cheer. "I just . . ." She looks over at Shanna's empty chair, and I wonder if she's disappointed that I sat here instead.

Dad clears his throat, "How was your day, honey?"

Mom and I are both so surprised we look at each other, not sure which of us he's speaking to. We're off script. Dad stopped asking me how my day was after one time in junior high when I answered with a real-time explanation of tuning my clarinet.

"Uh . . . fine," I say. It wasn't fine. I lost first chair and a friend defected. But it's the answer I'm supposed to give, so I do.

Dad sucks in a breath and I wonder if he's about to ask me how Shanna's day was, when Mom reaches out and brushes her fingers against my cheek. "Everything okay?"

My phone vibrates and I slide it out of my pocket to see a text from Isaac.

Sorry. See you later?

"Yeah," I tell her, a piece of reed still jammed inside my cheek. "Everything is good."

sixteen

I power up my laptop, happy enough to forgive Lilly now that I know I'll be seeing Isaac later. Brooke calls first. She's wearing a sports bra and has her hair up in a wet ponytail.

"Are you going to put a shirt on?"

"Why?" She looks mystified as she bites into a pizza pocket. "Oh, there's Lilly."

Our friend pops up on the other side of the screen. She's got on a hoodie from last year's band camp and too much concealer around her eyes. I personally think the mea culpa would go over better if she went ahead and let me see she's been crying, but whatever. Isaac texted me again to say he'd be over in about an hour, so she's got plenty of time to apologize.

"Hey, Sasha," Lilly says cautiously. "How's it going?"

"Fine," I tell her. "I came home and practiced a ton. Charity's only keeping the seat warm for me."

"Damn straight," Brooke says, some pepperoni falling out of her mouth to land in her bra. She fishes it out and pops it back in her mouth.

"Oh my God, Brooke," Lilly says, ignoring my jab at her cousin. "You're so gross."

"Whatever, dude. I was looking for some pumpkin recipes for foods class last week and typed *pump king* instead. Skewed my results. Now *that's* gross."

"I don't want to know," Lilly says, but I think maybe she does.

"Seriously, Sasha, you doing okay?"

Brooke asks this while holding her pizza pocket up into the air and examining the remaining contents as if they might be more interesting than my answer.

"I'm fine. Really, guys." I look at Lilly, but she only nods. Apparently I'm going to have to dig for this admission of wrongdoing the way I fish for compliments from Heath.

"So did you know?"

Lilly doesn't feign innocence or pretend she doesn't know what I'm talking about. I'll give her that.

"Yeah." She drops her eyes, and Brooke pops the rest of her dinner into her mouth.

"And you didn't tell me Charity was going to challenge?"

"Sasha . . ."

I'm so tired of hearing an ellipsis after my name, as if everyone is trying to be delicate with me. Isaac certainly isn't, and I'm so distracted by the idea of him being here soon that I have to mentally review what Lilly says next before I realize she's not following the script for making up with me.

"Charity's trying to get into Ashland. Her GPA isn't that great but if she takes first chair it might help."

"You mean *usurps*," I correct her. "*Usurps* first chair."

"It's not yours," Lilly shoots back. "She beat you in the challenge, fair and square. You couldn't have landed a spot in a church choir with that performance."

My heart clenches in surprise, a surge of rage is injected into my veins along with blood. "And you can't land Cole," I tell her.

"Hey, whoa, ladies," Brooke says, the conversation clearly taking a turn from what she expected as well.

"Screw you, Sasha," Lilly yells, tears sending her makeup into a discolored flood. "Why do you have to be so damn mean?"

Next to the laptop, my phone lights up with a text from Isaac.

here

He's early. It's barely dark enough for us to slip out into the trees without being seen, and if he thinks he's coming inside to meet my parents he has grossly misjudged the situation.

"Lilly, where did you learn those words? Certainly not from me," Brooke says, trying hard to alleviate a situation that has gone all the way off the rails.

"Screw you too, Brooke," Lilly says, tears that match her skin now dripping onto her shirt. "If you won't tell Sasha what you really think of her, then you're a shitty friend too."

"Dude," Brooke's eyebrows have shot up to her wet hairline, mouth that typically has a retort ready to fire stuck in an open *O*.

here

Isaac's second text doesn't sit well with me, the inference that I'm supposed to leap at his call combined with Lilly's suggestion that perhaps Brooke has said some not-so-perfect things about me behind my back makes me take a pic of my middle finger as a reply.

THERE, I type.

"Who are you texting?" Brooke asks.

"Not your business." I put my phone in my lap so she can't see it. "But anything you said about me to Lilly is mine."

"You think everything is yours," Lilly says, before

Brooke can even open her mouth.

"Were backbones on sale at Walmart or something?" I ask.

"Fuck you, Sasha." Lilly's face is melting along with her clean vocabulary, streams of concealer now slipping into the sides of her mouth and coating her tongue when she speaks.

"Guys, I think we should—"

"No," I cut Brooke off. "I think you should tell me exactly what you think of me. Right now. To my face. Anything you can say to Lilly you can say to me."

Kinda what I had in mind but need you down here for that . . .

Isaac's text lights up in my lap, in response to my middle finger pic.

"Tell her, Brooke," Lilly says.

"Sasha . . ." Brooke's voice is unsure, watery, something I've never heard from her. "It's just that . . ."

"Say it," Lilly pushes. "Everyone thinks it anyway."

Brooke straightens and looks right at me, regal as hell even with a smear of pizza grease across her chest and a pimple in the middle of her forehead.

"You're a bitch," she says, just as my phone vibrates, tumbling from my lap.

Gotta go

I hear the low purr of a motorcycle as he fires up the engine, the noise sending my heart into a patter to match, black spots careening across everything I see as I push back from my desk, chair rolling across my phone and crunching the screen.

"A total bitch," Lilly agrees, her face briefly visible between flashes of black as I run to the window, my heart leading the way. It's pushing, beating frantically in a voiceless scream to tell him to come back, to stay, to lay with me in the moonlight and mold me into what I want to be.

The fastest way between two points is a straight line. Shanna knows this because I know this, and her heart feeds my brain, blood pulsing up and coming back down, knowledge and need combining to create the perfect storm as our body hits the window.

My head hits first, skull shattering the glass and making way for hands that search for purchase, feet kicking as if the air may suddenly coalesce. It doesn't, and I fall, branches tearing at my limbs, blood and blackness in my vision and two girls' voices from above calling . . .

Sasha?

Sasha?

Sasha?

I hit the ground and all the air is knocked out of me, a perpetual exhale that won't let me pull anything back in, my lungs flattened by the impact. I try but get only a hissing sound and the coppery taste of blood as I suck in streams of warmth running down both sides of my face. I try again to breathe, and this time it's a gurgle as blood surges up from inside as well, rising to meet what I'm swallowing.

I've managed a third breath when Mom and Dad come running, the side door slamming behind them. Mom's hands are on me, touching, pulling, pushing, grabbing, but they come back slick with blood so dark it's as black as the sky, fragments of glass sparkling with their own constellations on her palms.

"Don't touch her," Dad is yelling. "They said don't try to move her."

He's got one hand on his cell and the other on Mom's shoulder, but it's too late. She's already done everything she can think of: propped my head, wiped my face, told me it's going to be okay. All the things that got me through fevers and colds, chicken pox and strep throat. But I didn't have a tree branch stuck in my side then, or a flap of my scalp hanging to one side.

I move my hands, for what I don't know. I don't have the strength to raise my arms, so I dig into the ground, making ten tiny holes on either side of my body as I try to find something to root myself to. Mom is hurting more than helping, Dad keeps saying our address over and over, even though surely emergency services has got it by now, and still I can hear my friends through what's left of my window, vaguely calling for me.

What I don't hear is Isaac coming back.

I clench my teeth as Mom reaches for my face, trying to find some way to put my head back together. Maybe something she picked up in one of her crafting classes will finally be useful.

"Don't touch her," Dad says again, leaning over us both. "You'll make it worse."

"Jesus Christ, Mark," Mom says. "How? Look at her!"

"They'll be here," Dad says, repeating it as if it will make the ambulance come faster. "They'll be here. They're on their way."

"They're on the way." Mom puts her face right down to mine and says it a third time, in case I hadn't picked up on that fact.

The sirens can be heard from miles away. Dad leaves Mom and me under the tree to wave them down, just in case GPS fails them, I suppose. Mom puts her cheek next to mine, coating her own in blood and accidentally inhaling some of my hair, which hurts like hell when she finally pulls back and part of my scalp follows.

"Sasha," she whispers. "What have you done?"

My fingers dig deeper into the dirt, the cold solidness of it giving me more comfort than she can. I've done nothing, and I know it. It was Shanna who made this leap, her heart leading the way though our body shared the fall. Spasmodic light fills the yard, the branches of the tree we lie under dancing across the side of the house.

"Ma'am, we need you to move aside," a woman says, replacing my panicking mother with something I can relate to. She's all calculation, her eyes skimming over me in a moment, decisions being made immediately.

I like her.

Her partner hovers on the other side of me, his gloved fingers barely touching me as a cool assessment is made. They have their own language in glances and unspoken words, but the ones they do speak I must refute so that they will understand. Blood pressure. Heart rate.

"It's not mine," I say. These are my first words after falling, and they are tinged with copper. Still, the truth tastes good.

"Yes, it's going to be fine," the female medic says.

"No." I let go of a fistful of earth, grimy blood-streaked hand capturing her wrist so that she is forced to hear me. "My heart is not mine."

"Whoever's it is, it needs blood," she says matter-of-factly. "You don't have much left."

The pulsing light fades, the shadow branches taking over the dance being performed on the side of the house as black explodes across my vision. Dad is swearing, Mom is crying, but I . . .

. . . I feel just fine.

Because I didn't do anything wrong.

seventeen

The music my body makes is not appealing.

I'm in the back of the ambulance listening to a concert of beeps and buzzes, all of them discordant, my body the only blamable orchestra. I have so many extra things inside of me: a needle in my arm, tubes in my nose, a tree branch sticking from my side. I felt my sister curling up as the medics worked, retreating into the fetal position with each foreign object that is introduced.

I'm only able to stare straight above me because of the brace they put around my neck, the sterile ceiling of the ambulance the only thing I can see except for the medics' chests when they reach across me in response to some new wave of off-key noise. Their lanyards hang from their necks, one of them resting on my nose for a maddening instant, creating an itch I can't scratch.

"This is not how I sound," I tell the female, whose ID says her last name is *JONES* in all caps, an assertion of herself.

"What's that?"

"I don't sound like this," I try to say again, but the words are frightened things, not willing to come out into the chaos of lights and noises, strangers' hands becoming intimate with me in a matter of moments.

My eyes flick over to the male, *FABER*, whose jawline is tight in response to an erratic noise that won't settle down. I try to make it keep time with the muscle ticking in his jaw, but there is no pattern where the two find common ground.

There's an indignity to this cacophony, the idea that my body has created it an insult that goes deeper than the IV in my elbow. The music I create is breath exhaled into cold air, skin moving against skin, and the small noises Isaac makes in the dark to answer my own. Not this barrage that only rises with no falls, counter beats the only punctuation in a song with no rhythm.

I want to tell the medics this because I am embarrassed of my body's song, ashamed of the jarring quality that we all are being forced to endure in such a small space. But I don't get the chance. I'm whisked out of the squad and into a hospital, the sirens cut out to be replaced by my mother's sobs as she exits the front of the squad. I get a single moment of darkness and quiet, a breath in between an inhale where Mom isn't crying, and then the doors of the ER slide open and I'm plunged headfirst into sterile light and tightly controlled voices.

Mom disappears behind doors that my gurney crashes through, a lady wearing scrubs with kittens all over them forcing her back through when she tries to follow. The kittens are seriously misleading because the woman has a voice of steel and her biceps nearly pop the stitching right next to a fuzzy calico. I'm thinking about that sweet little face with a tear right down the middle of it when I realize I probably don't look much different right now.

"How bad?" I ask.

Jones glances down at me, a drop of sweat on her nose. She's running, the fluorescents flashing by above as I try to get someone to answer me. The medics are joined by people from the hospital, more hands are on me, new voices creating crisscrossing paths over my body as words are exchanged, most of them unintelligible.

"My face. How bad?"

"Don't worry about that right now, sweetheart," one of the women says, which as terms of affection go is a terrible choice in my situation. We come to a sudden halt that makes me woozy and a quarter turn that sends my head spinning even after the gurney stops moving, and then we're in an elevator being subjected to a truly abysmal rendition of Beethoven.

"I can't die—"

"You're not going to," Jones interrupts me.

"—listening to this music," I finish. "It's unbearable."

"That's the spirit, keep fighting," Faber says, but I see Jones glance over at him, eyebrows slightly pinched like maybe her internal bitch meter just pinged. It seems my so-called friends would agree with her, so maybe she's reading me right.

I can still hear Lilly's and Brooke's voices following me as I went down, tree branches snapping around me, the ground rising up—the only thing that's truly welcomed me in years. I covered the space in between me and it more quickly than any that's ever existed between myself and my friends, or my parents.

"I'm not a very nice person sometimes," I tell Jones, as the elevator moves upward. Whatever has broken inside seems to be leaking truth, words I've clamped my mouth shut over for years. I feel the dropping of my stomach, and hope that it's the movement causing it and not the organ actually falling out of me.

"Nobody's perfect," she says, but her eyes are on the bank of buttons, the light climbing as we ascend.

"I was close," I tell her. "Until now." I point to the flap of skin hanging against the side of my face.

"Sense of humor, that'll help pull you through," Faber says, but I ignore him. Everything he says ends with an upbeat, like he's making a car commercial.

"It's not me though," I go on, still trying to catch Jones's eye. "Whenever I'm not a nice person, or if I make a bad choice. That's my sister."

"Uh-huh," she says, and stabs a button as if that will make the elevator go faster.

"Are you in much pain?" Faber asks.

I don't answer him, because I am in pain. Rather tremendous pain, if I'm being honest. I'm breathing, but never enough, like a balloon that only fills halfway and then ejects everything in a halfhearted wheeze. My lungs feel like a cheap party favor, my head the piñata that took the brunt of the hit, my heart the soundtrack that keeps skipping.

The only thing still working well is my mind, and whatever part of the body willpower is located in. I won't lose consciousness again, won't switch off and let others discover all the hideous things inside of me. I take a deep breath and try to focus, causing a bubbling noise from my side.

The elevator doors open, and we're greeted by a wall of people in white, and finally, some consistency. There's a deep *thwump-thwump* coming from somewhere, methodical and perfect. I relax as it fills my ears, my chest cavity, the hole where my sister's apology should be, still vacant. Voices are lost, like mutterings in another room that are easily dismissed. I've left the elevator music and senseless sounds of the ambulance behind me to come to this point, a helicopter on the roof creating the great, deep pulse of sound, a black mechanical heart to lift me into the sky.

I go willingly, some of the people in white climbing in beside me. Jones and Faber are left behind as we lift off, this feeling of weightlessness so different from my fall to the ground. From the corner of my eye I can just see Jones turn to Faber, spinning her index finger next to her ear.

I'll have to try harder. Argue louder. Explain better. Maybe someone has to know me before they can see that I would never do these things; use a boy for sex, throw myself out a window to keep him from leaving, have friends who hate me. Sasha Stone is not that person; Shanna Stone is.

But Shanna has been terribly quiet since we landed, as if the fall knocked her into silence. If she's anything like me at all she's putting together the right words for an apology—or as I like to call it, an explanation. She'll find the right things to say, just enough to make it better without actually humbling herself. And when that happens, we're going to have a long talk about personal safety.

And hopefully punctuation.

I can't hear anything except the rush of wind outside and the constant *thwump* of the blades, but one of the women in white looks down at me and rests a hand on my cheek. I smile at her, even though I know there's blood in my teeth.

I smile because everything is going to be okay.

Shanna will be back.

eighteen

When I wake up things are missing: the branch from my ribs, the hair on the right side of my head, my sister's voice. There are things to take their places: a chest tube, catheter, stitches, and the serious face of a woman sitting by the side of my bed. She doesn't know I'm awake yet, and she's reading a yellow file that's resting on her crossed legs, her nose crunched in concentration and her eyebrows stuck in a permanent worried position.

I'm not wearing the neck brace anymore but I quickly find out that moving my head isn't the best option. My scalp feels stretched tight, as if there wasn't enough skin to make ends meet but they sewed it together anyway. The music of my body is silent, but I can see a heart monitor by my bed, the sonic waves it makes erratic in places.

"Sasha?"

I turn back toward the woman, amending my earlier assessment down to *girl* when I hear her voice. It's hesitant and unsure, with none of the conviction of an adult.

"Yes?" I ask, ignoring the feel of the pillowcase against my bare scalp, shockingly cool.

"I'm Amanda Cargrove, with family services," she explains.

"Oh," I say, closing my eyes. "That's nice and everything but my parents have jobs. I've got insurance. The hospital doesn't need to worry about how all this will be paid for."

I make a small circle with my hand to indicate "all this," an IV trailing in its wake. But even if I could make a big gesture it wouldn't be able to cover everything, the squad, the helicopter, all the worried faces hovering over me that need to be compensated for their time.

I'm probably in a lot of trouble.

Amanda clears her throat. "I'm actually with mental health services," she says.

"Oh," I say again, but nothing else follows.

"Would you like to tell me about what was going on right before your accident?"

No, I would not like to tell her about the boy I was meeting who is not the boy I am dating, or the friends who called me a bad word. I would not like to tell her about the panic in my chest at the thought of Isaac leaving, angry with me, or the sound of glass breaking when it connected with my skull. I would not like to tell her about losing first chair and who knows what else in the small period of time it took for me to fall twenty feet.

I would not like to tell her these things, so I say nothing and stare at the blank gray screen of the TV mounted directly across from my bed. I can see myself reflected there, badly. I'm amorphous, a vague lump with no clear outlines of where I begin and end. I don't know how much of that is because of the surface, or because that's what I really look like right now.

Amanda flips over a piece of paper. "Your first responders said that you fell out a window. Can you tell me if that's true?"

"Are you even supposed to be talking to me?" I ask her, the first synapses waking up inside my head to fire in irritation. "I'm a minor."

"I have permission from your parents to be here," Amanda says. "They're very worried about you, Sasha."

"Where is here?" I ask, glancing around the room again. I appear to have it to myself, which is a blessing. I don't think I could stand listening to someone else's noises with only a length of curtain in between us.

"You're in the trauma ward at Stillwell Hospital," she says. "Life flight brought you here from county. They didn't have the necessary equipment to—"

"Put me back together again?"

Amanda only looks away from me, back down at the file balanced on her knee. She's even blushing a little, like maybe she shouldn't have said that.

"How old are you?" I ask her.

"Twenty-two," she says, as if the gulf between seventeen and twenty-two is a vast thing I can't possibly comprehend.

"Did you always want to be a social worker?" I ask.

"We really should be talking about you instead," she says, eyes still on the papers as if they might provide a question for her to blurt before I come up with another one.

"What kind of a degree do you have? Where did you go to school? How long does it take to get certified in what you do?"

I know the answers because it's something Lilly considered. They are: associate's, community college, and not long. Someone with that kind of pedigree is not going to sit upright while I'm on my back and grill me about my personal choices.

Amanda clears her throat, going for a do-over. "Your parents know I'm speaking with you, and they're very concerned about your fall."

She says *fall* like I'm supposed to correct her.

Someone who is being evasive would concoct a story of how it happened, impossibly, while brushing their hair, tripping on piled clothes, or while performing some complicated dance move that built up speed right before meeting resistance. But I'm not a liar, and I'm not ashamed of what I did.

Because I didn't do it.

"I didn't fall out the window; I jumped," I say, watching as her pen scratches across the file still on her knee, the writing a sloppy mess she'll have to type up later. I could offer her the little table on wheels by my bedside, meant to hold nothing more substantial than cups of Jell-O. But I don't.

There's a knock on the door so tentative it has to be a nurse and not a doctor. Amanda looks to me for approval before giving permission for her to enter. This nurse is wearing scrubs with superheroes all over them, a mix of DC and Marvel that would have Heath declaring blasphemy if I didn't shoot him a death glare first. He and his friends have been banned from geek philosophy in my presence.

There's a second stab in my middle, like the tree branch might have scraped across organs before they took it out, microscopic cells rebuilding what Mother Nature damaged in my fall from grace.

"Are you sure that I'm okay?" I ask the nurse, her

mouth opening in no doubt what was going to be an obvious statement like, "Look who's awake," as if she or Amanda have narcolepsy and were surprised to find themselves conscious.

Instead of answering, the nurse glances to Amanda for guidance. To her credit there's no good way to handle that question. I have more things inside of me right now than the last time Isaac came over, and by the feel of it, my right ear is about half an inch higher than my left. Also the only person who has entered my room so far is a mental health worker so the safe answer probably is that no, she's not sure I'm okay. But you don't just say that to someone.

You also don't just call people female dogs, but I'll bring that up with the interested parties later.

"How do you mean, Sasha?" Amanda asks, sparing the nurse.

I wave the question away, suddenly tired. My head feels like a half-full water balloon, the kind you can squeeze really hard on one side but the other bulges out, ready to burst. I can open only one eye, the other swollen and heavy, my pulse a distinct beat coursing through puffy flesh. The nurse smiles at me and hooks a bag of something clear into my IV.

"For the pain," she says.

Pain. It was an echo when I woke up, a voice already

spent in an empty room. But it's been growing while I talked to Amanda. I settle into my pillow as my vision grows fuzzy, noticing the tiny professional frown on her face when the nurse glances at my heart monitor.

"What——" I begin.

"I need you to rate your pain on a scale of zero to ten," she says, pulling a rectangle of cardboard from the plastic holder at the foot of my bed.

The diagram she's holding shows a series of faces, the one on the far left the ubiquitous happy face seen on everything from denim jackets to bumper stickers. His smile flattens as the faces evolve on their journey to the right, heating from a mellow orange to a burning red, mouth a wide O of pain, eyes squeezed shut like bird tracks in the snow. I can't help but notice that the red face with the number ten underneath it has a worn spot on its cheek from years of people touching it, maybe mistaking it for a cherry scratch and sniff.

"Five," I say blithely, settling on the one that seems as if it would smell like peaches. That face is mildly concerned, but it could be distracted from its pain by decent conversation or maybe some chamber music. It has no bearing whatsoever on how I actually feel. Zero is Isaac under the trees and ten is a bad name from my friends, in stereo. But they don't have that diagram here.

The nurse makes a note in her chart, and Amanda

in hers. "We'll do this again in about ten minutes to see how you're reacting to your pain meds and adjust accordingly," the nurse says.

But I'm already reacting, sliding down the irritation scale of red to the sunny haze of yellow, ten to zero in sixty seconds, a C minor scale even though it only has eight notes and this is definitely a double-digit process. I'm at a negative two on the pain scale and sliding into the black when I remember Amanda is still in the room, and maybe she's okay.

"I'm high as fuck," I tell her.

I smile and falter on the last step into unconsciousness, until I wonder why I haven't seen my parents yet.

Or Heath.

Or Isaac.

Or Brooke.

Or Lilly.

Or if there's anybody left who gives a shit.

A crack of light in the darkness, the creak of hinges.

I'm awake, what should be the monotonous tones of my heart monitor nearly on tempo but not quite. It will never be fully black in this room, I realize. Too many machines, shiny with reflective surfaces. Too many lights blinking. Red. Green. Orange. Stop. Go. Slow. The light widens, a form slipping through.

"Mom?"

Funny that I know this from her shadow, a less dark patch in the room, vague yet familiar.

"Shh . . . ," she whispers, moving toward my bed. "I thought you'd still be asleep."

It feels like I might be. My tongue is as heavy as my eyelids, but they're all pulling toward a central point—it stuck to the roof of my mouth, then sliding inexorably down.

"Slept enough," I say, managing to flick one finger toward the windows. It'll never be dark out there either, I suppose. Headlights. Lamplights. Streetlights. Halogen. Fluorescent. Radiating.

"How are you feeling?" Mom asks, flipping on the lights. She drags a chair to my bedside, its legs scraping on the floor. I close my eyes against the sound, and my head tilts to the side, tiny pinpricks of hair already growing back in.

I want my hair back. I want my scalp in the right place and my eyes both able to open all the way. I want there to be something in my middle instead of nothing, a blank cavity that only negative things swell from. I want there to be an easy answer like when I was a kid: a Band-Aid, some ice cream. I want to cry.

That's how I'm feeling.

So I just do, because I can now. My mom is here, and

somehow that makes me feel safe and terrified at the same time. Safe enough to cry but terrified I won't be able to stop. Tears slide out from under my swollen eyelid, the pressure of more liquid adding a new vibration to the constant thumping in my head, the barometer of the pressure inside of Sasha Stone rising even higher.

"Honey, honey, honey," Mom says, pressing as close as she can to me without getting hands and arms and fingers tangled in all my cords. I cry into the crook of her arm, my pulse a hot thing in my face, pressed against the coolness of her skin.

I finally pull back, dried out, lips cracked and tongue still sticking to everything inside my mouth as if it were flypaper. As I do, there's a new sound, like packing tape being peeled off the roll.

This new sound came from me.

"Whoops," Mom says as one of my machines begins to beep hysterically. She reaches down the front of my shirt as if it were the most normal thing in the world, and presses a sticky pad back in place, covering an irritated patch of skin where it had been before.

"What?" I look down at my chest, fascinated. I'm dotted with them, pale gray pads with wires that spool down my front to crawl out from under my gown, winding their way around each other back up to the heart monitor.

"And Dad always says I'm disconnected," I joke, and it's Mom's turn to cry. She does it quietly, holding my hand while I take inventory now that I'm fully conscious.

There's a tube in my nose, an IV in the top of my left hand, and while the heart monitors on my chest aren't exactly in me, they're definitely violating my privacy.

"Can I have a mirror?" I ask Mom. She wipes away her last tear using my hospital gown, and shakes her head.

"Not yet."

"That bad?"

"Yeah it's . . . it's pretty bad, Sasha."

"The nurse said she'd be back in ten minutes to check my reaction to the pain meds," I tell Mom.

"You had a reaction, all right," Mom says, smiling a little. "I didn't think you knew some of those words."

"Oh . . . was it . . ." I try to remember, but those moments must be kept somewhere else, stored away for Shanna. "Was I bad?"

Mom waves away whatever potty mouth I grew while medicated. "It doesn't matter, honey. You were out cold by the time the nurse got back. Dad and I were here, and that girl from the county . . ." She fades out, like someone popped a mute in her horn.

"The social worker," I finish for her. "Amanda."

"The medics called her in because they thought

you . . ." She doesn't finish, eyes searching my face like maybe I'll volunteer a word that isn't *suicide*, something much closer to the sane, well-adjusted daughter she thought she had.

I don't say anything.

"We'll get you a real therapist, honey. Someone older, with more experience."

I think about Amanda and her ink-stained pants, the little sore in the corner of her mouth where she poked her tongue while she was thinking. Then I think of a lined face, a wood-paneled office with rubber plants and leather-bound books. A place where I'm not in charge and can't outwit anyone.

"I want Amanda," I say.

"But, Sasha, she's barely an adult herself. She's not qualified to—to—"

"To fix me?" Mom drops her gaze, her thumbnail sliding under mine as if I were still a child needing someone to clean them.

"I thought you believed me about Shanna," I say, watching as she rolls a bit of dirt out from under the nail, a piece of our yard that I managed to bring with me here to this forever-lit, sterile place. "I don't need fixing. There's nothing wrong with me, Mom," I say, my voice rising.

"Sasha, please," Mom shushes, glancing toward the

door. "If the nurses think I'm upsetting you they won't let me stay."

"She's here, Mom," I say, pulling my hand away from her and reaching for the heart monitor. "I'll show you."

I find the time stamp, figure out the controls and scroll backward to where I was talking with Amanda.

"There," I say, stabbing a finger at the blip on the screen, a valley out of concert with the rest of the terrain. "Shanna's right there."

Mom takes a deep breath, eyes closed. "No, honey," she says finally, letting the words out with the exhale. "The doctor said it's called dilated cardiomyopathy."

nineteen

I. Things I Know

   A. dilated cardiomyopathy: *a heart muscle disease in which the left ventricle stretches too thin and cannot pump blood properly*

      1. *Symptoms*

        a. Fatigue (Checkmark)

        b. Shortness of breath (Checkmark)

        c. Reduced ability to exercise (Band camp is over, so checkmark.)

        d. Swelling in your legs, feet, or abdomen (Checkmark)

      2. *Complications*

        a. Heart failure (Some would argue that happened already.)

        b. Regurgitation: blood flows backward into the heart

when the ventricle fails to expel it (so your heart throws up back into itself)

c. *Edema: fluid buildup (only after Isaac visits, ha-ha)*

d. *Arrhythmia: abnormal heart rhythm (So, like the sixth-grade band, but in my chest cavity)*

e. *Cardiac arrest: your heart suddenly stops beating (So . . . dead)*

f. *Blood clots: can form inside left ventricle, if they should enter the bloodstream may cause stroke, heart attack, or damage to other organs (Yes, this is what an embolism is. By my count, second mention of sudden death.)*

II. *Things I Don't Know*

    A. *What Shanna has to say about all this*

Shanna has been silent since the diagnosis. Dad follows her lead, his jaw wired shut as I sit in between him and Mom, one facial muscle trembling as if it doesn't quite have the strength necessary to do its job—much like my left ventricle. We've faced multiple doctors and specialists in this way in the week following my accident.

Mom is his polar opposite. She asks questions, repeats the answers, and has even begun to take notes as the doctors talk about treatments, tests, therapies, transplants. When she asked for my input I told her I'd noticed everything starts with a *T*. I don't know what else to say. I am of no use in this situation that exists only because I have failed at something.

I take tests, sit, stand, walk on treadmills, raise my arms. Things are inserted and removed, radiation passes through my body with X-rays, and blood leaves in little tubes. But lots of little tubes add up, and I spend most of my time resting; the fatigue that I had noticed earlier seems to have tripled. Whether because there's a reason for it now, or because it's actually worse, I don't know.

As soon as my chest tube and catheter are out I go to the bathroom on my own, making the trip the second Mom and Dad say good night and close the door behind them. My IV is still in, so I have to take the tree along, little bags of liquid that follow me as I go to empty a different bag of liquid that's inside.

Nobody looks good under fluorescents, and bathroom tiles are probably the worst background for anyone other than a police lineup, so I avoid looking in the mirror as much as possible. I suppose I look like death. True death, not just the expression.

Judging from the initial reactions of everyone who walks into my hospital room I'm assuming if I'd died it would be a closed casket. I can feel hair growing back in on the side of my head that was shaved. It will be a while before it's long enough to cover the fault line I can feel running from the middle of my forehead to behind my right ear. I touched the stitches briefly once, fingers exploring in the privacy of my room. The stitches holding my face together are close and thick, and I imagine the curvature of the wound makes my head look like a baseball.

I hold my hand up like a blinder so I'm not tempted to glance in the mirror as I use the bathroom. I run my finger over the rest of the wounds on my face, counting the stitches as if they might have changed since last time. Six trace my left jawline, three seem to be attaching my earlobe, and I've glimpsed at least eight curving from above my collarbone to disappear behind my back. It could go all the way down my spine like a zipper, for all I know. The wound in my side I've seen plenty, every time my shirt was lifted so that people could listen to my heart, my lungs, my failure to operate correctly.

It burns when I pee, the catheter leaving behind a trail of swollen tissue. I go back to my bed, careful not to tangle my IV in anything as I slide under the sheets and push buttons until I have the bed the way I want it. The lights are off, and I can just see the outline of myself in the black reflection of the windows. No details. No stitches. Just a girl, with holes where her eyes and mouth are.

"Shanna?" I say quietly, but she remains voiceless

without pen and paper, or a phone.

And maybe it's easier for her that way, not having to own up to the reality of the situation. I may have killed her, but she'll be responsible for both our deaths when they come, her brag of a stronger heart clearly being in error. We'll have plenty to talk about once I find a way for us to communicate again.

I look at my heart monitor, the irregularities frighteningly obvious.

I better hurry.

Everything has fallen away.

I ask Mom if she's been in touch with my teachers about makeup work. She puts down a medical manual about the structure of the heart and pats my hand.

"Don't worry about that right now."

I look at Dad, but he's studying the pain chart my nurse keeps referring to, his own mouth in a flat line that reflects the number four face.

"What about Oberlin?" I push. Mom waves her hand like my further education is a fat housefly with an errant flight pattern that might land in her hair.

I realize that it might be more fitting to be looking at caskets than curriculum, but my goals have faded drastically in a short amount of time. A week ago I was creating a spreadsheet of courses that I could take in order to get my bachelor's in three years. Now I'm focused on my heart continuing to beat.

Shanna's heart.

It's her faulty heart impeding everything, fluttering into helplessness right when I need it most and fast-tracked to flare out long before my mind. All the work I've done, every breath my lungs forced into a clarinet, every note my fingers mapped, every piece my brain has memorized is useless without a heart to fuel them. I'm getting angry and Shanna chides me for it, the monitor at my side emitting a bleep.

Mom and Dad both tense, eyes going from me to the monitor, unable to read either one.

"I'm fine," I tell them. "Shanna just doesn't like my train of thought."

They exchange a glance.

"What?" I demand.

"Honey—" Mom begins, but I cut her off with a raised hand. She's a nice person, which means she's really terrible at delivering bad news, all the candy-coating making you not notice the rotten center of the words coming out of her mouth. Dad has his uses, the deep practicality I inherited making even bitter truth a quick process.

"So what is it?" I ask him.

"The doctors are concerned that your heart condition

is urgent enough for you to need a transplant," he says.

My hands go up to my chest in reflex, fingers curling into small fists. "But that would mean Shanna—"

"Shhhhh," Mom hisses at me, and gets up to close the door to my room. "Don't."

"Sasha," Dad says carefully, using the same tone I've heard over the phone with people who made rather large income tax return errors. "You probably won't last long without a heart transplant, and there are certain conditions you have to fulfill in order to be eligible for a donor organ."

"You have to be healthy—other than your heart, of course," Mom pipes up.

"Check," I say, hands still covering my chest where I can feel my sister beating erratically, her tempo lost.

"You can't abuse alcohol or drugs," Dad says, avoiding my eyes.

"I don't," I say. "What? I don't!" I insist when I see Mom frowning at the floor like maybe it had suggested otherwise.

"The last thing . . . honey," she says. "You have to be mentally sound."

"Check," I repeat, daring them to contradict me.

They share another look before Dad clears his throat.

"There's some concern about how you came to fall out the window," he says. "But your mother and I talked, and we think we've managed to convince the doctors that it was an accident."

"Okay," I say, deciding not to tell him I already informed Amanda otherwise.

"It also means you can't talk about what you think is going on with your heart," Mom says. "To anyone."

"I said something to the medics," I admit.

Dad shrugs. "You were in shock."

Mom nods in complete agreement. "If they suspect you're not mentally competent, you won't get a transplant and—"

"And I die," I finish for her. "And if I do get a transplant, Shanna dies." As do nights sitting on trestle bridges, and moonlit meetings with Isaac. Will I even have the memories of what we did together, if Shanna goes?

Mom sighs, looks to Dad for help.

"See that, right there?" He points at me, as if there's an incriminating word bubble hanging over my head. "You can't do that."

"I've been doing some reading. . . ." Mom rustles in a bag at her side, pulling out some pages covered in her handwriting. I notice it's a different bag than the one she put the heart structure brochure in, which makes me wonder if this is going to be like my childhood: music lesson bag, pool bag, a briefly used karate bag. Except now one has copies of my X-rays and the other a well-thumbed *Diagnostic Stastistical Manual*.

"Delusional disorder," she begins, touching the tips of her fingers to the paper to following along, "is one of the less common psychotic dis—"

"Psychotic?" I yell just as a nurse sticks her head in my room.

"How are we feeling today?" she asks.

I've always hated using plural pronouns to reference a single person. It feels especially irritating right now since it might actually be accurate, even if I can't convince anyone else of that fact.

"Psychotic," I answer, repeating myself.

The nurse smiles as if I'd said *just fine* and pulls my covers back. "Let's see about that echocardiogram," she says, as if we were all curious about it in the first place.

Dad clears his throat and leaves the room. Every time I have to get out of bed there's a juggling of priorities where I have to decide whether to use my hands to keep my gown from flapping open in the back or stop all my cords from getting tangled in the bedrails. When Mom and Dad traverse the halls with me to different areas of the hospital for testing, I look like a jellyfish that has caught medical equipment and two confused adults in her tentacles.

Dad displays his solidarity by making the trip with

us down to the lab, but exits again when the front of my gown is unceremoniously untied by a guy who is less interested in my body than even Heath ever was. His clinical eye and glancing touch is so much like my boyfriend's that I feel a prickle in my eyes, unshed tears gathering.

I don't even know if I can still call Heath my boyfriend, since I've had zero contact with the outside world. My phone is presumably in pieces on my bedroom floor, shiny reflective plastic waiting to stab into the soft sole of my foot when I get home.

The sonographer tells me the gel will feel cold, then squirts it right onto my boob. It makes an indecent noise and I stifle a giggle as he puts the probe next to my skin. Shanna shows up on the screen, a thumping mass of black, white, and gray. Mom leans in, studying the image as if her glancing experience with cardiac medicine has enabled her to understand what she's looking at.

"Mom, can I get a new phone?" I ask.

She looks up, surprised. I must look pathetic as hell right now, hospital gown gaped open, a stranger putting things on places nothing unnatural should be. It's a good time to ask.

"Is that smart?"

I drop my eyes. We haven't talked about the why of

my launching myself through the window. It's taken a backseat to figuring out how we're going to keep me alive long enough to explain it.

"I'll talk to your father. And maybe that social worker."

"Amanda."

I nod as if grateful, but she just put two human hurdles in between me and phone ownership. "What about my laptop?"

Mom's already shaking her head, but I keep talking. "I've got a lot of ebooks on it, Mom. I need something to read other than two-year-old issues of *Seventeen*."

She bites her lip, fading against my argument because what kind of mother denies her terminally ill daughter reading material?

"You can take the internet applications off it," I keep going. "I won't even be able to use email."

"I'll think about it," Mom says, just as the sonographer starts lacing up my gown, our oddly intimate and impersonal encounter at an end.

"Reading material!"

Mom's chirpy greeting first thing in the morning matches some of the beeps from my bedside, a grating soprano of cheer that borders on panic. I toss aside a copy of *People* that's three months out of date.

"Finally," I say, hands out for my laptop. Instead I get a brochure with a smiling Asian kid on the front and a helpful-looking white doctor in the background. *The Children's Cardiac Center* is written across the top, supposedly made endearing by primary colors and crayon print.

"What is this?" I ask as Dad comes in carrying a box of granola bars that I asked for.

Mom sits down next to me, putting her bags down on either side of her chair. I notice she always keeps the one that holds her notes about mental disorders on the far side where I can't reach.

"It's a program from the children's hospital," she explains. "It's a really nice place, honey. You'd have your own room and—"

"I have my own room," I interrupt. "It's at home."

Mom looks to Dad to deliver the bad news, her optimistic vocabulary not able to compute what comes next.

"You're not going to be able to go home," he says, leaning back against the wall. "Your heart rhythms haven't been stable on the monitor and your blood pressure has been barely in the normal range. You're going to need to be under constant care until—"

He breaks off so abruptly that I feel a spike of fear. "Until what? I die?"

"No, honey." Mom's hand shoots out, fingers on my

wrist as if the simple act of feeling my pulse will keep those words at bay. "Until we're able to find you a transplant."

She says it as if search and rescue is out looking for a heart that may have been misplaced, not that we're waiting for someone else to die so that I can live.

"How did I go from fine to needing a new heart?"

"You weren't fine," Dad says. "This . . . this . . ."

"Dilated cardiomyopathy," Mom supplies.

"It's always been there," he goes on, not even attempting the pronunciation. "Your mom said you passed out the other day in the living room and that you've been sleeping a lot."

I don't point out that he's only listing things Mom has told him, nothing he's witnessed himself. I wonder how loudly Mom had to scream to call the ambulance in order to get past his earplugs.

"Your dad is right," Mom says, her hand tightening on my wrist. "The signs were there, we just didn't know what they were pointing to. So in a way, it's a good thing that—"

"Patricia," Dad warns, his voice tight.

"Well, maybe it is," Mom shoots back. "Otherwise we might not have known until she . . . she . . ."

"Until I had an embolism or massive heart failure." Leave it to Mom to find the silver lining of me propelling myself outdoors through plate glass.

"We met with a heart specialist yesterday," she goes on. "The team decided it would be best for you to be under constant care for your heart in the cardiac center. They're concerned about the conditions surrounding your fall from the window but are willing to admit you to the center as long as you have regular visits from a mental health specialist. I told the team that you and Amanda had really hit it off."

The team. I picture a line of cheerleaders, some with hearts next to the deep-V neckline of the uniform, some with brains. Me and Amanda really "hitting it off" while shaking pom-poms. Rah-rah. Go team.

I flip open the brochure to see a shiny reception area with fresh flowers and a smiling woman waiting to check me in. On the top of the page it reads, *Welcome*, not *Abandon All Hope, Ye Who Enter Here*. I bet if I set this next to a brochure for an indoor water park there wouldn't be much difference. All the language is comforting, using words like *care*, *comfort*, and *convenience*. Nowhere do I see *surgery*, *scalpel*, or *sedative*.

There aren't pictures of crash carts or red alarm lights going off, there's no blood spatter on these gowns, or exposed organs. Everything that happens in this place for the dying looks like a good time, closely watched over by smiling people who only want me to enjoy myself.

"So I live there?"

"Yes," Mom says. "There are plenty of kids your age

there," she adds as I glance at a shot of toddlers in a finger-painting class. None of them have IVs in their arms or machines attached to them.

"You'll be able to keep up with your schoolwork, too," Mom goes on. "There are online classes you can take so you'll graduate on time, or they can arrange for tutors on site if you'd like."

I've gone from valedictorian to hoping to graduate on time. I flip to the back of the brochure, which has driving directions and a map of their campus, probably the only one I'll ever see.

"What do you think, honey?" Mom asks, her hand on mine once again. "It looks nice, doesn't it?"

The brick facade of the cardiac center does indeed look nice, very much like an admissions center for a college. But I'm willing to bet there are panels with hidden defibrillators everywhere, and that all the doorways are wide enough to admit wheelchairs. I put the brochure down, resting beside my knee.

"I don't understand how this happened," I say.

Dad shifts against the wall, his eyes on the ground. "It happened because of me," he says.

twenty

I. Things I Know

    A. 30 percent of dilated cardiomyopathy patients inherited their disease from a parent.

    B. Mine came from Dad.

        1. He didn't know he had it, and only found out after both he and Mom were tested to determine the origin of mine. Now Mom has two silver linings to be thankful for.

        2. He'd been ignoring his own symptoms for years, attributing them to stress and not wanting to upset Mom.

        3. His isn't as bad as mine and will be treated with a pacemaker.

II. Things I Don't Know

    A. How many silver linings it takes to bring the whole cloud
      crashing down

I wait until Mom and Dad are gone to plug in my lap-top, it being the consolation prize for learning I won't be going home. As promised, they'd taken all the inter-net browsers off it, but they don't know the first thing about messaging services. I pull up the one I use most often, weighing the pros and cons about who I should reach out to. I choose Brooke, because she's online at the moment, and settle for something simple to announce my continued presence among the living.

    Hey.

    Holy shit that really u Sasha?

    Really me. Still in the hospital.

    I won't ask if ur ok b/c I know ur not but I am so so so sorry
      about what we said. U don't even know.

I didn't throw myself out the window because of my friends, but if Brooke wants to keep apologizing for it, I'm going to let her. I take a pic of my busted face with the webcam, closing my eyes. I send it to her without a caption.

    FUCK

I rest my fingers for a little bit so that she can stare at what's left of me before I let her off the hook.

You would love it here. Lots of stitches and open wounds.

Ha ha. Really Sash we're so sorry, we set up a thing at school
     and people have been giving money.

I glance at the cardiac center pamphlet. It's going to
take more than a bunch of kids giving up their lunch
change to even make a dent in that bill, insurance or not.

Isaac stopped me in the hall and gave me some money and
     it smelled like cigarettes and is probably from drugs but
     whatever. I washed it and put it in the jar.

Isaac's name in black and white sends a jolt through
my system, a tiny stutter on my heart monitor.

That's nice of you. Thanks.

Np. I feel really bad.

Not your fault.

Can I call u?

Don't have my phone.

When are you coming home?

My heart stumbles through another beat, not liking
the answer any more than I do.

**I'm not. I have to go to live in this cardiac center where
     they can keep an eye on me until a transplant becomes
     available.**

That's how the doctor had put it to me when we
talked earlier, after Mom and Dad broke the news to me
about my new living arrangements. Transplanted hearts
don't come into use because of a traumatic accident

that ended someone else's life; they *become available*, like a hotel room when someone else checks out. There's a whole language used here that I have to get used to, words that they use so that it never sounds like you're weighing one life against another.

Cardiac center???? Transplant????!?!? WTF??????

They found out I have a heart condition and I need a new one.

There's a long pause before she answers me, and I imagine Brooke composing more apologies. What I get is:

Do they let u keep the old one & can I see it?

It's so Brooke that I laugh, and my breathing tube pops out of my nose. I leave it lying on my chest, a cool whiff of oxygen hitting my chin.

I don't think so, but if they do it's all yours.

She answers with a smiley face and a thumbs-up.

Do you still have your old phone?

Yeah. Why?

I need you to do me a favor.

After talking to Brooke I open up a blank document and stare at it for a few minutes, not knowing how to start the conversation. I settle for something simple, and close the laptop. It whirs at me as I settle into bed, rolling onto my side so that my stitches are faceup, the prickly new hairs of my scalp not rubbing against the pillowcase. I can just see my outline in the window, a white smear with black holes where my eyes and mouth belong. I reach toward myself, the hand coming into detail, the IV cord trailing behind.

"I'll talk to you in the morning," I say, and drift off to sleep.

Are you still there?

I am (her)e. S-(or)-ry. -Am [?-

Not funny.

Prog(no-sis) = Not good.

You could have killed us both.

(you too?)K my life, st(ill) had [non]e. 1 + 1 = 0 Two lives, n/ever/ lived.

Why do I even try to talk to you?

I listen.

"Welcome to the cardiac center."

The woman at the front desk isn't as pretty as the one

in the brochure, but given that none of the children looked ill and all the staff had perfect teeth, I assumed they were models anyway. This woman's teeth aren't that great, but she smiles like she means it, so she either is truly happy to greet me, or there's a pull string in her back.

"Thank you," Mom says, dropping one of my bags to the floor with a huff. There's a fine sheen of sweat on her upper lip. It must be exhausting carrying around all my issues.

My scalp is still prickling from a brush with the sun, warm fingers touching parts of my skin that have never felt its rays. I hold on to the last gasp of fresh air that I have inside me, knowing that once it's expelled all I'm pulling in is recycled exhales of sick people made pleasantly cool by air-conditioning. I don't know what I'm breathing in, but I know I'm letting out my last taste of the outside world. It leaves me in a rush and I feel its departure like an energy drain.

I'm just like them now. And I don't even mean the people in the pamphlet, because they clearly did their photo shoot and promptly vacated. The girl who wanders through reception has a nurse on each arm and an IV tree so loaded with bags it probably weighs more than she does. She puts each foot in front of the other with grim determination, even though the best thing she's possibly headed toward is her favorite flavor of Jell-O.

I get an ID bracelet with my name, birthdate, and blood type neatly printed. The letters that make up my name have never looked so dark, fresh toner bleeding onto the whiteness of the paper. I am Sasha Stone, a name that used to mean something, a girl who got what she wanted, a force to be reckoned with. As the pneumatic doors shut behind me and Mom tells the receptionist how nice she thinks it is that I can wear my own clothes at the center I become simply:

STONE, SASHA (O NEG)

This is all that matters now, a quick identification for when I finally have that embolism, or complete cardiac failure.

"I can't do this," I say, staring straight ahead at the duffel bag Dad has flung over his shoulder. It's packed to bursting with all the clothes they thought I could use, loose-fitting, for easier access to all the parts that might need to be poked, punctured, or simply torn open to get everything working again should all systems fail.

"You have to, honey," Mom says tightly through her teeth, as if I might be embarrassing her.

But I don't have to, that's the thing. I thought it through a few nights ago, weighing the pros and cons of asking Mom and Dad to just take me home and let me die. Maybe I could go out while blowing on the high end of a Handel, my heart exploding at the perfect time.

Maybe I could die under the pines, Isaac's hair swaying in my face and the moonlight surrounding us as everything I had in me left in a breath. Maybe I could have an embolism sitting right in front of my computer, a sudden, stone-cold death for my friends to witness.

I open my mouth to make the suggestion, and the receptionist pops a party favor into it, a ridiculous paper thing that creates something north of an F sharp and then splits down the middle to die, making a fart noise. It's so ludicrous I start laughing, and Mom squeezes my hand.

"Your room is this way, Sasha," the receptionist says, like she's the concierge somewhere really expensive. On second thought, I guess that's exactly what she is. We walk down the hall, me now wearing a paper tiara that reads "WELCOME" in turquoise, Dad carrying a balloon bouquet that no one ordered and probably cost more than we want to know.

"Karen." The receptionist nods at a nurse coming our direction. "I want you to meet Sasha, our newest resident."

"Hello, Sasha," Karen says, and comes in for a hug without asking. Luckily someone opens up a door and my balloons get caught up in a cross draft, a wall of rubber and helium protecting me from overenthusiastic friendliness.

"Hi," I say, giving her a nod and keeping the balloons between us. She gets the point and settles for nodding back.

"You're going to be very comfortable here," Karen says, and I wonder if that's the highest thing I can aspire to now. Dying in comfort. "Your room is right down this wing with the other girls your age."

She motions toward a corridor painted sky blue, and we all head that direction, a funeral procession missing the coffin. I glance into the other rooms as we pass, but I only see a patient in one of them, lying on her side, back to the hallway, arms curled protectively around herself.

My room is 211 and I pause in front of it, noticing the scratch marks where the name placard underneath has been changed many, many times. Did this room open up for me because someone got better, or worse?

"This is nice, isn't it?" Mom waltzes past me to push open the curtains, the outside light flooding what I have to admit is, in fact, a pretty nice room. They've gone out of their way to make it look more like a hotel and less like a hospital. I have a sofa and a dresser to put clothes in. The sheets on the bed are extra long so that they touch the floor on both sides of the mattress, which makes it look luxurious but will also hide all the cords attached to me. Finally, the TV isn't mounted on the ceiling, which instantly makes any room feel institutionalized.

"Yeah, not bad," I have to agree.

Dad plops onto the sofa. "Better than at home," he declares. And he would know, since Mom put him on it the night after I threw dinner at the wall.

I find the most important thing first—an electrical outlet—and get my laptop hooked in immediately. Mom busies herself putting away my clothes, and I take my little bag of toiletries into the bathroom, where the decorator didn't try as hard. I guess there's no real way to dress up handicap rails, but there's something stark about the frank admission in this room that I might not be able to stand up and sit down without assistance.

There's also a phone right beside the toilet.

I think I'd rather die than call for help with my pants around my ankles.

I go back out to the bedroom to find Mom and Dad looking helpless. All my things are put away, a framed picture of them from the last time they really seemed to like each other—about ten years ago—is sitting next to the TV. With my clothes out of evidence and my laptop tucked under the pillow, there's nothing in here that says this is my room.

Until I hear the sound of the name placard being changed outside.

Now this is where Sasha Stone lives.

And probably where she'll die.

twenty-one

I decide ten minutes into our first session at the cardiac center that I'm going to buy Amanda a T-shirt that reads, *And How Does That Make You Feel?* That's been her response to everything so far, from my reaction to a very permanent-looking plastic nameplate being inserted into the Room 211 slot, to the fact that the password to the WiFi is *hearthealthy.*

"So yesterday was your first day here," she says, her ankle tapping against one leg of the rolling chair she's wheeled into my room for what she calls a sit-down even though I'm lying on the couch. "Have you met the other residents?"

I shake my head, not wanting to go into detail. Mom and Dad left after getting me settled, like this was fourth-grade camp and it would be easier for everyone if they cut the cord fast. Except at camp we were all lost and bewildered, forming groups for safety right away. Here the packs are already in place, and I'm wandering among them with half my face sewn back on, which automatically made them close ranks. I ate my dinner in a corner while pretending to read the menu that informed me how everything I eat here is perfectly calibrated to not make me spontaneously die.

"This must all be coming as quite a shock," Amanda goes on, after making some sort of note on her pad, probably about my antisocial behavior.

"No," I deadpan. "I've been expecting it."

Amanda uncrosses her legs, and I notice that her socks don't match. "Look," she says, "you asked me to be here. The therapist who usually covers ER on-call would have taken one look at you and dished you off to a four-letter without thinking twice."

"Four-letter?"

"Someone with a lot more credentials than me," she explains.

"You're turning into a complicated case, Sasha Stone," Amanda goes on, chewing on the end of her eraser while she looks over her notes. "The night of the accident you told me you jumped out your bedroom window. But I'm seeing in the notes from your cardiac team now you claim it was a fall?"

"It was a fall," I repeat the end of her question as a statement.

She looks up. Her face would be cool and collected if it wasn't for the bit of eraser hanging off her lip. "You sure about that?"

"Yes," I say.

"You wouldn't just be changing your story because a suicide attempt would automatically bar you from receiving a new heart?"

"No."

"Okay," Amanda says agreeably. She looks back down at her notes, which I'm sure is a ploy since there are only a few lines written there.

"So . . ." She turns a page. It's covered in writing; I spot the names *Jones* and *Faber*.

"You talked to the medics?" I blurt. Shanna's sudden charging inside me forces the words out before my brain pulls the plug.

"Yes," Amanda says. "How do you feel about that?"

"Fine," I lie. I'm very good at keeping a straight face under all circumstances, but since my face's new default is definitely un-straight I have no idea if I look confident or not.

"How would you feel if I told you that as an advocate for mental health, I'm not in agreement with the

concept of those with mental issues being denied working organs?" Amanda asks.

I shrug. But I'm listening.

"Sasha," Amanda leans forward, drops her voice. "You
need a new heart; that's the cardiac center's job. My job
is to help *you*, and judging by what you said to the medics, you could use it."

"And whose job is it to monitor you?" I ask. "Someone who wouldn't be cool with you withholding such
information, I bet."

"That's true," Amanda says casually. "But to be honest, I'm not terribly happy with my boss right now.
Apparently your dad made a sizable donation to the ad
campaign for our next tax levy. I get to rearrange my
schedule—and my other patients—to fit yours."

Amanda says *get to* in a tone that informs me she's
not thrilled about it, and I get the feeling Dad probably
made that donation out of my college savings once he
realized hospitals were my better bet in the short term.

"So I was reassigned from a court hearing today for
someone I've been working with closely for six months
to be with Sasha Stone, who answers my questions with
monosyllables and sarcasm."

"Also, I requested you," I say quietly, eyes on the
floor. I'm guessing Amanda hasn't been requested for
anything since eighth-grade lab partners, and I'm right.

Her anger deflates like one of my welcome balloons, now hanging limply around knee height.

"I know," she says, but her voice has a key change, the sharps removed. "Which I would assume means you'd rather talk to me than someone else. So let's do the actual talking part, and skip the bullshit."

I like the way she swears; it reminds me of Brooke.

"Okay," I say.

Amanda resituates herself on the chair and looks back at her notes. I'm expecting her to come at me with something impressive next, a bit of medical terminology or something self-affirming to show me that she knows what she's doing. Instead she snaps her folder shut.

"So what's going on with you?"

It throws me. I had my shoulders squared, ready for a verbal sparring match in the thirty minutes that are left in our session. Instead she asked me a simple question, and while my mind ponders the longer answer, my mouth pops out the simple one.

"I'm dying."

Amanda nods, doing me the courtesy of not insisting along with the rest of the cardiac center that everything will be all right if we put a happy face on.

"A week ago I was alive, and now I'm dying," I go on. "In a few days they're putting a machine in me that will do what my heart won't."

"Yes," Amanda says, flipping her folder again briefly. "An LVAD. It's to assist your left ventricle with pumping."

I feel a small smile, maybe a three on the pain scale of happiness. Amanda smiles back. "What's funny?"

"I was thinking of my friend Brooke and how she accidentally googled *pump king* instead of *pumpkin*. Or maybe it wasn't an accident. It's hard to tell with her."

"Brooke?" Amanda repeats. "She's a friend of yours?"

"Yeah, she's . . . yeah." I think she is, anyway.

"Can you tell me about your sister?"

Amanda's folder is shut, her eyes on mine. But I'm willing to bet she's got every word of my conversation with Jones and Faber memorized.

"I don't know." I say. "Can I?"

"Yes."

I study her, something most people can't take for long. A liar is easy to spot, and lying is easy to do once you've learned how badly others do it. But Amanda isn't a liar, and all the truth that's in me comes out, heading for her like a magnet.

"I did jump out the window," I say. "But it wasn't me, it was my sister."

Amanda opens her folder again, writing perfectly on the lines even though she keeps her eyes on me.

"My sister was upset about something and she felt

that was the most logical reaction. She's very emotion-
ally driven. Her name is Shanna," I tell Amanda, and
spell it out for her. "I absorbed her in the womb and her
heart took the place of mine."

Amanda glances up at me, pen still. "What can you
tell me about Shanna?"

I feel a small shudder deep inside, a life stretching
back into wakefulness at the sound of her name. I hold
Amanda's eyes, waiting for her to contradict me as I
speak.

"She likes sex and boys who will give it to her; she
likes the smell of cigarettes and beer mixed with exhaust
fumes. She likes to be shocking and say lewd things. She
likes cold night air. She likes to have her way."

"Is that the only thing you have in common?" Amanda
asks, head still down. I stare at the uneven part in her
hair, wondering if she knows it looks bad or just doesn't
care.

"Other than an entire body, yes," I say.

"But only the heart is hers?" Amanda's pen scratches
away, the pad of paper shifting up and down on her
knees.

"Yes, only the heart, but sometimes she uses our
whole body for whatever she wants."

"And she wants things like . . ." Amanda's pen hovers,
ready to record my sister's dark leanings with cheap ink

and a yellow legal pad. It feels good to see it there, an inanimate object about to take witness to my truths.

"A boy. Isaac."

"Isaac," Amanda repeats, tongue sticking out of the side of her mouth while she writes.

"He's why she jumped," I explain. "They got into a fight. I guess. Kind of. He wanted something more from me—her—than I was looking for with him. And then we—*I*—sent him a nasty text while he was waiting for me down in the driveway and he took off. So she kind of panicked and . . ."

". . . and took the fastest route down," Amanda says. Which actually makes my sister sound logical.

"Shanna's bones come up out of my gums sometimes," I tell her.

Amanda nods like that's to be expected. "Tell me more about Shanna's bones."

"I used to think they were pieces of clarinet reed," I tell her. "But then Shanna said it's actually her bones working their way out of my system from when I absorbed her."

"Shanna *said* this?"

I consider my answer for a long moment, wanting to get it right. "She didn't say it. She wrote it down."

"That's how you two communicate?"

"That and when she throws us through storm

windows to express dissatisfaction."

Amanda raises an eyebrow to let me know I've violated the sarcasm rule. I have to admit she's got the eyebrow raise down.

"Yes, that's how we communicate," I amend.

"And when did this begin?"

Like everything else it falls somewhere on the time-line of my life where the biggest demarcation is losing my virginity to Isaac Harver. "I think it was after," I say.

"After?"

"No, sorry—just before."

"Before what, Sasha?"

I feel a flush, my heart still capable of shoving all the blood up to my face. "I'd rather not say."

"That's fine," she says agreeably. "But if you're not open with me I'm not going to be a terribly effective therapist."

I think I'm going to be very open to plenty of people next week when they put the LVAD inside me, so I leave that barrier in place. Amanda allows it, giving me the space of a quarter rest before continuing.

"Do you want to add anything more about Shanna right now?"

There's a blip on the screen, my heart rate monitor disagreeing with this line of questioning. "No."

"How about Brooke?"

"I miss her," I say, apparently an embolism not being the only spontaneous thing that can happen.

"When is the last time you saw Brooke?"

I can fudge this one a little, since I last *spoke* to Brooke the other night over messaging, but I haven't technically *seen* her since . . .

"The night of the accident."

"So she knows about it?"

"She saw it happen," I tell her, gratified by the surprise on Amanda's face as the professional mask she was attempting to mold slips a little.

"She was there?"

"No, I was Skyping with Brooke and Lilly," I explain. Amanda nods and leaves space for me to go on, but I don't know what to say.

I've thought about it while I stared at the reflective roof in the back of the squad, the cracked ceiling above my bed at Stillwell, and now the artfully decoupaged tiles of the cardiac center. I don't know how I had my laptop tilted, if my friends would have only seen me run off screen and heard the crash, or if they actually saw me unravel right before their eyes, leaving behind a chunk of my hair on the remnants of the broken window.

"Did something happen during this chat?" Amanda asks.

"Lilly said something I didn't like, and Brooke agreed," I say stiffly.

"And what was that?"

"A word I won't repeat."

"Was it directed at you?"

"Yes."

"And how did that make you feel?" Amanda pauses. "Is that really why you jumped out the window?"

"No," I tell her. And it's the truth. "Because I didn't—"

"—jump out the window," Amanda finishes for me. "Shanna did."

I nod in agreement. "And trust me, Shanna doesn't care what those two think."

"What does Shanna care about?"

I glance at the clock just as the second hand ticks into place.

"Time's up," I say.

twenty-two

I. Things I Know

    A. An LVAD looks like plumbing around my heart, plumbing that requires a power source.

        1. I will have a power cord exiting my body near my belly button.

        2. I will wear a controller and battery pack at all times, which looks like backpack straps, minus the backpack.

        3. "I will continue to lead a full and rewarding life." (This is a pull quote from the brochure.)

    B. LVAD is close to Vlad and is fitting since it will in fact be impaling me.

II. Things I Don't Know

    A. If it will hurt Shanna

B. *If I'll ever see Isaac again*
C. *If he'll find me disgusting when I do*

(on)c(e) there was a girl[s] made of (me)tal—is it me or is it y-ew-?

Amanda very helpfully left the activities schedule with me after our therapy session, a list of the varying social and recreational opportunities that promise to be invigorating but better not go too far or else it could kill the participants. I give it a hard look, well aware that between her and the nurses I'll be pestered into doing something, and trying to figure out which will require the least of me.

TODAY AT THE CARDIAC CENTER!
9:00 a.m.——Fun with Watercolors! Local artist Shyane Wergei shows you how to take what's inside and get it out using a paintbrush.

Probably not the best wording for a heart transplant center.

11:00 a.m.——Bond Over Books! Bring your favorite book and share a passage that matters to you with the group.

I'll take Mom's *DSM* that I swiped and read everyone the entry about my supposed psychotic disorder.

> *2:00 p.m.—Share the Love! Hop in the cardiac center van for a trip to the Humane Society, where a special dog or kitty is waiting to steal your heart.*

Seriously, whoever wrote this did not consider their audience. Also most of us are medically prohibited from hopping.

> *4:00 p.m.—Meditation with Melody! Relax before dinner with guided meditation.*

This one actually has my attention, although I'm not sure an exclamation point has any place near the word *meditation*.

As predicted, my nurse makes a big show of talking about how bored I must be "all cooped up" in my room all day with "no one to talk to." She has no idea that I'm continuing to carry on plenty of conversations with both Brooke and Shanna over the laptop, and I'm not in a hurry to enlighten her either.

After my daily maintenance is attended to—weight, blood pressure, temperature—I'm given my privacy back, but Brooke is at school and Shanna won't answer direct questions so I'm faced with the fact that it's time to go make some friends.

I'm not good at this. Lilly and Brooke are my friends, but I'll be the first to admit that this may be a force of habit more than anything. We bonded in kindergarten because Brooke liked to find dead birds at recess, Lilly liked to scream about it, and I liked lecturing them both about germs and keeping their voices down. We were odd children, effortlessly seamed together by our oddness, our parents relieved that we'd found each other, even if our combined personalities alienated everyone else.

Everyone here is dying, which means I have to be nice to them. It's not one of my better areas, and I know it. I waste ten minutes getting dressed even though I'm wearing nothing more complicated than pajama pants and a hoodie, try to part my hair so that some of the damage is covered, take a deep breath, and pull open my door.

There's a girl sleeping in a wheelchair by her doorway, legs off to one side, knees pressed together, IV tree keeping guard. I'm untethered, no longer needing constant hydration or pain meds. In their place I have a lineup of orange pill bottles in the bathroom, the myriad of sentinels required to keep me going every day.

I slip past the girl in the hall, making my way to the

common room where I find one girl teaching another how to play chess, and a third patient curled into an overstuffed armchair with a novel. I walk over to one of the bookshelves to pick through the offerings, surprised to find some books that would be more appropriate on Mom's nightstand.

"Careful with that one," someone says, and I turn to see the girl who had been reading has joined me. "It'll get your blood pressure up and you'll be on a low-salt diet. I tore the cover off so it wouldn't be taken away from us, but if you have to explain your spike and blame the book I won't forgive you."

I watch her carefully, trying to figure out if she's serious or not while I fan the well-worn pages under my thumb.

"You're new," she goes on, her eyes roaming my face until they settle on the stitches I couldn't quite get my hair to cover. "Oh, you're *that* girl."

"Which girl?"

She snorts. "We all come in here looking like we're dying. You're the only one to show up looking like somebody tried to kill them."

I put the book back, my hand going up to finger my stitches.

"Hey," she says. "What's the difference between this place and a nursing home?"

"I don't know."

"Everybody in a nursing home is waiting to die. We're all waiting to live."

One of the girls playing chess turns in her wheelchair. "Layla, how many times do I have to tell you that joke isn't funny?"

"How many times have I got to tell you it isn't a joke?" Layla shoots back, and the chess player huffs, returning to her game even though it looks like her opponent might have hit the painkillers a little hard and blacked out early.

"What about, everybody here is waiting for someone else to die?" I suggest.

"What's that?" Layla's attention is back on me, her eyes following the curve of the stitches that arch around my neck as my hoodie shifts.

"Your joke," I explain. "What's the difference between this place and a nursing home? Instead of 'Everybody at a nursing home is waiting to die, and we're all waiting to live,' you could say, 'we're all waiting for someone else to die.'"

I wait for a reaction, but she's still staring. "You know, so we can get their heart."

"Right," she says. "I get it. I just think it's even not-funnier than my version."

"Oh." I go back to looking at the books.

"Which means Nadine over there will hate it," she adds. "So I kind of love it. Hi, I'm Layla by the way." She offers her hand to shake.

"I gathered," I say, taking it. "Sasha."

Her hand is bony in mine, and I find myself making a terrible assessment of how long she has left, how much time I should invest in this friendship. Then I see the belt around her waist.

"Is that an LVAD?"

"Yeah," she says, lifting her sweatshirt so I can see. "Mark of the last resort."

"I get mine next week," I tell her, and I swear I can see the same computation going on behind her dark brown eyes, a weighing of the free time she has left and if she wants to spend it with someone who won't be around to remember anything she said or did.

"Dilated cardiomyopathy?" she asks, and I know we're going through our second round of introductions, an exchange of diagnoses and not names.

"Yeah. Sickle cell?"

Her eyebrows shoot up. "Just because I'm black you think I've got sickle cell?"

"No, I . . . no," I say, immediately backpedaling and trying to name any other heart condition I can think of, and coming up with none. "I'm . . . did I just really screw this up?"

"No, you're just really white, that's all."

"Sorry," I say. "It's not like I'm racist or anything."

"Not on purpose anyway," she says, but her eyebrows have come back down so I think I might be forgiven.

"So . . ." I dig into the waistband of my pants to pull out the folded schedule of the day's events. "Are any of these actually decent? I was thinking about the meditation one."

Layla looks it over. "If we're lucky, the watercolor lady might smoke a joint before she comes in and we can try to get a contact high off her hair. She thinks we like her a lot because we invade her personal space."

"I think I'll pass on getting high."

"The Humane Society trips seem cool but I'm allergic, so I can't go." Her eyes shift to me, maybe hoping that if she's out then I am too.

"What about the books thing?" I ask.

She shrugs. "It's okay. Mostly a lot of people bring stuff that's got to do with somebody dying and talk about how they can relate. I'd rather read about people falling into crazy love, something I don't know the first thing about."

She lets the sentence fade out, eyes still searching me. "You ever been in love?"

I let a little smile answer for me, no words necessary.

"So . . . the meditation?" I say.

Layla nods at me. "Meditation it is. You get breakfast yet?"

And suddenly I have a friend.

Meditation with Melody! turns out to be guided by a cassette tape player, not someone actually named Melody and certainly nothing resembling real music. Layla takes a mat next to mine, and we lie side by side, staring at the tiled ceiling. Another girl joins us, the one who Nadine had been attempting to teach chess. She takes a mat to the right and promptly goes to sleep. A nurse comes in and starts the tape, dimming the lights and clicking the door quietly shut behind her.

Something like a pan flute begins, tripping over a few bars to be joined by a soft male voice that encourages us to picture a safe, quiet place in our minds. Over by the wall, the girl who joined us lets out a long, protracted fart.

"Oh my Lord, Josephine," Layla says, but the other girl doesn't respond.

The voice from the cassette player urges us to concentrate on a calm memory, but my entire focus is on the fact that the pan flute in the background wasn't tuned properly. It's soon joined by the sound of running water.

"Great. Now I've got to pee," Layla says, and I turn

to look at her. "I don't think I can meditate myself out of peeing."

"You're not into this at all, are you?" I ask her.

She sits up, her LVAD cord slipping out from under her shirt. "Nope, but you seemed interested so I thought I'd give it a shot."

"I thought it would be better," I admit. "Like with real music."

"You into music?"

"It's my whole life," I tell her, my fingers going to the edge of the mat where some stuffing has poked through. "Used to be, anyway. I played the clarinet."

"So what happened to your face?" Layla asks, waving away my startled look. "The other girls have a dessert bet going and if I can get the real info and an extra sugar cookie out of the deal, I'll split the cookie with you."

"My sister threw me out a window," I tell her. "And you can keep the cookie."

Layla lets out a whistle. One that starts high and ends low, like a bomb falling. "Damn girl. Is she your stepsister, half sister?"

I shake my head. "Twin."

"No shit." Layla crosses her arms, resting her head on them. "Is she in juvy now?"

I pick at the hole at the edge of my mat where the seams have come apart, digging my index finger inside as I wonder how much to tell her. "I don't really like to talk about it."

"Ohhhhhh . . . ," Layla says, her voice making the same high pitch to low that her whistle had earlier. "She dead?"

"Why would you think that?" I ask.

"Honestly?" She cocks her head to the side like the question is more for herself than me. "Josephine read your visitor's name badge the other day and we googled her. Didn't take a genius to put together that a mental health worker coming to talk to a girl who was Humpty-Dumptied back together again means you've got issues. That's still a doozy of an issue though, I'll give you that."

"My sister's not dead," I say, the warm pulse in my wrist agreeing.

Layla lowers herself back down to the mat, throws an arm across her eyes. "What's her name?"

I pull my finger out of the mat and blow away some of the stuffing that snagged on my jagged nail. I lay back down next to Layla as the meditation tape switches over to the tide and seagulls, interrupted occasionally by Josephine's snores. I swear I can feel the hollow bit in the mat under my shoulder blade where I pulled stuffing out.

"Shanna," I tell her, thinking of darkness and sounds

my throat can't possibly have ever made, but my ears miss hearing.

"So you've definitely been in love before," Layla says, and I start, wondering how she followed my thoughts.

I look over at her and she shrugs. "It's all over you. Moony looks, vacant stares. You might be in a safe place right now, but I bet it's not quiet."

I laugh, causing Josephine to roll over in her sleep, arms covering her ears.

"Sure," I admit. "I'm probably in love."

"Nope. It's you are or you aren't," Layla insists. "My mom always says you just know, and you can't *probably* know something. You know it or you don't."

I think of all my lists of things I know, and things I don't know. I don't have a list for maybes, so Layla could have a point.

"Then how do you know?" I ask.

"According to books I have to tear the covers off of, or according to my own personal experience?" Layla asks. "Because I can tell you anything you want to know about the first. The second . . . guess I need a working heart first."

"Why's that?"

"Being near death scares them off."

I giggle, my noise blending in with the pan flute. I do her the favor of not arguing with her about being near death. I could probably pick Layla up and throw her, and I'm not exactly the picture of health myself.

"So you know by"—Layla takes a deep breath, and closes her eyes—"feeling a little empty if you're apart more than a day or two, like half your self wandered off without permission. By needing them closer even when they're right inside you, by knowing the smell of their skin and being able to sort it out from your own, by sharing a glance and saying the world, by feeling like nobody will ever know you like they do, but being a little sad that there's nothing more you can share. Because in the end it's just you who has to be enough."

She opens her eyes and smiles at me, slow and quiet, and I think she's either read all the romance books in the world or there's someone out there she needs to say something to before she dies. Either way, she's put words to something I couldn't, no matter how many lists I made. And maybe I need to add something to my last column of things I know, and that is that I messed up everything.

Heath didn't want me by his side; he wanted whoever the girl with the highest GPA was, something to balance his own with. He wanted a girl who wanted the same things he did—to look like the best, the brightest, a clean, shining example of a good teen.

Isaac didn't care about that. He wanted me, actually

me, with the hard edges and all. He wanted it enough to scratch our names in rock next to pictures that had lasted a thousand years. And our names probably would too, for the people after us to read. And the people after them. Isaac and Sasha, next to each other. Forever. It looks like that's the one bit of me that is going to be around for a while; all the supposedly good things I've tried to do are captured on a grade card for a girl who won't make it to college, while a bad thing a boy did for me is going to say I existed beside him.

And I tried to erase it.

Layla is still watching me, waiting for an answer.

"Yeah," I finally say. "I think I am in love."

The words feel heavy, like a deep B flat. They're powerful and all-encompassing, demanding my throat close up, threatening to make me cry. They matter more than a lot of things, I realize now. More than the bloodred As on my papers or a weighted GPA or Sasha Stone always being number one.

I smile again, thinking of Isaac with his middle finger up in the air, which leads to thoughts of his hands, and my mind wanders further. Future Sasha Stone and all her plans have been derailed, a train gone off the track as surely as if it tried to use the trestle bridge and collapsed into a burning heap of twisted metal at the bottom of the ravine. And if Sasha Stone doesn't need

to worry about being rewarded for anything, maybe
Shanna Stone should have her way, in the little time we
have left.

My breath catches in my constricted throat, a small
sob emerging. Layla reaches over to squeeze my hand in
the dim light, and I finally do relax, sliding down into
meditation not to the sound of the sea breeze, but the
quiet clicking of her mechanically pumping heart.

Will the LVAD hurt you?

Don't K[no]w

Are you scared?

Not s(ur)e.

twenty-three

"Holy shit balls, dude."

Brooke's voice is loud in the cardiac center common room, like it could knock over furniture. Josephine looks up from her laptop, Nadine from a game of solitaire. Layla jumps, almost knocking over her bottle of nail polish. I'm on my feet in a second, highly aware that my friend from the outside is too alive, too vibrant for them. Already the room seems small with Brooke in it, her ponytail thick and healthy, her legs strong and sure underneath her.

"Hey." I grab her by the elbow and steer her down the hall toward my room.

"I mean, your face," Brooke keeps going. "Dog turds on a stick. I thought I was ready for it, but . . ."

"Thanks a lot," I tell her.

"Can I touch your stitches?" she asks as I close my door behind her. "I'll wash my hands first."

"Sure," I tell her. "As long as you brought it."

Brooke flops onto my bed, her face suddenly serious. "Yeah, we've gotta talk about that."

I cross my arms. "What? It didn't work?"

Mom and Dad still have me on a no-phone diet, and they're stricter than even the nurses with our individual nutrition plans. But Brooke's old cell was the same model as mine, and she should've been able to power it up, call an activation line, punch in my number and passcode and voilà—my phone is restored to me without parental assistance or permission.

"It worked fine," Brooke says, reaching into her pocket to pull it out.

"So what do we need to talk about?"

She switches it back and forth in her hands before answering me, her teeth clamping on her bottom lip. "I read your texts."

I sit down on Amanda's rolling chair, hard enough to send it back into the wall. "You did what?"

"I thought it might be smart, after everything that happened," she says. "I didn't know if there might be anything on here that would . . . upset you."

"You didn't pause to consider that maybe you reading

my texts might be equally upsetting?"

"Sasha . . ." Brooke lets my name out in a sigh, like she's giving something up. "I saw. When you went out the window. Lilly and I both, we . . . we saw you reading a text and then you—"

"And then I jumped out the window," I interrupt. "I remember. I also remember that you called me a bitch."

Brooke picks at the case on the phone, an older one of hers that she had made. Me, Brooke, and Lilly at band camp sophomore year, arms around one another, sweaty tank tops stuck to our skin in patches.

"I'm sorry about that," she finally says. "But you know what? You kind of are a bitch, dude. But I don't care, because you're also smart and funny, and kind of a musical genius. So whatever. If you're a little bit of a bitch too, then fine, I'll take you that way. Because honestly the person you're the biggest bitch to is yourself, Sasha Stone.

"You've always pushed yourself to your limits and never cut yourself any slack. I think you demand perfection out of yourself and everyone around you, and sometimes we fail you, and sometimes you fail yourself. And I think you hate that more than anything."

We sit quietly together for a minute, the clock ticking off our breaths. Mine are coming in short bursts, analyzing the portrait of the person Brooke just painted for me. This is how I look to her. This is what a bitch is. Maybe being one isn't such a bad thing after all.

Brooke powers on the phone, finally looking up at me.

"So you and Isaac Harver, huh?"

I feel a tick in my chest, the upbeat of a tempo change. "Did he text me?"

"Um, like a hundred times," she says, thumbing through my messages.

"And you read them?" I feel a flush rising, embarrassment beating out anger.

"Yep," Brooke says. "The newer ones aren't all that interesting. But some of the old ones . . . I mean, wow. Who needs YouTube?"

"All right, enough," I say, making a swipe for the phone. Brooke is quicker, pulling it out of reach.

"I'll give this to you, but only if you promise me it's not going to get you hurt again. You're still my friend, and I got enough on my conscience as it is."

I lick my lips, eyes on the phone. "I promise."

"Okay." She hands it to me, and I jam it into my waistband, the plastic case absorbing my body heat in seconds.

"So your mom said you're having some kind of surgery in a couple of days?"

"Yeah. It's called an LVAD. You should google it,

right up your alley. I'll have a cord coming out of my belly. My friend Layla out in the lobby, she's got one."

Brooke's eyes go to my door, all calculation. "Do you think she'll let me see it?"

"We can ask," I say, twisting the knob.

"Listen." Brooke stops me. "There's something I want to tell you before you hear it from anyone else, and I don't know how you're going to take it. So . . . I don't know, should you be sitting down or something? Do I need a crash cart?"

"Brooke, I found out my heart could stop working at any moment and I'll drop dead. Nothing you can say is more shocking than that."

"Heath and Lilly are together," she says, closing her eyes and then screwing one back open slowly when she doesn't hear a body hit the floor.

My hand grips more tightly on the door handle, and I wait for the shock, a wave of anger or jealousy, maybe the cold touch of wrath. But there is nothing, not even a jolt of surprise that spikes my blood pressure. Shanna rests, unperturbed, beating a steady rate that seems completely nonplussed by this turn of events.

"How'd it happen?" I ask.

"They were both pretty torn up about you, and everything. I guess they were comforting each other and got a little too enthusiastic or something, I don't know. I wasn't thrilled about it when she told me, but if it means anything to you, I think they're both happy."

"No," I say, opening the door. "That doesn't mean anything to me at all."

twenty-four

My texts are a history of everything I've missed, my responses as absent from the record as I was in the world.

From Brooke

Dude? WTF? Did that just happen?

OK u need 2 call me I can hear sirens.

There's a chunk of yr hair hanging from the window.

Screencapping.

Like, b/c u can explain how u made it look real. Not b/c it's awesome.

Alright. It happened.

WTF?

From Lilly

Sasha?? Sasha??

U NEED 2 ANSR ME! U R FREAKING ME OUT!!

Not funny

Now it's really not funny b/c ur not at school.

Tlkd to ur mom. Will try to come and c u.

I can't help but smirk at Lilly's assertion that she's only going to *try* to come see me, as if my fall from grace had bumped me down on her priority list a few notches. Or maybe she was already making out with my boyfriend by then.

From Heath

Talked to Lilly and Brooke. Don't know what's going on.

Please call me.

At school. Everyone is saying different things and asking me questions. I don't know what to tell them. Call me.

Got home and my mom said she talked to your mom. I don't know what to think.

That's the last text I have from my boyfriend, that he doesn't know what to think. I'm sure it was excruciating for him.

From Isaac

Sorry had to go, dad's truck wouldn't start needed a ride to
  work

Hey lady, where are you?

hearing things @ school call me

You need 2 answr me crazy shit going on

where the fuck r u?

went to your house yr mom not happy to see me

WTF?

Is it b/c of me?

My eyes fill up at his last text. The others asked if
I was okay, wondered where I was, or wanted the truth
about what actually happened. Isaac was the only one
who had the guts to ask if it was his fault. And it wasn't,
even if him leaving that night is what pushed Shanna to
great lengths for his attention, it's not his fault.

It's hers. It's the fault of a girl who doesn't know how
to live what little bit of a life she's been given, a small
space tucked into the dark cavity of my chest. It's the
fault of a girl who doesn't know how to be a real person,
the fault of a girl who maybe already knew that she only
had so much time left.

I run my thumbs over the phone, not sure who to
answer first or what to say to any of them. Brooke is the
easiest, so I tackle that first.

From Brooke
WTF?
Phone works—ty!

From Heath
I don't know what to think.
I talked to Brooke. Sounds like you figured it out.

I'm surprised when three little bubbles pop up right away, which means Heath is typing an answer.
Will come visit. You can be mad at me then.
Maybe I will be and maybe I won't be. It's hard to say. Whatever corner of my heart was reserved for Heath has been subsumed by Shanna, and she has no use for him. Even though he's only coming to officially dump me to my face, I have to give him credit for making the drive and being a gentleman. Or maybe he just wants it on the official record for when he runs for governor that he didn't abandon his terminally ill girlfriend. I can picture him as an adult wearing a three-piece suit, holding up one of my senior pictures and the cardiac center's visitors' log at a press conference. He might even manufacture a tear.

I ignore Lilly's assertion that she will *try* to come see me. If she brings it up I'll tell her I *tried* to text her, but I had a lot going on in between therapy and surgeries.

Which leaves me with the last text that came in, from Isaac. I tap my thumbs against the screen.

From Isaac
Is it b/c of me?
Hey. Not your fault. I'm at the cardiac center in the city.
Surgery scheduled for tomorrow.

Just like with Heath, my response is immediately followed by the ellipsis inside a bubble. But I don't picture him the way I did Heath, someone looking to be absolved. Instead I can see him keeping his phone nearby, needing to hear from me because he actually cares. And that's kind of terrifying.

What kind of surgery? U scared the shit out of me.
I'm getting an LVAD...it helps my heart work. Mom says
it's a good thing I fell out the window b/c that's how we
found out I need a transplant.

My answer to Isaac is longer than my texts to anyone else, mostly because there was no planning involved. With everyone else what I texted was designed to procure a specific response. A breezy thank-you to Brooke so that she wouldn't worry, a quick jab for Heath, one he could choose to respond to or not. If I ignore Lilly completely she won't have the guts to text again, easily excised from my life. But with Isaac I'm just typing, saying what I think, and he's answering the same way.

U gonna be ok?

**Don't know yet...I have to stay here until I get a heart and
don't know when that will be.**

I pause, thumbs hovering over a new text, unsure
whether I'm giving up on future Sasha Stone, waiting
on rewards that I might not live to reap. Like with my
clarinet, my hands make the decision.

Come see me?

Tonight? Can be there but it'd be late. Have to take dad to
work.

Visiting hours are over at five, but rules are the last
thing on my mind when I reply. Tomorrow morning
Mom and Dad are coming to help me pack up loose
clothes and my toothbrush, all the little things that
have become my life. Then we're going to drive over to
the hospital and a doctor is going to slice open my chest
and put a machine in my heart. After tomorrow I'll have
a scar between my breasts and a power cord underneath
them. I have to see Isaac before then.

Yes. Text me when you get here.

And while I know it's Shanna's heart that wants him,
it's my fingers shaking when I hit send.

Layla is stirring her oatmeal with suspicion, as if it
might have an ulterior motive, when I sit down next to
her at lunch.

"I am so sick of this," she says, watching a chunk slide off her spoon to plop back into the bowl. "Every night I tell God that if I'm going to go, make it before another bowl of oatmeal, not after."

"I need to ask you something," I say, cutting right to the chase.

"Yes, you can have my oatmeal," she says, shoving the bowl toward me. "Done."

I push it back. "I want to know how to get out of here after hours."

Her eyes get big, and she lowers herself to taking a bite of oatmeal in order to buy time before answering. She chews with exaggeration, holding her finger up to let me know to wait.

"Was that good?" I ask, when she finally swallows.

"As an evasive maneuver, maybe. On the acceptable food scale it's like a two."

"It's a bad evasion too," I tell her. "I'm still here."

"Uh-huh, I see you."

"So?"

She takes a drink of milk, eyes on me over the rim of her glass. "So why are you asking me?"

"Because you've been here the longest, I know you the best, and you like a good romance story."

She puts the glass down with a thump. "Oh, you do know me. You want to get out and see a boy before you get your LVAD, don't you?"

I nod and she glances around the cafeteria. Some of the smaller kids are huddled in a corner peering over one boy's shoulder at his iPad, but other than that we're alone.

"Okay, here's the deal," she says, leaning in closer. "If all you want to do is get outside, that's easy enough, because Angela's the nurse on duty tonight. But I'll do you one better, since I know where there's an empty bed maybe you can make good use of. No dirty sheets to explain in your room, right?"

Before Shanna I would've told her to shut her dirty mouth, blushed, dropped my eyes, done anything to keep a veneer of cleanliness and respectability about myself. Now I just nod, all pretenses dropped. I want to know where this bed is and how I can get Isaac into it without getting caught.

"So Angela," Layla goes on. "She's got a brother who pulls in some decent cash on the side by selling off pills. She gets them to him, he splits the profits with her. This is a fancy place we're in, but that doesn't mean the nurses make bank. I heard Karen telling somebody just the other day she could probably make more at McDonald's if she didn't mind the grease in her pores, and at least there the teenagers aren't dying."

"She said that?" I'm surprised, remembering the hug Karen went in for the second she met me.

"Hell yes, she said that. Sucks to be us, but how would you like to be our nurses? Once we die we're gone. They've got to stay behind and look at the next face, smile at us the whole time until a new one comes in needing to be told everything is going to be okay when everybody knows it isn't."

"Point taken," I say. "So Angela makes cash on the side by selling off our pain pills, and I can bribe her to look the other way. But the only thing I'm on right now is antibiotics and immune-suppressants. I doubt they have a high street value."

"Got you covered," Layla says. "I'll slip you a couple of Oxy, but you've got to tell me your love story. And don't leave the good parts out either."

"Done."

The text comes in from Isaac that he's in the parking lot, and I slip down the hallway to the back exit, shoving a stone in the crack between the double doors so they don't lock behind me. I'm wearing the best thing I could put together in my limited wardrobe, a pair of pajama pants that hang a little low on the hips and a worn T-shirt thin enough to be kind of sexy. I don't have real shoes, just the flip-flops Mom gave me for the shower, so I'm smacking my way across the parking lot toward him when he looks up.

He's leaning against his bike, backlit by a security light and a halo of smoke around his head. He looks like everything I should never want, but somehow I'm walking faster, my mouth splitting into a smile.

"Hey," I say, as I step into the circle of light he's parked in.

"Hey," he says back, his eyes roaming over my face.

I still haven't looked in the mirror, because if I did I know I would have told him not to come. The nurses keep telling me it's *improving*, but I'm nowhere near what I was the last time he saw me. I can part my hair so that the half that's still growing in isn't as obvious, but the stitches across my forehead can't be hidden. So I don't even try, instead meeting his eyes boldly.

"Shit, lady," he says, his hands going to my face. He runs his thumb over the stitches softly, and I lean into his touch. "You look badass."

"Badass, huh?" I say, a tear slipping down one cheek. He wipes it away without comment.

"Thought it'd be worse, after everything I heard."

"And you still came?" I ask, wondering what he could have imagined that looked worse than I do now, yet still brought him here in the dark of night.

"I'm here, right?" One hand slips under my cascade of hair to feel the bristles underneath. "What's going on with this?"

"They had to shave a lot of my hair off," I tell him. "Part of my scalp was just . . ." I stop talking as his thumbs brush against my lips, his forehead touching mine.

"Why'd you go and do that?"

I press back, our faces close. I want to tell him that I didn't do it, Shanna did. Then I think of our names together at the glyph, my sister nowhere in between them. "I know where there's an empty room," I say, tugging on his hand.

He follows, but there's enough hesitation to make me wonder if he was only being polite about my face. I slip through the door, kicking the rock aside and still holding his hand. We tiptoe through the darkened hallway, and I wave at Angela when she looks up from the station desk.

"Um, is this a good idea?" Isaac whispers.

"It's okay," I tell him. "I paid her off with Oxy."

I find the room number Layla told me would be empty, a transplant patient who had come back to the cardiac center for her recovery time and shipped out before I showed up. We go inside, and I leave the lights off, leading him over to the bed.

"Listen to you, Sasha Stone," he says, as I wait for my eyes to adjust to the dark. "A punk haircut and bribing people with drugs. What's next?"

"This," I say, and press myself up against him. He kisses back, his hands wandering under my shirt for a second before he pulls away. My body knows what to do because it's done it before, but I've never been fully present in these moments with him. My skin wants to leap off my skeleton, wrap itself around him.

"Is this a good idea?" he asks again.

"I told you, I took care of the nurse. She's on shift for the rest of—"

"No," he cuts me off. "I mean this. You and me doing . . . this." He tightens his hands on my body like he's not sure what he wants the answer to be.

"Yeah, it's fine," I say, leaning in again.

"I won't hurt you or anything, right?" he asks, pulling back.

"No, it's okay," I tell him, and then I'm on the bed and he's with me.

We've never done it in a bed, and it's different. All my hazy memories from Shanna are desperate, wind in our faces and dirt on our backs. But here and now Isaac is different with me, like maybe he knows it's actually me, not her. He's cautious and sweet, gentle in a way that changes how I respond. It's not the crazy, grasping, defiant competition like it is for Shanna. It's soft and kind and we lie together afterward, something new as well. I curl against him, the prickles of my shorn scalp probably tickling his chest, but he doesn't ask me to move.

"This is nice," he says, one hand toying with the hair I have left.

"Yeah," I have to agree, even though part of me doesn't want to. I feel like every time before this was for Shanna. But what I just did . . . that was for me. And I liked it. Sasha Stone liked having sex with Isaac Harver. It feels like graffiti in my mind, something I can't unsee.

"So what's the surgery tomorrow?"

"It's called an LVAD," I tell him. "Basically it's like a pump in my heart they put in to keep me going until a transplant becomes available."

"How long does that take?"

I shrug, my naked shoulder moving against his chest. "Depends. You've got to have the same blood type as the donor, and be roughly the same age and weight. Plus the heart can't be far away, because it can't have stopped working within the last four hours. So you have to hope that someone near your age, weight, and with your blood type within a certain mile radius dies, and agreed to be an organ donor when they got their driver's license. Even if they did, their family still has to approve and agree."

"That's fucked-up."

"Yep," I agree. "I have a pager that will go off if a heart becomes available for me, and I get rushed to the hospital for the transplant. I'm supposed to wear it at all times."

Isaac's brow furrows. "At all times?" He lifts our blanket to peer underneath.

"I think it's in the pile of clothes on the floor," I tell him.

"I guess you better go get it then," he says, rolling over to pin me to the bed.

"You get it," I tell him.

Neither of us gets it.

I walk Isaac to the back door afterward, where there's a bit of lingering and kissing despite the cold rain starting to fall. I say something about him riding all the way back home in the weather but he shrugs it off, tells me it's worth it and disappears into the dark like the antihero I have to remind myself he is. There's a light coming from under Layla's door, so I keep my promise, knocking before slipping into her room.

"Hey." She looks up from her book, eyes heavy with the sleep she's denying herself as she waits up for me.

"Hey," I say back, trying to keep my tone light as I take the chair by her bed.

Layla looks awful. I didn't know black people could go pale, but she definitely isn't her normal skin tone, and her fingers are trembling in a way I don't like as she sets aside her bodice-ripper paperback.

"So, dish," she says, but I shake my head.

"You sure? You . . . sorry, but you look rough."

"Says the girl with half her face sewn back on," she shoots back.

"Which should carry even more weight," I say.

"Meh." She waves aside my concern. "I stayed up too late last night. Had to see if the heroine got her hero. Same story tonight, just in real life."

"If you're sure . . ."

"Yep, but first things first. Did you take care of the dirty laundry?"

"Literally and figuratively," I nod.

"Okay." She leans back in her bed, eyes closed. "Tell me your love story. What's his name? How did you meet?"

I start slow, telling her about how my sister fell for him first, but I might be following suit. Her eyes get big and I know she assumes that's why my twin threw me out a window, and I let her think it. I talk about Heath and our antiseptic relationship, how nothing he ever did touched me—and I mean that in all the ways.

Layla smiles at that. "So this Isaac, he your first?"

"Yeah," I say, laying claim to it. "You ever?"

She smirks. "I wish. Mom's been helicoptering me since I was in fifth grade. Even if there was a boy interested in having sex with a flat-chested girl who might die right in the middle, he'd also have to be okay with my mom standing right there with a defibrillator."

I snort—there's no other word for it—and Layla laughs along with me, though it leaves her short of breath.

"There's somebody though, right?" I ask, and Layla shrugs, her stick-thin shoulders poking against the blanket as she does.

"Maybe there's a boy," she says. "Maybe I met him at a camp for kids like me, the kind where you don't go for long hikes or do trust falls, because we were all fragile things. Maybe we write each other letters instead of texting, so that we've each got something that the other actually touched, in case it's the last one that'll come. Maybe he got his heart, and it's a fine, strong one. Maybe he's waiting on me so that we can meet again someday, the same people we were before, but now with more time ahead of us than what's behind. Maybe that's why I haven't decided to die just yet. Maybe that's my love story."

"Yeah," I say, thinking about my life, two stark columns of *good* and *bad*, *yes* and *no*. "Yeah, maybe."

twenty-five

I could die today.

Technically I could die any day, for no reason at all, so it seems like the chances will be much higher when my veins are full of chemicals, my senses unresponsive, and my torso splayed open like the frog I dissected in seventh grade.

Mom and Dad do a great job of not talking about it when they pick me up from the cardiac center, grabbing my bag like we're going on a camping trip, except this one happens all indoors and under sterile conditions. Nobody says this could be the last time I am outside, this could be the last time I ride in a car, this could be the last time I bite my fingernails, this could be the last time I take a drink of water.

But I'm thinking it with every small thing, all the little insignificant moments that make up an hour, a day, a life. All those things I took from Shanna with a kick of my fetal foot, tearing her umbilical cord away from her body and making sure she never had any of those moments. Until she took them back from me. A life for a life. I'm angry with my sister and her crappy heart, but I'm worried about her too. I don't know how the LVAD will affect her, if it will give her strength or sap what she has left.

Dad proudly shows me his own scar, somehow thinking that seeing a red streak across his white, fish-belly, weird-hair-patterned chest would make me feel better. His pacemaker went in last week and he keeps insisting to me that it works like a charm, and he feels better than he has in years.

He might feel better, but he looks like hell; Mom too. Between me and Dad she's been living in hospitals and drinking bad coffee since my accident—which is what they keep referring to it as. Like a crane falling, or a car hydroplaning. Certainly not their only child choosing to jump through glass and fall to the ground.

They're doing what they think is best, putting on brave faces and manufactured cheer. But it's still a relief when the doors to the surgery wing swish shut behind me and I'm left alone with strangers who are all business.

The anesthesiologist does give me a quick smile, asks me to count backward from ten. I start, thinking how ridiculous it is that with everything I know, all the things I've accomplished in my life, the last thing I might say will be an exercise from kindergarten. It's not fair and I don't like it. So instead the last thing the world gets from me is a plea, something I hate myself for as I sink into oblivion.

"Ten . . . Nine . . . Wait . . ."

When I wake up I am high and freezing. Recovery rooms are cold by design. Bacteria and viruses can't breed as easily, and my incisions won't bleed as easily either. People always say the room is spinning when they're screwed up, but I feel quite the opposite, bolted down through my chest, as if a rod ran through the ceiling down into the ground, me halfway between.

My mind is liquid, sliding from present to past, this place to others. I remember freshman science and a bug project we did. I partnered with Brooke because I knew she would have no problem catching them, and she knew I'd have zero compunction about jamming needles through their slim thoraxes, pegging them in place just as I have been here in this room.

They were anesthetized first, of course, just like me. For them it was a cotton ball in their glass jars, a hazy death before being impaled. Except for one; a huge beetle Brooke snagged off the sidewalk as she came into school. I hastily scrawled a tag for it, plunging the pin through its chest before the teacher came in before the first bell. No time for pity.

It wiggled. All day. Some of the kids poked it to watch it squirm, but most held back, eyes on me. They said things, I remember now.

Said I was terrible.

Said I was psychotic.

Said I was heartless.

There's a sound, a whir I can't place. I turn my head and my brain feels like it will keep sliding, pool out of my ear and provide a second pillow. The one I have now is flat, shapeless, cold. My brain would be warm, soft, and comfortable. An excellent pillow.

I am very, very fucked-up right now.

The sound comes again, and I turn the other way to see a nurse reading a book, and the world must be a very small place because it is the same one Layla had last night. Either that or I am both here and there at the same time, but that is not true because I am held in place by this great weight on my chest. Amazing that I can breathe. That my lungs can go up and down against this impossible pressure.

Maybe I'm not breathing, or perhaps my brain isn't

getting the signals because they were never my lungs in the first place. Maybe they were always Shanna's too. How much of me is her? What can I lay claim to when we move with the same body, talk with the same mouth, bleed the same blood?

I don't know if I'm thinking these things because they are true or because I am high. I will ask the nurse; she will know. It is her job to assess how messed up I am. Layla told me that. She said the person sitting with me in the recovery room will gauge when I can be wheeled out, trusted to not tell my parents that they are robots and daisies grow from my face, that my lungs are now my sister's too and the tombstone needs to have both names on it, but no birthdate for Shanna.

They definitely don't want to hear that.

I try to say something to the nurse, make a noise, hold my breath, wiggle a toe. My mouth falls open and a wheeze comes out, similar to the sound I'd heard before. The weight on my chest shifts with the exhale and I feel something new, the flutter of a small butterfly trapped inside my chest, a piece of my science project resurrected and left behind when they sewed me up. It's in there with Shanna, wanting out.

My hands go to my chest to help it, to tear open myself and make amends for the beetle. But they are weak things, my fingers, and all they can do is feel the stitches, follow them down. Down to the cord that exits my body, right below where the butterfly is trapped.

And it's not a butterfly after all, but the new pieces of my heart, which was never mine in the first place. It pumps away inside me, whirring and working, making noises and pushing my blood, wrapped around Shanna in this life-giving embrace that she must endure to keep us going.

I don't know what is her and what is me, what is us and what is machine. I don't know. I don't know. I don't know.

I. *Things I Know*
    A. *N/A*
II. *Things I Don't Know*
    A. *If Shanna hurts*

/Fuck/ing hurts / you asked w!t! password hea©th-urts. Pocket full of posey. You're high I'm /hil/gh We all fall d-ow-n. what now? This now. (ME)TAL

From Brooke
How'd it go? Ansr if u didn't die
PS send pic of ur cord

From Isaac

Thinking bout you

C you soon

From Heath

I hope all went well today.

Whether you believe that or not.

My phone is a weight in my hands, one I can barely lift. I stashed it in my hospital bag, tucked into a side pocket with tampons on top of it so no one would go digging. It's dead by the time I'm out of ICU, five days after the surgery. I've been moved to a regular room in the hospital, and much like my phone I have to be near a power source at all times.

I've been complimented on odd things since coming out of surgery, how quickly I learn how to clean the exit cord on my own, how good my appetite is, how often I poop. I am like a baby, except one who menstruates, which is terribly inconvenient, though it does drive Dad out of the room at the mention of it, taking his pacemaker with him.

Mom asks if I need help, which creates an awkward moment when I ask exactly how she expects to help me putting a tampon in, and she follows Dad, telling me she'll see if she can find more ice chips. I take care of everything in their absence, my IV tree and heart monitor following close behind, as I am once again part of a system and not whole on my own. My phone is charging and hidden under my pillow by the time they return, its cord anonymous among the many that create a web around me.

There is a line down my center, like a fish that has been gutted and then someone changed their mind, tried to fix everything with needle and thread. The stitches are very dark against my untouched skin, the wounded flesh an angry red. Now I understand why they would not let me see my face right away. Mom keeps redirecting my hands, my gaze, anything to keep me from touching and looking at where I once was open and am now closed again.

She asks me how I am feeling constantly, and I answer. I consider showing her my sister's messages, scattered things that they are. But to do so would mean showing her the phone Brooke smuggled to me, or the laptop they think I only use for reading. I don't tell her that we're both still sulking a bit from the use of the word *psychotic*.

Because if that's accurate then I'm crazy and she doesn't exist.

Unacceptable.

For both of us.

My heart is still working in the morning. I know because I can hear it.

Mom is asleep in her chair, folded over to one side with her finger stuck in the pages of the *DSM* I slipped back into her bag during a visit to the cardiac center. I don't know if she's searching for more things that might be wrong with me or if she's just one of those people who can't not finish a book.

Dad is at the window, watching the sunrise. His eyes flick over to me when I move, and we stare at each other for a second.

"How are you feeling?"

"Like a machine," I answer. "How are you feeling?"

"Like a human, but with a pacemaker," he says.

I'm the first to look away.

"I thought it was my fault," he says, his words directed at the window and the people pouring into the building to come and see their loved ones. The sick and the dying. The new ones who just came out of other people. Ones who haven't done anything irrevocable yet that they can't be forgiven for.

"It's genetics." I shrug.

He shakes his head. "I'd like to say that you'll understand someday, Sasha. But I don't know if you will."

I press the button on my med line, the one that gives

me a little more painkiller if I think I might need it. Dad's talking, so I definitely think I might need it. He's still looking out at the parking lot, like maybe someone out there is holding up cue cards.

"You've really done a number on your mom. You have no idea what it was like for her, losing that baby."

"Shanna," I correct him.

"And now you're putting her through it again," he plows on. "Twice over, because she could lose you too."

I notice he doesn't mention that he could lose me, maybe because that's already been done.

"Technically you're putting her through it," I say. "If we're operating under the assumption that my heart problems are from you."

"Jesus." Dad puts his head in his hands, and is so still that I wonder if he got too upset and the pacemaker blew.

"How did you get to be so cold, Sasha?" he asks.

"How are you just now figuring it out?" I shoot back.

"I knew," he says quietly. "Your mom, she doesn't want to see it, but I've always known. For your fourth birthday we took you to the zoo, and in the gift shop all the other kids were grabbing stuffed animals, hugging them, naming them right there on the spot. You picked out a set of dead bugs, suspended in glass cubes. It came with a magnifying class so you could study them."

My pain meds are doing their job, floating my body away from the whir of my heart, my mind unmoored and fixated on odd things. The bell of a lily that faces me; the flower of resurrection. The baby's breath nestled next to it. It's all very nice except someone needs to invite an exterminator to that flower shop because there's a stinkbug nestled deep inside the lily. Also, baby's breath is poisonous.

What an odd name for poison.

Dad said something, and I should answer him. The thing about the bugs and the magnifying glass. I remember that toy, remember peering down at little body parts for hours, trying to figure out how they worked.

"So I can manipulate them," I say, not realizing my thoughts are flowing outward now. "If I know how they work, I can make them do what I want."

Dad sighs, rests his forehead against the window.

"You graduated to people though, didn't you?" he asks. "When you found out about . . ." He doesn't finish, doesn't say her name, whoever the woman is that he's cheating on mom with. "When you found out you didn't get mad, didn't run to tell your mom. You held on to it, used it against me.

"I don't know how many surgeries it would take to make you a nice person," he says, his voice a whisper that comes back from the glass, as cold as the surface they just hit. "How many hours of therapy. They can give you a new heart, but they can't fix something that isn't in there. What's missing from you, Sasha?"

My tongue is a lead weight, so I can't ask him if there were cameras in the surgery, or if someone in there ran their mouth. Everything I was afraid of has come to pass. They opened me up and found nothing inside.

"Dad," I say, forcing my breath to come, my tongue to work, my trachea to vibrate. The drugs are strong, but my brain is stronger and I will speak. "Can we talk about this sometime when I'm not fucked-up?"

"And when will that be?"

I have to admit as I slide into unconsciousness that it's a valid question.

twenty-six

"Last time we saw each other you were telling me about Brooke and Lilly," Amanda says, scanning her notes. She's wearing corduroys today, but they're about an inch too short so when she sits down she looks like a little kid in time-out. Her hair is up in a messy bun that some girls can pull off. She is not one of those girls.

"And what did I say about them?" I ask.

I've decided to try a new tactic with Amanda, answering her questions with a question. She complies, flipping a few pages back in her notebook, which kind of makes me uneasy because I know I didn't say that much during our session at the cardiac center.

"You had some concerns about the fact that they may have witnessed your fall."

I snort at her choice of words, and she lets the pages fan back into place.

"I understand that Brooke came to see you at the cardiac center before your surgery. How did that make you feel?"

"Did my mom tell you that?"

"Yes. Were you glad to see Brooke?"

"Why wouldn't I be?"

"And what did you two talk about?"

"What do friends usually talk about?"

"So you consider her a friend?"

"Is there a reason that I shouldn't?"

"Who else is your friend?"

"Not Lilly."

Whoops. She got me on that one. It was like a hammer into my kneecap and I reacted. I should probably give Amanda more credit. Just not when it comes to personal grooming.

"Why isn't Lilly your friend? Because she called you a name?"

"That, and she stole my boyfriend."

Amanda nods at me, and I know I'm supposed to say more. I don't want to, but apparently the void inside me that Dad is wising up to filled with words while I was dead to the world.

"Heath," I explain. "He's the guy I've been dating

forever. And apparently he's with Lilly now. So no, not my friend. Either of them."

Amanda nods and makes some sort of note on her legal pad. As usual it's very short, which makes me wonder about the pages and pages that she references later on. When she writes them. What she writes.

"And how does that make you feel?"

I don't have a good answer for that. Well, I actually do, but I know it's not the right one.

"I've got a lot going on right now," I say instead.

In the big picture, this is true. In the day to day, this is a patent lie. I have very little going on other than ice chips and IVs.

"Your mom says a boy came to the house looking for you after the accident. Was that Heath?"

"No." I shake my head. "That was Isaac."

"So the LVAD surgery was successful," she says. It's a good tactic. She just changed subjects and made a statement instead of asking a question.

"Yes." I lift my shirt to show her my cord and the little battery pack at my side.

"Was this the first time you had surgery?"

"No," I tell her, easily pulling all my medical data up since it's what I'm quizzed about most these days. "I had my wisdom teeth out when I was in junior high."

"And how does the LVAD make you feel?"

I consider telling her about the butterfly in my chest that needs electricity to work, how it reminds me of the beetle with a pin through its living body, something I did, the big, bleeding red *A* on that science project. How that wasn't terribly fulfilling because it was just another in a long line, before and after, my grades a long vowel-filled exhalation of superiority.

But she's waiting with her pen and paper, ready to put it all down permanently. And these are dark things that need to stay inside. So I lie.

"Alive," I say.

Alive Awake Aware /Alpha\ Aspire Atone Alone

I have the weirdest sensation when I finally return to the cardiac center: I'm glad to be back.

The heart wing of the hospital I had my LVAD surgery in was nice enough, as hospitals go. Which means that the floors were even and most of the nurses didn't use scrunchies to hold their hair back. Other than that it was greatly lacking. By my second day in recovery they informed me they were short on space and I was going to have a roommate.

The first part of that compound word is correct. The second carries an implication of affection that was inaccurate at best. I shared a space with another person; we listened to each other breathe, roll over, and urinate for a period of two weeks. I can't say that I would recognize her on the street, and we didn't share so much as a good-bye as I was rolled past her bed in my wheelchair on the way out.

I spot a new girl in the cardiac center common room as I make my way down to 211, the SASHA STONE nameplate still in place there. The new girl is folded into an armchair, staring out the window like someone has appointed her to that task. I don't know if she's here because she already got a new heart and was moved here for rehab, or if she's like the rest of us: waiting. She doesn't notice me, but I knock on Layla's door the moment Mom and Dad are convinced that I am appropriately settled and I won't die from sadness the second they leave.

"Who's the new girl?" I ask.

"Brandy," Layla says. "And hi."

"Hi." I settle onto her bed, since she's on the couch, tablet across her knees. She looks better than she did when I left, which isn't saying a lot, but I won't have to worry about my supply of Oxy for Angela running out anytime soon.

"What did I miss?"

"Not a lot. Nadine lost three more pounds. She's not allowed to give her desserts away anymore, so all the underground calorie betting has been shut down pretty hard."

"Nuts," I say, wrinkling my nose. Our entertainments are small but we cling to them.

"And the new girl doesn't have a foot."

"That's—wait, what?" I immediately hate myself for stealing Lilly's stock phrase but there are times when it's appropriate.

"A foot," Layla holds up one of hers to clarify. "She's missing one."

"How did that happen?"

Layla looks at me over the edge of her iPad but I push. "You asked me on my second day here what was going on with my face, so I'm guessing you went after someone's missing appendage with equal grace."

She tries to look offended but can't hold on to it long. "Okay, yeah. And I got a cup of peaches off Josephine for being right about the cause before Karen shut down the illegal food swapping."

"And the cause?"

"Not all that exciting. Nadine bet that she lost it in an accident of some sort, but I made her get more specific in case she tried to plead technicalities when it came down to parting with her sugar-free cookie."

Layla has a point. People use the word *accident* for all kinds of things. Death. Betrayal. Peeing your pants. Babies.

"So she said car accident, Josephine went with bear attack—which was a stupid bet, but she said she doesn't like peaches anyway—and I chose the obvious."

I spin my hand in the air.

"Bad circulation," Layla says with a shrug.

"Ouch."

"Yeah, so like, no foot plus no good story to go with it." Layla flips the cover shut on her tablet. "So how do you like the LVAD?"

"*Like* is a strong word," I tell her, and she smiles.

"Hey, it's keeping you alive."

"Yep," I say, suddenly conscious of the straps across my shoulders that hold my battery pack in place, and then even more irritated by the fact that I've grown so accustomed to them, I had forgotten they were there.

"You staying here?"

"What do you mean?"

"Your LVAD," she says. "If you respond well, they might let you go home until you get a heart."

"Doubt it" is all I say as I keep my face straight, ignoring the rest of my body as it descends into panic. The flutter in my belly. A muscle jumping in my back. My throat closing up.

The last time I left my house was in the ambulance after exiting through a window. It feels like an irreversible act, something that can't be undone simply by walking in through the front door and announcing that

I am home, if I can even claim that space anymore. I try to imagine climbing the steps, stopping to catch my breath every few, and easing open my bedroom door. In my mind there is still glass on the carpet and a tree branch has grown through the unclosed hole, a leaf brushing against the strands of my hair clinging to the sill.

"No, I don't think I'm going back," I say.

"You have to eventually, you know." Layla's voice is quiet, barely louder than the combined noise of our mechanical hearts.

"Unless I die," I tell her.

"Weird goal."

"So what's Brandy like?"

Layla rolls with my subject change. "She's pretty cool. Didn't get huffy about me asking about her foot. Oh, and she beat Nadine at chess first night here, and insisted on calling it *chest* instead. So she's my new best friend. Sorry."

"So she's better at chest than Nadine?"

"Way. Better." Layla holds her hands about three feet out from her top.

I laugh, the sound bouncing around inside me, scratching against the soft tissue still swollen around my sternum.

"I miss anything else?"

"Josephine's parents said she sleeps too much and that she needed to come off the intravenous painkillers, so she was switched out to pills instead. She woke up long enough to be pissed off and say some words that I hope they didn't hear down in the kids' wing."

"What's she on?"

"They gave her Xanax for her fibromyalgia, and she said it was like using a cotton ball to soak up Niagara Falls, but Karen put her foot down and her parents started tossing the a-word around so she shut up."

"They called their own daughter an"—I glance around and drop my voice—"asshole?"

It's Layla's turn to laugh, the sound much larger than her sickly frame. "Addict. But are you even serious right now? You can't say *asshole* in a normal voice? Oh no, wait, let me guess." She raises a hand to stop me. "You're the good twin."

I feel a finger of anger worming through me, burrowing down next to my LVAD.

"Sorry, sorry, sorry," Layla said, but she's still laughing a little. "I've just never met someone so lily-white, and I don't mean your skin."

"Thanks," I say, snuffing out the anger.

"And FYI Angela's brother already has a good line on Xanax, so I wouldn't bother trying to bum any off Josephine in the name of your illicit love affair. Besides,

I doubt she'd give them to you anyway. Brandy told me she walked into Jo's room to say hey one day while Jo had the bottle out and she basically hunched up over it and started growling like a dog with a T-bone."

It's a funny visual but raises a question.

"Brandy *walked* in? I thought she was missing a foot."

"She's got one of those fake things."

"A prosthetic?"

"Yeah, pretty realistic too. First time she pulled her foot off in the lounge Nadine screamed so hard her oxygen nodes popped out."

"Nice," I say. "Sorry I missed that. Why would she take off her foot though?"

"She wanted me to paint the toenails."

"Huh." I think about that while Layla yawns and stretches out, wondering what it would be like to just take out the part of you that doesn't fit.

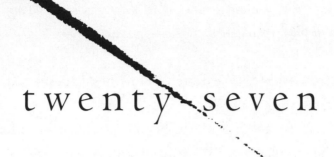

twenty-seven

TODAY AT THE CARDIAC CENTER!
11:00 a.m.—Stitch in the Snow! Join a knitting class with
Nurse Karen by the windows in the common room and celebrate
the first snowfall of the year with a new scarf! (Note: This is
an indoor program.)

In case you were wondering.

2:00 p.m.—Scrap your Crap! Crafty Nurse Karen continues
to share her skills in this scrapbooking class. Turn your pixels
into pics and make something to remember.

Or, leave behind something for others to remember
you by.

*4:00 p.m.—Meditation with Melody! Relax before dinner
with guided meditation.*

Apparently Nurse Karen's craftiness doesn't extend
to cassette tape players.

I put my schedule on the breakfast table next to Layla
as she stirs her tea. "Want to meditate again?"

She pulls it toward her and glances at it before taking
a sip of too-hot tea and having to spit most of it back
out. "I will if you will."

"Deal," I say as we're joined by the new girl.

"Hey," she says, pulling out the chair across from me.
"I'm Brandy."

"Sasha," I tell her, giving her a once-over. She's pale
and skinny but doesn't have an IV tree following her
around or any permanent machines attached to her like
Layla and me. And Layla wasn't lying about her having
Nadine beat at chest.

"Want to do meditation with us later?" I ask her.

"What's it like?" Brandy picks up a piece of her
unbuttered toast and eyes it the same way she had been
the window the first time I saw her, like maybe it has
something important to share with her and her alone.

"Lame," Layla warns her. "But Nadine doesn't go, so
I never miss it."

"Sure." Brandy reaches across the table and snags my

schedule, turning it around so she can read it right side up. "Except it can't be that lame. There's an exclamation point in the title."

"Makes it even lamer," Layla says around a mouthful of apple.

"No, you've just got to say it emphatically," Brandy says. "This is meditation with MELODY!"

She yells the last word, slamming her palm when she does. Over at another table, Nadine and Jo both jump and Nadine knocks her plain yogurt over.

"Footless freak," Nadine mutters toward us as she goes to get some napkins.

Brandy ignores her, pulling out the pager that we're all too familiar with and setting it on the table. She's decorated hers with sugar-skull stickers.

"I hate carrying this thing around," she says, spinning it with one finger. "It's like waiting for a boy to call, but if he never does it will actually kill me."

My hand goes to my hip, where my own pager is pressed against my skin. Like my LVAD, sometimes I forget it's there, but for a different reason. I can still feel the flutter in my chest, but that along with the low hum of the motor have faded into the white noise of my daily life. I forget about the pager because it is eternally silent.

"Does Sasha know the game?" Brandy asks Layla.

"What game?" I ask, but Layla's mouth is full of tea, and she points me over to Brandy.

"I came up with something to kill some time, so to speak," Brandy says, tipping me a wink. "It's a little twisted, but if you're not into knitting or scrapbooking it does the trick."

"Uh, it's a lot twisted." Layla tosses the rest of her apple across the cafeteria to land in the trash. "But if Karen comes in here with puppy dog eyes and tries to hand me knitting needles I might cave."

We slip out through the common room, avoiding Karen's glance from the windows, where she is surrounded by the preteens and a few of the littler ones. Layla's room is warm, and I strip my sweatshirt off as soon as we're inside, realizing the cardiac center is probably the only place I'll ever be able to wear a tank top in public again without my scars and LVAD attracting stares.

Layla sprawls onto her bed and I follow, tucking my legs in so Brandy can fit too.

"If there's not enough space I'll take my foot off," she offers. "Perks of the prosthesis."

"So what's the game?" I ask.

"All right." Brandy hands Layla her tablet. "Layla said you've got a fussy side. So don't get all puffed up on me."

"A fussy side?" I ask Layla, who shrugs, flipping open the cover.

"You'll see. This game, it's not . . . well, it's like fun, but not funny. Get it?"

"Like my joke about all of us waiting for someone else to die?" I ask.

"That's so dead—bang on," Layla says. "You don't even know." She pulls up the local news station, scanning through recent articles. "Two dead on interstate crash this morning," she reads aloud.

Brandy whips out her phone. "Where?"

Layla scrolls a little more. "Vinton County."

I watch as Brandy pulls up a map on her phone, her eyebrows drawn together. "Probably too far away. Time?"

"Uh . . . six thirty-eight this morning."

Brandy checks the clock and shakes her head. "No good, even if they were donors we're past the four-hour beating-heart limit, and that's not allowing for travel time."

"Travel time?" I ask, though I'm pretty sure I know what she means.

"Yeah, for one of those poor bastard's hearts to come to us," Brandy says, nodding toward Layla's screen. "Next."

"This one looks promising," Layla says. "Shooting in the suburbs, one dead, one in critical condition. Younger guys in their twenties."

Brandy tilts the tablet toward her. "Does it say where the dead guy was shot?"

"Reynoldsburg."

Brandy smacks Layla lightly in the back of the head. "No, like his body."

"Uh . . . it just says gunshot wound."

"Assume chest then," Brandy shakes her head. "No good. Got the name of the guy who was in critical?"

"Lawson Harris."

"Spell the first name," Brandy directs Layla while she taps out a text.

"Who are you texting?" I ask her, but she shields her phone away from me.

"Friend of mine at the DMV," she says. "He can tell me if this guy is an organ donor."

I glance at Layla, who is scrolling for more fatalities. "Isn't that kind of illegal?"

"Probably more than kind of," Brandy says, tapping her phone when it buzzes in her hand. "Nope. Not an organ donor. Next."

In my waistband, my own phone vibrates.

From Heath

Coming to see you today after school.

Oh boy.

I have a twinge of regret after I send the text because I need a favor from him.

Hey could you bring me my clarinet that's at school?

Cage 22 Combo 9-15-5. Don't want to get rusty.

Sure.

"That your lover?" Layla asks.

"Ex-boyfriend," I correct her.

"Where we at here?" Brandy nudges Layla with her fake foot, but Layla minimizes her news feed.

"I got nothing. Just the two on the highway and the guys who got shot."

"Slow day," Brandy says, tossing her phone aside. "So how screwed up are we?"

"Very," I have to admit, but there's a methodology at work here that appeals to me, an arrangement of facts and figures that my bored brain reaches for. I mentally scan the available information, looking for holes.

"If you don't know their blood type, it doesn't matter anyway," I tell the girls. "We don't know if the heart will be a match. And technically agreeing to be an organ donor at the DMV is an advance directive, but the family has to agree at time of death."

"Facts, facts, facts," Layla teases me, shoving my arm. "It's just something silly to pass the time. Don't make it all serious, or I'll unplug your LVAD."

"Actually . . ." My voice fades out while I ponder, and Layla leans in toward me.

"Uh-oh," she says. "That's the thinking face."

"Which side?" Brandy asks.

I pull my phone back out of my waistband, tapping in some searches. "There's a relationship between blood type and ethnic group, so if you know the race of the person in the news story we could probably take a decent stab at their blood type. I might even be able to find a distribution map of blood types in the area of the accident if I dig. Combine that with travel time from hospital to hospital, factoring out any major heart transplant facilities that are closer to the accident than we are . . . and yeah, we might actually be able to come up with a viable percentage on whether one of us gets the heart, as long as I know your blood types."

I look up to see both of them staring at me, mouths open. "What?"

"She's way more twisted than she looks," Brandy says to Layla. "Or, how I imagine she looked before, you know"—she points to my scar—"that."

"So are you going to tell me your blood type?" I ask, phone in hand.

"A positive," Layla says.

"B positive," Brandy says. "And I can't tell you how many jokes I get."

"Lucky," I mutter under my breath, plugging in their types beside their names in my Notes app.

"Why, what's yours?" Brandy asks.

"O neg," I tell her, not looking up.

"O neg as in *oh shit*," she says.

"Yeah, pretty much."

There's a tentative knock on Layla's door and Josephine pokes her head in. "What are you guys up to?"

"Life and death situations," Layla says. "Close the door behind you."

We all scoot in even closer as Jo joins us on the bed.

"No knitting for you?" Brandy asks.

"Not sure I want to be around that many kids with sharp objects," Jo says. "Plus Nadine is being a bitch today."

"Just today?" Layla asks, then looks to me before asking her next question. I nod.

"So what's your blood type, Jo? And don't say Xanax."

A ping goes off on Layla's tablet, an alert of a fresh news story. Brandy gets to it first and flips it open, her face lighting up.

"Yes! Suicide by hanging. We can work with that."

twenty-eight

Heath shows up about fifteen minutes before we're supposed to start meditating, so any kind of zen I might have achieved is instantly screwed. I'm in the common room in an overstuffed chair, my legs hanging off one side. Layla sits on the couch next to me, reading another trashy romance that her mom brought her. I'm swiping through my notes and running averages on blood types in my head when he finds me.

"Hey," he says, setting my clarinet case on the floor by the chair.

"Hey," I say back, and sit up. I still have on the tank, since they keep the heat pumped pretty high in here for the comfort of everyone with poor circulation. I know my chest scar is bright and eye-catching, but I still hate that it's the first place his eyes go.

"You, uh . . . you doing okay?" He points at it like I don't know what he's referencing.

"No, you idiot, she needs a heart transplant," Layla says.

"Heath, meet Layla," I say. "Layla, Heath."

"Hi." He nods at her, and she nods back.

"So what are your odds on getting one?" he asks, and while others might find it insensitive, it's a huge relief for me.

This is Heath and me, facts and figures, streams of data. We rely on the concrete and let the impulsive evaporate, which explains a lot about why we were together so long, an investment of our time we weren't willing to bail on yet.

"It's complicated," I tell him. "We don't really know the actual algorithm they use, but when a heart becomes available it's determined by blood type, greatest need, and proximity of the recipient."

"Oh." Heath's face falls a little bit. He knows I'm O neg because we coordinated the local blood drive for the past three years, the Red Cross volunteers' faces lighting up when they saw my paperwork.

O is the universal donor, but O neg can only receive from other O negs, which make up about 7 percent of the world's population. So they'd treat me like a queen and pump me dry. Getting that attention seemed cool then. Now it's a death sentence.

"How's Lilly?" I ask, and he has the grace to blush.

"She's good."

"Is she?" I say, and Layla makes a noise in her throat. "Well, thanks for bringing my clarinet."

"Sasha, listen. I . . ." Heath looks around the room. "Can we go somewhere and talk?"

"I have to meditate in like five minutes."

Heath's jaw tightens, something I'm familiar with. "Then give me the five minutes."

I get up and he sees the LVAD battery pack at my side. "What's that?"

"Life support." I slip past him and he follows me to my room, where I close the door behind us. We stand, awkwardly facing each other.

"So Brooke told me about . . . him." He can't say it, and I'm not helping him. I stare blankly.

"About who?"

"Seriously, Sash? C'mon. This isn't easy for me either, you know."

I'm about to tell him that it isn't my job to make it easier, but whatever there was between us, no matter how thin the string, it pulls taut in the moment that I see tears standing in his eyes. Somewhere, my heart responds. But I can barely feel it.

"About Isaac?" I provide.

"Yeah," he says. "I didn't think you were the cheating type."

I'll be sending Brooke a text later. But right now Heath is the one in front of me, and the rational part of me knows he deserves an explanation.

"Do you want to sit down?" I ask him.

He shakes his head. "You said five minutes."

"This will take longer than that," I say, and motion him toward the bed. He sits and I remain standing, eyes closed, hoping that somehow not looking at him will make this easier.

"I don't know if this will help at all, but I think it explains a lot," I say, pushing the chair in front of me and spinning it with my hands while I speak.

"What do you mean?"

"You know how I passed out at school?"

"Yeah, it was your heart."

"Right," I say slowly. "Except it's not mine. I had a twin, Heath. I absorbed her in the womb, but her heart took the place of mine. Her name is Shanna, and I think she knew she only had so much time left. She fell for Isaac."

I open my eyes to see the strain on Heath's jaw has only increased.

"The heart wants what the heart wants," I finish. "I had no say."

"Are you serious right now?" Heath slams down a hand on the desk chair, and it stops midspin.

"I—I . . ." It's my turn to stutter.

"Because it couldn't possibly be *your* fault, right, Sasha?" His perfect complexion is red, his manicured finger sticking in my face. "*You* would never cheat on your boyfriend. *You* would never sneak out of the house. *You* would never have sex with Isaac Harver, would you?"

The butterfly in my chest is panicked, trying to fly away. I grip the chair in front of me, my knuckles white, my breath coming in short stabs.

"No," I say, my voice shaky. "I wouldn't."

"Jesus Christ, Sasha," he says. "Wake up."

"I am awake!" I yell, the rabbit tempo of my heart beating in my ears. "Why can't you just believe me? Ask my mom; she listens when I talk about Shanna."

"Does she?" Heath asks, his own voice quiet now, hand at his side. "Or is she trying not to upset you and make you have a heart attack?"

"I guess you're not worried about that."

Somehow we've changed places. His anger evaporated his tears, while one has come from somewhere, sliding down my cheek, hot and salty. His hand is on the door, and he walks away from me as the chair rolls out from under my hands and I slide to the floor, more tears following me down.

"No," he says. "I don't give a damn."

He doesn't even look back.

The clarinet is waiting for me by the chair in the common room, a constant that has held for me in even the worst of times. Now, in the great tempest of my life, I am the one that abandoned it. I suspect that's how it began, me denying music my talent and instead giving that time over to Isaac, forsaking my mind for my body, not knowing that the last did not belong entirely to me. And so Shanna erupted, tearing into my life as she destroyed it.

I walk into the meditation room, ignoring Layla's questioning glance and Jo's squeak of alarm as I kick the cassette tape player into a corner. My clarinet slides together reluctantly, punishing me for weeks of disuse. The cork is dry, the reed chipped and broken. I replace it, wetting a new one with my tongue, sucking on it to draw out the familiar taste of resin.

This is me, this is who I am. This is Sasha Stone, who would have graduated as valedictorian and gone to Oberlin, who would have been on a dark stage in a few years, wearing black, unable to see the audience because of stage lights but feeling them there, their eyes on her though an entire orchestra was onstage. Sasha Stone

always garnered the attention. Sasha Stone stood out in
a sea of stars.

But somehow I am here, not on a darkened stage but
in a badly lit room with flickering fluorescents that
hum to match the mechanical hearts of my audience
members. I am here, with a harsh line down the middle
of my face to match the one on my chest, a line that—
should I ever make any stage—could never be covered
by makeup. The light would seek it out. Illuminate it.
All imperfections glare in the spotlight.

I tune up, the B flat scale dancing out of my fingers
with ease. I see Layla draw a mat near her own, encour-
aging Brandy to join her. Jo does too, after a moment,
her usual mat in the corner abandoned. I fly through
another scale, second nature taking me through the
warm-up I have done a hundred thousand times, my fingers happy to dance yet a bit stiff. I glance up to see that
Layla and the other two have laid down on their mats,
hands at their sides. I turn off the rest of the lights, the
only illumination in the room coming from the rectan-
gular window in the door. It lands at my feet, daring me
to step inside.

It's quiet in here, the girls' breathing and our hearts
the only noise. I give them something they'll recognize,
Pachelbel's Canon, and even though it's never been a
favorite of mine I see faces gathering in the window,

Nurse Karen and then Nurse Angela peeking in to see where the music is coming from. My fingers breeze through it, the notes familiar. Between my own breaths I hear the other girls' evening out.

I finish off and ease into Schumann's "First Loss," a simple but elegant piece in E minor. It's always been a favorite of mine, and though it's written for children, there's a true sadness in this song, followed by what feels like a paroxysm of rage at the end, a denial of what will happen, or perhaps already has. This song is about death, and while I've always known that, I never played it like I understood. Until now.

I wet my lips at the end, tightening the mouthpiece and checking the reed. I have to take a break before I launch into the next song. I'm out of breath and nearly wheezing when Jo's voice rises from the darkness, surprising me.

"Hey, do you know that one song that kinda goes like this . . ." She hums a few bars of "Memory" from *Cats*, which takes me totally off guard but I gladly play it, stumbling over the bridge because I don't have any music in front of me. The Sasha Stone of a few months ago could have improvised the entire piece, but that was a different girl, one whose fingers would never be tired after only three songs. One who could have played for hours without gasping. I flex my hands, easing out a cramp at the end of Jo's request.

"How about . . . uh, the song they always play at grad-uations," Brandy says.

"'Pomp and Circumstance'?" I ask, and riff a few bars for her.

"Yeah, I kinda like that."

"Sure," I say, and this comes easily, branded onto my memory since freshman year.

The requests come quickly after that, with lots of guesses on my part and humming on theirs, but we piece together music in that cold room, musty mats underneath us, the air around us heavy with darkness and minor keys. My mind is agile, my fingers keen to play, and as I claim back this small piece of my life, I begin to plan how I will claim it all, once again.

?sister? talk to ME.

I am —her-e

My answer, written so that she will understand.

U had y/our/ time (minetime). Over [no]w. I need a F(u)t(ur)e.

To Brooke
Thanks a lot.

???

You told Heath about Isaac

Yep But I told you about Heath & Lilly

Found a great subreddit with gifs of blisters bursting

Staying mad at Brooke is impossible. I want to throw my phone, but instead I end up texting her back about Heath coming to give me the official shove-off and asking her to send pics of some sheet music I know she has stashed away. She says she will in exchange for shots of Brandy's stump if she's cool with that.

I'm doing a silent walk-through of some Brahms I think would work well for our next meditation when Layla and Brandy burst into my room.

"Who's the douche?" Brandy demands, taking the spinning chair while Layla takes the couch.

"The douche?"

"The guy who walks like he stores the family Christmas tree in his ass," Brandy elaborates, spinning first one direction, then another.

"Oh, Heath." I snap apart my clarinet and take my time doing it. I don't know what to say about him. He's a chapter in a book I've already read, but one I'd keep on my bookshelf for a rainy day if I were desperately bored.

"Uh, yeah, Heath," Layla says, mocking me. "What's the story there?"

"He's the guy I fit with," I say as I snap my case shut.

"Like fit, fit?" Brandy asks, making a fist with one hand and jamming her index finger in it.

"Ew, no," I say automatically.

"Then you don't fit," Layla says. "I don't care if your clothes match or what. If the thought of bumping uglies with him makes you barf a little, it's a no-go."

"Can we talk about something other than my ugly?" I ask.

"How about a crane falling across three lanes of traffic on the eastbound?" Brandy offers. "Probably a few possibilities there."

I shake my head. "Doubt it. Any life-threatening injuries probably involve crushing, ribs puncturing organs, and so on."

"Bummer," Layla says, and picks up my nail file.

"Although I guess there could be amputee situations, possible bleed-outs . . ." I tap my fingers on the bed railing, my eyes drifting to Brandy's prosthetic.

She stops spinning in the chair. "Look, I'm kind of over it. So if you want to ask me stuff about my foot, go ahead."

Layla tosses aside the file and moves over to the bed to join me. "Is it weird?"

"At first, yeah," Brandy says. "But you just get used to it. Like, you wear glasses, right?" She points at Layla, who nods. "So when you get up first thing in the morning, what do you do?"

"I put my glasses on so I can see," Layla says. "Otherwise I'm blind."

"Right, so same thing. I get up and put on my foot so I can walk."

"Wait, do you get half off on pedicures?" Layla asks, and I whack her on the arm. "Ow! What? She said she's over it."

"Want to hear something cool?" Brandy asks.

"Yes," Layla and I say at the same time.

"So I sleepwalk, like, a lot," Brandy says. "And after the amputation it was this big problem. Dad lined the floor around my bed with pillows every night, because I'd forget I had only one foot, and I'd try to get out of bed in my sleep."

"Sucks," Layla says, but Brandy shakes her head.

"I only fell a few times before my brain figured it out. So now I put my foot on in my sleep. Except once I put it on backward and it got stuck, and we had to go to the ER. That was not awesome."

"How did you even explain that?" Layla asks.

"Wait, so even in a semiconscious state you knew to put your foot on?" I ask, redirecting the conversation before they start trading ER stories, which I've learned can quickly become a thing in the cardiac center.

"Yeah, I guess it's kind of like people putting on clothes before they walk outside even when they're sleep-walking. They just know."

"Does it hurt?" Layla asks. "Like your . . . I don't know, do you call it a stump?"

"Yeah, stump," Brandy says. "It doesn't hurt so much, no. But my foot still does sometimes, which isn't so bad. But the itching makes me crazy."

"Itching?" Layla sits up. "The foot that isn't there can itch still? And you can't scratch it, like ever? That is the literal worst."

"Yep," Brandy says. "The doctors tried to explain it to me. Basically what happens is my brain still gets signals from that foot, even though it's not there. So sometimes it'll hurt, or itch, or burn. It took a while for insurance to come through with my fake foot, so they tried mirror therapy for me first."

"Explain mirror therapy," I say.

"So, it's like a box," Brandy says, rolling the tray table over to put it in between her and us. "And there's an opening on each side, and one on the top. If you've got your right hand, you stick it in that hole, okay?"

She pretends to stick her right hand into the imaginary box and we both nod.

"And the inside of the box has mirrors facing each other, so if you're missing your left hand and it itches, you stick your right hand in there and look down through the top and your brain sees two hands and you scratch the one that looks like your left hand."

"How does that work?" Layla asks.

"It's a mirror image," I tell her. "It tricks your brain into seeing the reflected image of your right hand, which it believes is the missing left. Then you scratch the hand you're missing and your brain gets the visual signal that the itch has been scratched."

"Thanks, nerd, I got that part," Layla says. "I'm saying how do you scratch any hand at all if you're missing the other one?"

"Oh, um . . ." I look to Brandy, who shrugs.

"I don't know. I always just stuck my foot in it."

"Wait, so if my left tit is bigger than my right and I stick it in there will my brain think I have two big tits?" Layla asks.

"Neither one of your tits is bigger than anything," Brandy says.

"Plus you wouldn't be able to look into the top window anyway," I tell her.

Layla puts both her hands in the air and sighs. "You two are killing my dreams."

"Once I got the prosthetic it kinda worked the same way," Brandy goes on. "My eyes see me scratching my right foot and thinks it's taken care of."

"So your brain was still getting signals from your missing limb? That's why it would itch?" I ask Brandy, trying to get back on topic.

"Yeah." She nods, her hand subconsciously dropping to her foot to give it a scratch. "It's called phantom limb syndrome."

Medicine can't explain why a phantom limb itches in the night, fingers scratching for skin that isn't there. They don't know how to silence the burn in a foot that doesn't exist, the tingle in a hand rotting elsewhere. There is no answer for how a muscle not attached to the body can cramp, causing familiar pain in a limb long estranged from its owner.

They've tried. Severed nerve endings have been cauterized, stumps shortened, entire areas of the brain deadened to stop signals from nowhere. It doesn't work. Instead of relief, the afflicted receive fresh pain to compound the suffering, scar tissue piled over trauma.

I don't know how my heart left me, only that it did. Slipping from my fetal body as Shanna's pushed it aside, the cells broken down and absorbed into Mom to be shed with her skin, contributing to a layer of dust somewhere in our home before I even arrived.

It has tried to reach me since then, sending signals like phantoms through my veins, pulsing toward my brain to tell me what I care for and who I love. It has succeeded, mostly, even what small strength it retained overpowering Shanna's inadequate organ. She might be pumping our blood, but my wants and needs prevailed, until she knew there was only so much time left for her.

This is why Heath never felt vibrant to me, my feelings for him dulled by space and time, the signals from my rightful heart barely reaching me. This is why Isaac has fallen into me like a meteor, hot and fast, unavoidable, Shanna's heart making demands as it winks out of existence. And while I can't deny that my body enjoyed participating in her choices, it will come to an end.

I know I am the stronger of us, have already proven it by simply existing while she is merely clinging to life by my permission and only with the assistance of a machine that penetrated both of us, leaving metal entwined with our soft tissues. I will shed it, rid myself of the cords, the metal, the machines, the needles, the endless cheery faces asking what I need but not able to give me anything.

I will restore Sasha Stone.

I will be me.

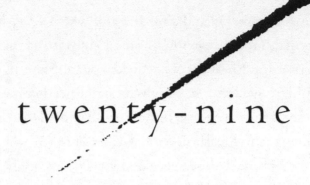

twenty-nine

"The nurses tell me you've been assisting with the meditation classes?"

I try to look away from Amanda's double-knotted shoes, wondering if her mother tied them for her before she went out the door to work this morning.

"*Assisting* is one word," I say.

"How would you describe your involvement?" Amanda asks.

"I run it. Before I showed up a boom box ran it."

"So you've improved the class?"

I let that one go unanswered. Amanda's pen fills the silence, scratching across the paper.

"I understand you have a new friend?"

Amanda's voice is an endless lilt, as if her vocal cords

are tipped in a way that makes it impossible for her to make a statement instead of asking a question.

"Yes. Brandy," I say. "She's an amputee."

"And what's she like?"

"She's like a regular person with just one foot."

Amanda's pen is still moving, but I can't imagine she's trying to capture the amazing insight I just imparted.

"And I understand your ex-boyfriend came to visit?"

"That was unexpected," I say, and she finally stops writing.

"Because?"

"He found out about Isaac."

"And how did he process that?"

I think about Heath's finger pointed at me, his face red and hot behind it. "Not well," I admit. "I tried to explain about Isaac being for Shanna, and her attraction to him not having anything to do with us."

"He didn't accept your explanation?"

I remember the muscle ticking in his jaw, anger I didn't think him capable of filling the space between us.

"No, he didn't."

"And how does that make you feel?"

I know how I felt in that moment, as my door shut behind him. I stayed on the floor for some time, curled over my LVAD as if it were my actual heart and needed protection. There was pain, but dull and far off, my broken heart keening elsewhere, the feeling barely reaching me.

"I can't really feel anything," I tell Amanda. "Not my feelings, anyway. It's like Brandy's phantom pain from her foot. My brain picks up signals from it still, but they're very weak. She told me about this mirror therapy thing they did to show her the inverted—"

"Yes, I know about mirror boxes," Amanda interrupts, putting her pen down. "And you came to this conclusion concerning signals from your heart after talking to Brandy about her foot?"

"Yes. I'd never considered it before, but it makes sense. Shanna's feelings take precedence because her heart is here, inside me. And my own is gone, a phantom heart."

"So what would you see if you looked into a mirror box?" Amanda asks.

It's a good question, and I give it time to circulate. "Well, it's not quite the same thing," I say. "I can't put Shanna's heart in there and see my own reflected back."

"No, you can't," Amanda agrees, but in a way that makes it sound like her question still stands.

"Do you know the difference between the mind and the brain?" I ask.

Amanda blinks quickly a couple of times, and I can't tell if she's surprised that I know to ask in the first place or insulted that I am putting the question to someone with a degree. An associate's degree, anyway.

"Yes, I know the difference," she says. "Do you?"

"Your brain is an organ. Your mind is your consciousness, your thoughts, the definition of who you are." I close my eyes, hoping that the words are right, the logic inside of me finding a channel out that others will comprehend. "The brain is a physical thing, but a mind is separate and indistinct. Like a soul. An identity."

"Okay." Amanda nods.

I keep my eyes closed, the darkness helping me draw sense into my words. "So . . ." I go slowly, not wanting to confuse Amanda. "I have Shanna's self inside of me, wrapped up in her heart. If I look at an inversion of myself, like the mirror box, I guess . . . I guess I'd see her."

It feels right, like I've done it. Unwound another problem put in front of me and come up with the answer. I open my eyes, and Amanda stares back at me so long I have to resist the urge to tell her that her glasses are crooked.

"I spoke to your mother yesterday," she finally says.

Amanda is smarter than she looks. This is her first non-question, and she vocalized something meant to throw me off guard.

"Okay" is all I say.

"She's made some progress in therapy sessions with her own doctor."

I keep my face stiff, hoping she can't tell I didn't know Mom was in therapy. Ever since Dad cut his losses with me he's re-upped his investment in her, which I imagine is where this is coming from. I picture them stopping at Starbucks on the way home from her appointments, sitting by the lake in the park we used to picnic in together. Except now there's no space between them on the bench where I used to be. It would almost be romantic if it didn't leave me stranded.

"She said I could share some things with you that you might find helpful. Would you like to hear them?"

I try to want to. I think Sasha Stone would want to. Somewhere, her heart cares that her mother has been destroyed by this, and that the little pieces are being put back together by a stranger while she's being sidelined. As if Sasha Stone were an impediment to her own mother's improvement.

"Yes, tell me," I say.

Amanda flips some pages in her notebook, and I wonder where the demarcation is between the pages that are about me, the pages that are about Shanna, and the ones about my mom, and if the ink bleeds through, one page to the next.

"She told her doctor that she was worried about

weight gain when she found out she was pregnant with twins, and that she was determined to remain active throughout the pregnancy. But that she may have overdone it."

"Okay," I say again, keeping my face blank while Amanda waits for me to interpret.

"Sasha, your mother blames herself for your sister's miscarriage. She always has."

I nod to encourage her to go on, not because I agree.

"Your mother has been carrying the guilt for years, and the chance to right the wrong to the unborn child inside her living daughter made her want to believe you."

Amanda leans forward in her chair, which should be dramatic but she loses her balance when it rolls a little.

"Sasha, I've spoken to quite a few doctors on this topic and all of them say that there's no way to effectively determine what causes a miscarriage that early in pregnancy. Your mother didn't cause the miscarriage, and neither did you. You don't owe her anything."

"Well, she gave birth to me, so . . ."

"I mean Shanna," Amanda says.

I lean toward her as well, because I think she would like that. "I know," I say.

What I don't say is that I'm starting to think Shanna owes me.

Big-time.

I am (here you are) you (there? goes my heart)
attack—serious as (a little birdie told me that
you hate me).

And I believe that little birdie.

From Isaac
How you feeling?
Sasha?
Sasha?

I. *Things I Know*
    A. *Mind over matter is not only a saying.*
    B. *Buddhist monk Thích Quang Duc set himself on fire in*
        1963, meditating peacefully while he burned alive.
II. *Things I Don't Know*
    A. *How far I can take this*

thirty

TODAY AT THE CARDIAC CENER!

Apparently not proofreading classes.

11:00 a.m.—Civil War Reenactment on the Lawn! Get hooked on hoop skirts as the Historical Society brings us their best! Note: The cannon will not be in use due to last year's pacemaker incident.

I would rather hear about that incident than attend the event.

2:00 p.m.—Wild for Woolies! The zoo brings in their cuddliest cuties for some special playtime in the common room!

To be followed by earnest hand washing so that our compromised immune systems don't collapse.

4:00 p.m.—Songs with Sasha! Who knew such talent walked these halls? Come hear resident musician Sasha Stone in the meditation room to get those toes tapping!

"You're famous," Layla says as I take my seat at lunch.

"Only in the Cardiac *Cener*," I say, and she rolls her eyes.

"Yeah, I knew you'd catch that typo."

I try to act like I don't care, but the truth is that instead of ending up as a crumpled ball in my trash can, like every other day's schedule, today's is tucked in between the pages of the only romance novel Layla's mom could bring me that didn't have three inches of cleavage and some side boob on the cover.

"Wild for Woolies?" Brandy asks, eyeing the schedule. "Do they even know?"

"No," Layla says with conviction. "They don't know."

"Know what?" I ask, peeling a banana.

"Lily-white," Layla singsongs under her breath, so I look to Brandy for the explanation.

"A wooly is a big old joint laced with crack," she says.

"I'm definitely not wild for that," I tell her.

"No shit," Brandy says, managing some fake shock.

"We should write our own schedule," Layla says, pulling the sheet back from Brandy.

"Dead-on," Brandy says. "Um . . . give me a sec . . . Fondle the Furries!"

"Wait, wait, wait, I got it," Layla says. "Meet your favorite mascot in the laundry room to get down in kinktown."

"A furry is—"

"Yeah, I actually know that one, thanks," I stop Brandy from explaining.

"Roll Your Own," Layla goes on in a fake radio announcer voice. "Nurse Karen isn't the only one with skills! Joints with Angela meets before dinner!"

"You guys . . ." I try to shush them, but Layla holds her hand out.

"Okay, okay, I know. Belt the Bitch! Nadine will be grabbing her ankles—"

"GUYS," I say, and they understand two seconds too late.

Brandy sighs. "She's standing right behind us, isn't she?"

Layla and Brandy turn to face Nadine, whose face is white with anger, her lips a flat line.

"Hey, sorry, Nadine." Layla at least has the grace to look guilty; Brandy is just glancing between the two of them like she's gauging how much time she needs to get away on her gimp foot.

"I didn't mean anything by it," Layla goes on. "We got carried away."

Nadine shakes her head. "No, I'm the one who's sorry, Layla."

"How's that?"

"Sorry for you that the organ donor registry isn't an equal-opportunity employer," she says, and Brandy stands up. I think she's going to run for it, but instead she plants herself firmly in between the two of them.

"Shut your face," Brandy says, low and quiet.

"What are you going do, crip? Chase me down?" Nadine says, stepping in toward Brandy.

"I can't catch you," Brandy says. "But I've got a good arm, a decent aim, and this foot pops off pretty quick."

I can't help it, I snort into my orange juice, which is a mistake. Nadine looks over Brandy's shoulder to lock eyes with me.

"And you, Frankenstein," she says. "I don't care how good you are on that flute—"

"It's a clarinet," I correct her without thinking, and Layla covers a smile.

Nadine is shaking now, and we've drawn the attention of some of the ladies behind the lunch counter. I see one hurry off in the direction of the nurses' desk. Apparently they don't make enough to break up girl fights.

"I don't care how good you are on that *clarinet,*" Nadine tries again. "You're a whack job and everyone knows it. You should be in a mental ward, not here."

"Whack job, I hear you're good at those," Layla says.

"She's fucking crazy!" Nadine lashes out, pushing aside Brandy to stick a finger in my face. "I was outside your room the other day when you got into it with that douche face. That bullshit story about your sister's heart? That's not how absorbing your twin even works, dumbass. I googled it."

Everyone is quiet, the entire cafeteria standing to get a better look at what's turning into the best entertainment of the day. And as I take in the silence, I realize something other than the hum of voices is missing. My own heartbeat.

I focus on Nadine's finger, the tip of it shaking inches from my nose. It's vibrating with her anger, a steady jazz beat rippling off the end of her nail. I can't follow it, can't ask my lungs or my heart to maintain that pace.

"Shut up," I say, wanting only silence, something I can recalibrate in.

"You call me on out on my shit, I call you out on yours," Nadine says, but her voice is hollow, like someone yelling into the wrong end of a tuba.

Layla's hand is on my arm, dark on pale, like a clarinet in reverse. I want to tell her that, but there's no breath inside of me, nothing to push out and no need to pull in. My LVAD gives a pump, a tiny current in a sluggish river, and I hit the floor. I hear some of the smaller kids crying, feel a cold river of orange juice flowing down from the table to land in the middle of my back, but all I can think about as I lose consciousness is Brandy's prosthetic right foot in front of my face, and how nice the toes look.

It's a fresh coat, so slick I can see shadows dancing off them as nurses run to me. They roll me over, but there's only darkness in my vision as everything else fades out. Everything except Brandy's fake toes, bright and beautiful, perfectly painted because she doesn't have to do it upside down or at a weird angle. She can take her foot off and fix it any way she wants.

She's definitely onto something.

thirty-one

There is a small gathering of people in the hall outside my room. I hear Mom and Dad, their voices low
and muted. Amanda is out there too, her voice slightly
higher in pitch so that it carries. I can pick out a few
of her words, little accents to follow the low rumble

of Dad's voice. She's saying things like *anxiety* and *panic attack*, and I imagine the other girls in their rooms, ears pressed against their doors, sucking up the drama along with my diagnosis.

Nurse Karen is with me, recording my pulse, monitoring my heart rate, taking my temperature. "How you doing, honey?"

"You tell me," I say, watching her face as she types my data into the laptop she carries with her.

"Your temp is a little elevated," she says. "The doctor will probably order some blood work, see if we can find out why."

"Like an infection?"

I think of Shanna, curled inside of me, surrounded by metal, pockets of pus forming around her.

"Could be," she sets the laptop aside, reaches out to pat my hand. "Could be just a bug in your system."

"I need to get it out," I tell her. "I've got to be healthy if a negative Rh heart becomes available."

"One will, Sasha. I just know it," Karen insists, her optimism contrary to countless bar graphs and data tables. Karen's pie chart would be a happy face, a bright shining zero on the pain scale, defying reality on a daily basis.

There's a hesitant knock on my door and Mom pokes her head in. I get a glimpse of Dad in the hall, the knot on his tie pulled loose. Amanda stands beside him, spinning her car keys on her index finger. Everyone has dropped what they were doing and come here to support me, a girl full of metal and pus and infection and another girl.

"Hey, honey," Mom whispers, as if my eardrums were the problem and not my heart. "How are you feeling?"

The truth is that I feel empty, all the fullness of the altercation at lunch having overflowed and left me with nothing. I think the only thing inside me right now is an LVAD, pumping nothing into a void.

"I'm fine," I say. And I absolutely have to be. If I've been exposed to any pathogens or show signs of an illness when a heart with my blood type becomes available it'll go to the next person on the list. Nurse Karen pats Mom on her way out, and all the muscles in my face slide downward.

"It's all right," Mom says, which is a dumb thing to say because it's definitely not. My face screws up into a convulsion I hate, as uncontrollable as Shanna when she's made a decision. I'm crying against my will, dashing tears from my face and trying to avoid Mom's hug as delicately as possible because if I'm sick I could get her sick too. Never mind if it's a flu bug or the void inside me. If it makes the jump to her, Dad will never look at me again.

"I've got a fever; you probably shouldn't touch me," I say, so she settles for wetting a washcloth in the bathroom and wiping my face.

"Want to talk about what happened?"

"Some of the other girls got into it," I say. "Stupid stuff. I tried to stay out of it, but Nadine said that I'm crazy and Shanna didn't like that."

Mom's face stays neutral, but I feel the tiniest tremor through the washcloth as she pulls it away from my face. "Uh-huh," she says in a tight, controlled tone.

"You don't believe me, do you?" I ask, my voice cracking on *believe*. It's like practice sessions from when I was a sixth grader, but now it's my vocal cords, not my clarinet, that squeak because I don't know how to handle them.

Mom folds the washcloth into a square, as if having some form of geometric shape in this room can alleviate the situation.

"Honey, I've been seeing a psychiatrist, and Dr. Zhang thinks—"

But she doesn't get to tell me what Dr. Zhang thinks because there's an all-encompassing sound in the room, the moan of the low end of the B flat scale and it's spiraling upward, not missing a note. It's coming from deep inside of me, my own body the instrument and despair the musician. My own mother does not believe me anymore.

Our mother.

The door opens and Dad pulls Mom away from the bed as I grab for her hands, her fingers still cool and wet from the washcloth.

"Stop it, stop," Dad is yelling, and I think it's at me. "This was not a good idea. You shouldn't be alone with her."

I've got a good grip on Mom's wrist, and I'm not giving her up so easily. I yank her back toward me, and she knocks into my IV tree. It crashes to the ground, tearing the needle out of the soft inner flesh of my elbow and sending a spray of cold fluid and warm blood across all of us.

"You'll get sick, you'll get sick, you'll get sick," I'm screaming now, up on my knees on the bed, swiping at Mom's face with the washcloth, trying to get her clean so that she's not infected by me, by Shanna.

"Goddamn it, nurse! Nurse!" Dad is yelling as he pulls Mom, who has become a bag of flesh and bones that drags at his feet, out into the hallway.

Amanda pins my wrists above me on the bed as Karen rushes in, slamming the door behind her. I glimpse faces in the hallway, Brandy and Layla have their arms around each other, Jo's mouth is hanging open, and Nadine is standing on her tiptoes to get a better view.

"What the fuck?" Karen says, which goes so far

against everything I know about her that I start laughing.

"Sasha," Amanda puts her face down to mine, her voice calm and steady. "You need to listen to me. If you want me to let go of you, you'll have to calm down. I cannot let go of you until you're safe and everyone around you is safe."

She readjusts her grip on my wrists and leans in closer. I can tell she had a cheeseburger with onions for lunch, and I can't even be disgusted by her breath because I'm so jealous of the fact that she got to eat it in the first place.

"Got her?" Karen asks, and Amanda nods, not looking away from me.

There's a brush of coolness against my bicep as Karen swipes me with an antiseptic pad, and I get a glimpse of her frown as she stabs a needle in. I close my eyes as the sedative takes hold, not wanting to see how she's gone from a zero to a five on the pain scale, and I'm the cause. Usually I get a warning before the poke, but I must have really messed up this time because she didn't say a word, just jabbed me.

"It's not my fault," I tell Amanda, but her grip on me doesn't let up.

"She's causing a scene and—" Karen begins, and I squeeze my eyes shut even tighter.

"Stop," Amanda cuts her off, and the bones in my wrist are ground together a little bit but I don't complain. She's the only person on my side now.

"She's upsetting my other patients—"

"Stop," Amanda says again, leaving no room for argument. Karen makes a noise in her throat, and I wish I could close my ears too. I hear the door open, the sound of Mom's muted crying from down the hallway, and then it clicks closed again.

"Sasha, can I let go of you now?"

I lick my lips and nod. The pressure is gone, and the feeling of warmth emanating from her over me disappears.

"You can open your eyes," she says, and I do, peeling them open to see her sitting in the chair at the foot of my bed, her head in her hands.

"Oops," I say.

She looks up at me, spreading her fingers apart so that I can see her eyes. "Jesus, Sasha. What am I supposed to do with you?"

"I didn't do anything wrong," I say, and her head goes back down.

"Seriously," I tell her. "The other girls got in a fight and I . . . I . . ."

"You held your breath until you passed out because you didn't want to hear what was being said to you,"

Amanda says into her hands.

"*No*," I correct her. "That is not what happened."

She sighs and her arms flop into her lap, like they're too heavy for her to hold up anymore. "Look, I don't know if I can make a convincing argument to keep you here, not after what just happened."

"And what just happened, exactly?" I ask.

"You created a disturbance that upset other patients."

"Technically my dad created the disturbance. All I was trying to do was talk to my mom after having a medical issue."

Amanda nods slightly, and I feel myself nodding along with her to encourage the movement. "Okay," she says. "I might be able to work with that. But you're going to have to do something for me."

I'm still nodding so she thinks I'm agreeable.

"Remember the mirror therapy they used with Brandy's foot, the one you told me about?"

"Yeah," I say, ignoring the feeling of my phone vibrating under my pillow.

"Do you remember what you said you thought you'd see if you looked into one?"

"Yeah." The phone gives a last, insistent pulse and falls silent. "I said I'd see Shanna."

Amanda picks her keys up from the floor, where apparently she'd dropped them at some point in the tussle. "I made a mirror box for you," she says. "It's out in my car."

My throat goes hollow, my neck muscles stiff. I cannot agree or dissent.

"I want you to look into it, okay? If I'm going to put myself out on the line to keep you here I need you to do this for me."

"Okay," I say, the word coming from nowhere, an automatic muscle response of agreement.

Amanda stands up slowly, eyes on me. "I'm going to check on your parents and send Karen in here to sit with you."

"I'm fine," I say, another gut reaction. There is nothing wrong with me.

"I don't know if that's—"

"I said I'm fine, and I said I'll do it," I snap.

"I'll be right back," she says, and the utter silence of the hallway as she slips away reminds me of kindergarten after the teacher bawled somebody out and everyone else is trying to be really, really good to make up for it.

It's shock and I know it. Other people's shock gathers together and quiets them, a comfort of sorts, making it easier for everyone to process what happened, what I did, the cause and effect that probably sent the Civil War reenactors home early and canceled the woolies entirely.

There's a jingle of keys and Amanda is back, a cardboard box in her arms with a picture of a cheap microwave on it.

"Seriously?" I say.

"I'm working with available materials around my apartment," she says, and places it on my side table.

"You need to ask for a raise then," I tell her. "That's a crap microwave."

Amanda shakes her head. "Sasha Stone, you have no idea."

She smiles at me and I take a deep breath, my chest shaky. "Are my parents still here?"

"They're not far," she says. "Are you ready?"

I'm not, but it doesn't matter. I wasn't ready to fall for Isaac Harver or have my face smashed open or a tree branch in my lung or have my friends tell me I'm a bitch or Heath say he doesn't care if I die. I'm not ready, but I know what I'm supposed to do. I know what Amanda wants Sasha Stone to do. And Sasha Stone is a good girl, and I am going to be exactly that, again. I run my bed controls so that I'm sitting up as Amanda pulls the side table over next to me, swinging the tabletop so that the box is across my lap.

"Okay," Amanda says. "You look in that hole there."

There's a jagged circle she's made in the cardboard, a helpful duct tape arrow pointing at it. "It's just like

Brandy's box with the inverted mirrors. So when you look in—"

"I'll see my sister," I finish for her.

"Do you want more lights on?"

I shake my head, the heart monitor beside me sending spiky waves across the screen as I lean forward.

And there she is, staring at me.

I wish there were more holes so that Amanda could see her too and know I've been right all along, so that my parents could look in and see their dead daughter, so that Isaac could see her face light up at the thought of him. I wish Nadine could stick her head in this box, see this face and deny her existence. I wish that Brooke could meet her and be her only friend. I wish Layla could meet her and convince her there is such a thing as love and that she was in it.

Shanna is gaunt, eyes sunk into deep hollows, her cheekbones starkly prominent. Her teeth have shredded her lips, her hair limp and lax around her face. I'm looking at a life unlived, one passed entirely in darkness, her skin hanging from bones like loose clothes.

"Sasha?" Amanda asks.

"I see her," I say. "She's dying."

"Okay, I want you to stop now," Amanda says, but I can't. Shanna has locked eyes with me and won't be moved. She's angry about messages left unread, unanswered, a cord kicked loose by my foot, no matter what everyone else tries to say. I see it in her eyes. Eyes just like mine.

"That's enough." Amanda moves the box, and I scrape my chin on the edge of the cardboard. "Sorry," she says, but she's moving too quickly for it be a real apology, shoving the table out of the way and taking me by the hands.

"What are you doing?"

"I need you to get up now," Amanda says, as if it's perfectly reasonable. "I need you to come into the bathroom."

"I don't think—"

"Sasha, listen to me," she interrupts. "You said you don't want to leave this place and you said you would do this for me. Now it's time to get up and come into the bathroom."

I didn't say that; I told her I would look into the box and that was all I promised. But she wants more from me now, and Sasha Stone would do the right thing, would do what she was being asked, would be a good girl.

And I am Sasha Stone, so I get up, the floor cold on my bare feet. Amanda grabs the IV tree and follows me, one wheel squeaking as I pull the bathroom door open. She reaches past me and flicks on the lights, my eyes closing automatically in response.

"Open your eyes, Sasha," she says.

I don't want to. I don't want to, but she's asking me to so it must be what I'm supposed to do. It must be the right thing, so I do it.

I do it and I see.

Shanna is here too, in the bathroom. She looks like death in this lighting, the hollow at the base of her throat deep like a gouge. Her eyebrows are even thinning, tiny hairs gone entirely where the scar passes through her face, a red, heavy scar with pinprick dots still healing on each side of it where she's been sewn together again like a quilt.

My scar.

My face.

"Oh my God," I say, hand reaching up to brush against cheekbones close to the surface of my skin. "It's . . . that's me."

"Yes," Amanda says, her eyes holding mine in the mirror, our reflections honest and true with each other. "It's always been you."

thirty-two

The word *breakthrough* has been very important in the past few days, one that Amanda keeps repeating and saying forcefully, even though she treats me like I might shatter while doing so. She's been doing a lot of explaining, told me how I've used Shanna to allow myself a little room to "act out" without the guilt. She even said that the white things I've been pulling out of my gums aren't reed splinters or my twin's fetal bones—their mine. Apparently when your wisdom teeth are super deep your jaw gets chipped a lot while they're digging the teeth out, and those bits work their way up to the surface. Amanda has an answer for everything; she even explained away whatever Nadine thought she heard when I was talking to

Heath, asking the staff if they want to know what a conversation between a teenage boy and girl that uses the word *absorbed* is really about.

Nadine has kept a safe distance, Jo retreating back across whatever line exists between those two and the rest of us. Layla and Brandy have been supportive in the best way they know how—by keeping me up to date on deaths in the area.

"Shooting on the east side," Layla says, scrolling on her tablet.

"Read it to us," Brandy says, and Layla does, all of us getting a little excited when she gets to the part about it being execution style.

"Head shot, good for us." Brandy pulls out her phone. "There a name?"

Layla finds it and Brandy shoots a text off to her buddy at the DMV. "What are our odds, Sasha?"

I glance over at them from the window, where a solid inch of snow has fallen to top off the three that settled from last night. "It's impossible to say. There are just too many variables: blood type, Rh factor, tissue match, distance from donor to recipient, plus we don't know where we fall on the donor list, so—"

"Yadda yadda, blah blah," Brandy says, mimicking a hand puppet at me. "It's a game. You don't have to be right."

That's the thing though, I kind of do. All the time. But my friend wants me to say something so I'll do what I'm supposed to. I've learned that.

"One in eight," I say, making up anything to get her off my case.

"I'll take those odds," Layla says.

My phone vibrates in my lap, and I tilt it so I can read the message against the glare coming from the windows. It's a new message from Brooke, waiting underneath the one that came in right before Amanda made me find my soul in a microwave box.

> Assuming yu r dead. Pls spectrally instruct yur parents to give me my old phone back.
>
> **I'm here—doing better.**
>
> Snow day 2day. BORED. Send invasive procedure pics.
>
> **Snowing here too.**

My thumbs hover over the screen, wanting to say more, thank Brooke for being a real friend. I'm not good with those moments though, even when they're not face-to-face. Maybe I'll get a transplant and ask them to film my surgery for her instead.

A piece of paper slides under Layla's door, and Brandy snatches it up, waving it in the air. "Oohhh, TODAY AT THE CARDIAC CENTER!" she announces.

I groan, not even turning my head away from the storm outside. Snow is piling on the window ledge, each flake distinct until it smears into the next.

"There's not a whole hell of a lot going on," Brandy says, scanning the page. "'Scrappy Over Scrabble,'" she reads. "'Come to the common room to outwit fellow wordsters'—oh Jesus, never mind."

"'Outwit fellow wordsters'?" I repeat. "That's a mouthful."

"This bit must be in there just for us," Brandy says, still reading. "'Note: Please no actual scrapping.'"

"Sounds more like Karen's scrapbooking class," Layla mutters, scrolling through her news feed.

"Ooooo, burn," Brandy says, followed by, "Oh my actual God."

"What?"

But Brandy doesn't answer me, and her silence gets my attention as well as Layla's. Brandy is holding the agenda out so we can read it, because she's incapable of speech.

TODAY AT THE CARDIAC CENTER!
2:00 p.m.—Two Girls, One Cup! Join junior jokesters Paula and Mei as they entertain us with their stand-up routine. Note: The girls say audience participation is welcome, but bring your own cup! Can't wait to see what these krazy kids have up their sleeves!

"They can't possibly know," Brandy says.

"They don't know," Layla agrees.

"Two girls one cup is—"

"I KNOW," I stop Brandy before she can get far.

"We're definitely going to that," Layla says. "Those junior jokesters sound like some funny fillies."

"Punny preteens," I add.

"Clever cu—Ow!" Brandy yells as I throw a pencil at her. "You could've put my eye out."

"She's just trying to even you up. You're top heavy with two eyes and one foot," Layla says, and my phone vibrates again.

From Isaac

That wierd girl said you're doing better? Why don't you answer me?

I try to ignore the fact that he must have misspelled *weird* enough times that autocorrect gave up on him.

"Be right back," I tell the girls, unfolding myself off Layla's couch. "And I think the Scrabble thing could be cool."

Brandy makes a face. "For you, maybe."

I cross the hall to my room, shut the door behind me, and call Isaac. He picks up on the first ring.

"Hey." He's guarded, fences up in his voice that I've never heard there before. That's on me, ignoring his texts while I sort out Sasha from Shanna. But I can't explain, not right now, so I'll pretend I don't notice.

"Hey. So . . . you talked to Brooke?"

"The blond one?"

"Yeah." There's a hot spark of jealousy in my gut that he would even notice her hair color. What else did he notice? Her scarless face? No wires coming out of her torso?

"She told me at school you had some kind of attack but you're okay now, or something?"

"That's a bit of an overstatement. I've been running a fever, and they can't pin down the source." I take a deep breath, steadying myself to tell a lie. "They took my phone away because I'm supposed to be resting a lot. I just got it back but I didn't text you because I'm not supposed to"—I pitch my voice low and sexy—"get overly excited."

He doesn't say anything for a second, and I think either I really screwed up the vocals or we got cut off.

"Wouldn't want that," he finally says, sounding pacified. "Smart move."

"I am smart," I agree.

Smart enough to have taken apart Amanda's crappy do-it-yourself psychology project to find only one mirror when she left to talk to my parents after my supposed breakthrough. Smart enough to know it wasn't an inverted image because Shanna's scar was on the same side of her face as mine. Smart enough to pretend like I fell for it. Smart enough to say what

Sasha Stone was expected to say.

"Smart, but a little effed too, you know?" Isaac goes on. "And I kinda like it."

"A little effed?"

"Yeah, you know. With a shaved head and scars, the wild part of you is on the outside now too. We match."

"Yeah, match," I say, pulling a hangnail.

"So I been meaning to tell you . . ." His voice fades out like he's about to admit something heinous and my breath catches in my throat. Isaac Harver defaced petroglyphs without blinking so what he's about to say must be pretty awful.

"I read *The Divine Comedy*."

It's so unexpected that I burst out laughing, the sound so unfamiliar to my throat that it catches there, a jagged thing.

"What did you think of it?" I ask.

"It's not very funny," he says, which sends me into another bout of laughter. I consider explaining to him about how the ancient Greeks use the word *comedy* differently than we do, but since my life is currently measured by an unknown increment of time I decide not to bother breaking it down for him.

"So listen," I say. "If I called you suddenly and said I needed you here right away, would you come?"

"You know the answer to that."

I do know. And I know the sex is only part of it.

There's a lingering in his touch that goes past sensuality into affection, an edge of panic in his unanswered texts that is more than the loss of his go-to booty call.

"Good," I say. "Keep your phone close."

I hang up and slide my hand under the mattress to double-check that the knife I nicked from the kitchen is still here. I suck my lip in when the blade snags under my thumbnail, yanking my hand back to inspect the bloody half-moon forming. In my other hand, my phone buzzes with a text from Isaac, something he didn't have the guts to ask me over the phone.

The sister thing, is that bullshit? Is your heart yours or what?

. . . maybe it's yours ☺

Like the sound of that.

Talk later. Call whenever.

I drop the mattress, pressing down on my thumb until the drop of blood squeezes out the tip, my skin angry and purple. I wipe my finger on the clean sheet, leaving behind a streak of red, and glance back at the text.

Yes, this is probably going to hurt him.

But it's going to hurt me a hell of a lot more.

I. *Things I Know*
   A. *This will work.*
II. *Things I Don't Know*
   A. *N/A*

thirty-three

"Four-car pileup! Four-car pileup! Jackpot!"

I hear Layla yelling as I cross the hall, and open the door to find Brandy spinning a throw pillow over her head and making siren noises.

"Shut your hole. I'm trying to read," Layla says.

I move Brandy's foot to make room for me on the couch, but she promptly puts her legs back up once I'm sitting, her prosthetic a surprisingly heavy weight across my knees.

"Nice," I say, and she shrugs.

"Okay, breaking news," Layla says, while scrolling. "Four-car pileup on the eastbound . . . resulting in— wow—looks like two were life-flighted, three in critical condition . . . no names yet though."

Brandy puts her phone away. "Can't really know any-thing then."

"No," Layla agrees. "But, like, statistically speaking our odds have to go up the more people involved, right?"

She looks to me for confirmation.

"Sure," I say. "But—"

"No buts," Brandy says. "You still want to do Scrab-ble?"

"I don't know," I tell her. "I'm not feeling all that great."

"None of that," Layla says, flipping her tablet shut. "I want to see you spell Quetzalcoatl."

I shake my head. "That's a proper noun; you can't use those in Scrabble."

"Whatever," Brandy says. "I want to see Nadine try to pronounce it." She pulls her legs off my lap. "C'mon, girl."

I get up, ignoring the head rush when I do. Whether it's the flu or Shanna staging an uprising, I don't know. But I can't pass on the possibility of beating Nadine at Scrabble.

"Hey, can I use your bathroom real quick?" Brandy asks Layla, who nods and pulls a hoodie on over her LVAD before we leave. A prescription bottle falls out of the front pocket, rolling to a stop at my feet.

"Dropped this," I say, checking the label before I

hand it over. "You still on the Oxy?"

"Just to sleep sometimes," she says, tucking the bottle into her top drawer. "You need any for . . . you know." She grinds up against the dresser, her LVAD cord flapping at her side.

"Gross," I say.

"Uh, yeah, but do you need 'em?"

"I haven't seen him since . . ." I tuck my own cord up into my sweatshirt. "Since this. I don't know how I feel about him seeing me with it."

"Got you," she says. "But don't let it stop you. I'll give you a few so you have them if you change your mind."

"Later," I say, dropping my voice as Brandy comes out of the bathroom. The last thing I need is both of them making pelvic thrusts at me as I try to slip Angela narcotics so I can sneak out to see Isaac.

"The wordsters have arrived," Brandy announces when we get to the common room. "Well, one wordster, anyway."

Nadine rolls her eyes, but Jo makes a spot for me at their table. A couple of the smaller kids are at another table with Junior Scrabble, the winter day being boring enough to draw out a decent attendance at a cardiac center event, for once. Nurse Karen walks by and gives us a serious look before going over to sit with the littles.

"We know, no actual scrappin'," Layla says as she

pulls a stuffed chair over to our table to watch, though
it looks like Brandy is doing most of the work by pushing. I can't help but notice the sheen of sweat on Layla's
face as she flops into the chair, how shallow her breaths
are.

"Fine, I'm fine," she waves off my questioning look.

I draw my tiles, not thrilled with what I've got. Brandy
immediately leans over my shoulder and spells out *fuck-
ers*.

"Sixteen points," I tell her. "That's actually pretty
good. Sure you don't want to play, wordster?"

Somebody's phone goes off on vibrate, the hum filling the air.

"Nah," Brandy says, "I've got—" The phone goes off
again, and she pulls hers out to check it. "Not me."

Mine is back in my room, so I shake my head as it
goes off a third time. Layla digs into her hoodie pocket,
and Jo flips hers over from where it was facedown on
the table.

"Me either. Nadine? That you?"

She shakes her head, her eyes narrow and intense on
her tiles. "Mine's dead. I—Holy shit!" Nadine jerks her
arm, sending letters flying off the table as she grabs for
her side.

"Karen! Karen! Holy shit!" Nadine screams, yanking
her transplant pager from her belt loop and holding it

in the air. "It's mine! It's mine! A positive, baby! Holy shit!"

Jo claps her hands over her mouth, her eyes huge above her fingers. Karen runs from the kids' table, torn between getting Nadine to stop swearing and being happy for her. Brandy and I glance at each other, then look to Layla who is trying hard to smile, but she lifts her shirt up to double-check her own pager, just in case. I don't tell her the odds of two A positive hearts coming in at the same time.

"You see that? You see that!" Nadine is still shoving her pager in people's faces, jumping up and down and yelling. At this rate she's going to have a heart attack before they can get her over to the hospital.

"Nadine, honey. Get your bag, we've got to get you moving," Karen says, as the nurse managing the desk comes in, her smile blasting a number one on the pain scale.

"Ambulance is on the way," she announces. "It's go time."

Nadine does one last fist pump and slams Jo a high five before noticing Brandy and me being less than excited about her new lease on life.

"Hey, Layla," she says, jerking her chin. "Don't worry. Black lives matter, just not to the organ donor registry."

Layla goes a shade paler. Brandy jumps to her feet

and Jo covers her head as the Scrabble board goes flying, sending Nadine back a few steps.

"You bitch," Brandy says, her voice low and dark. "I swear to God——"

I reach out, grabbing Brandy's wrist. "Leave it."

"She can't just say shit like——"

"I said leave it." I grind her wrist in my hand and whip out my field-commander voice. She sits down slowly, pissed at me.

"Uh-oh," Layla says, digging deep to offer me a weak smile. "I see Sasha's thinking face."

I drop Brandy's arm. "Layla, get your bags packed. Leave me the Oxy."

"What?" Layla says. "That's not——"

"Do it." I toss the words over my shoulder as I head for the kitchen. The staff is a mess, the nurses gathering in groups to share the news or hurrying off to get everything in place for Nadine's exit. I spot the squad as I walk past the main doors, sirens off but lights flashing. The driver is leaning over the front desk, flirting with the receptionist.

The cafeteria is empty. I swipe a saltshaker from a table and slip behind the counter, turning on the hot water and opening cupboard doors until I find the cups. I screw the cap off the saltshaker and dump at least an inch into my cup, then fill it with hot water. It overflows onto my hand, hot and slick with salt. I close my eyes, take a deep breath, and chug it.

The saltwater hits my stomach like lead, a trail of heat following it down as it burns into my gut. I'm still swallowing, chasing the hideous taste with the sludge that sits at the bottom of the cup. It's more solid than liquid, a gelatinous mass that I have to make myself swallow.

But I do. Because I am Sasha Stone, who can force her bent and screaming hands to play for one more hour, who can choose not to breathe if she wants. This is mind over matter, and my mind is the strongest thing inside me.

The salt water is down, all bodily signals begging to let it retrace its steps immediately. But it's not time yet, I lurch away from the counter, water rolling in my stomach, and head down the hall. They've got Nadine in a wheelchair, her go bag across her knees. She's bright as a star, her face radiant and a smile so big it even includes me as she sees my approach. Nadine sees me coming with arms open wide, and opens her own, welcoming what she thinks is a celebration, her victory over a shared struggle.

She's still smiling up at me as I clamp my hands on either side of her face and puke into her mouth.

thirty-four

I'm in big trouble.

Brandy is still in the common room, pretending to read while she's actually eavesdropping on the front desk and texting me everything that's going on. I'm on my bed, reading her messages as they come in. I don't dare even crack my door. Karen pulled Angela from her duties and stuck her outside my room with strict instructions not to let me out under any circumstances.

> *From Brandy*
> Another accident on Wbound. Squad guy said not snowstorm but a shitstorm.
> Cops here. K says charge you w/ assault
> **Can't prove anything. I'm a sick girl. I puked.**

... that's what they're saying too

K totes pissed

LOL K jus tol them if Nadine dies b/4 next <3 comes up it's
    on you. that's manslaughter.

More like bitchslaughter

Layla get to the squad ok?

Y

We heard the screamin & she dropped half her shit but I got it
    all packed b4 they loaded her up.

She said you so lily-white to get that pissed. People say shit
    like that to her = just another Tuesday.

She left you the pills, btw

"Good," I say aloud. I didn't drink a whole glass of
salt water for nothing.

Ur like my hero right now

I don't have an answer for that one. Yes, I made sure
Layla skipped the line for an A positive heart, and maybe
she'll get to write another letter to her boy now, one
that sets up a time and a place to meet. But the most
important thing to me in this whole string of texts is
the mention of the Oxy.

I hear raised voices outside my door, Josephine arguing with Angela. I get out of bed and go over to it, ear
pressed against the crack.

"I just want to talk to her," Jo says.

"Nope," Angela argues. "Karen says she doesn't come out, and nobody goes in."

"This is a cardiac ward, not a prison," Jo says, and I crack a smile.

My phone vibrates in my hand.

Cops have to go, say roads r a mess, Another accident

OMG Karen just threw the pencil cup holder

Jo knocks on my door. "Sasha, can I come in?"

"I told you—"

"And I'm going to tell the cops in the atrium to check your purse if you don't let me talk to Sasha."

There's a moment of dead silence, followed by the click of a handle turning. I step back from the door and sit on the bed.

"Hey," Jo says, shutting the door behind her.

"Hey," I answer as she takes the desk chair.

"So, what the hell?"

"Layla wasn't going to last much longer," I tell her.

Jo hooks her feet around the chair, considering my answer while she swivels back and forth for a minute. "So you flooded my friend with possibly infectious pathogens so that yours got the heart instead?"

"Exactly." I also ensured that I'd have my own source of pain pills to slip Angela when I need them. If Layla gets a new heart she'll come back here for recovery, along with a whole new list of prescriptions, painkillers among them. If Layla dies, the Oxy goes out the door with her stretcher.

"Wow. Just, wow." Jo stares me down like I might flinch. I don't.

"Karen thinks you're crazy."

A gust of wind hits my windows, a total whiteout of snow coming with it.

"That sounds like an opinion, not a fact."

And that's exactly what it is, the opinion of an RN against the complete psychological evaluation I lied my way through to even get onto the donor wait list. So I'll hedge my bets waiting to see what happens first—an official diagnosis or the death of someone with an O neg heart. Someone who could be out there driving right now, in this snowstorm. Or shitstorm. Or perfect storm. In my lap, I cross my fingers.

Your mom just called in. K left her like 20 messages

Uh-oh K just called u the b word

To ur mom

TODAY AT THE CARDIAC CENTER—crafty Karen cusses!

Jo sighs and swivels in her chair some more. "I don't even know what to say to you."

"Then don't say anything."

Her hands clench on the seat of the chair, and I see her pulse racing in her throat, strong and hot. Jo gets up to leave.

"I guess I just wanted to tell you that I hope Layla makes it okay," she says, her hand on the doorknob. "And I hope you don't."

She's gone before I can tell her I understand why she feels that way, and honestly I'm learning to adjust to the fact that I might die.

As long as Shanna goes first.

thirty-five

She won't go easily, my sister. She wants me to see what I'll be missing without her and so as I descend into sleep she sends me Isaac, one of her memories tucked away that I didn't get to take part in.

"Hey," he says, the dark branches of a tree cast across his face in the moonlight. "You're up late."

"You texted me," I remind him, crossing my arms over my then-unscarred chest, trying to replicate anger when I'm actually elated.

"Didn't wake you up though, did I?" he asks, in a way that says he already knows the answer.

"No," I admit, stepping closer so that he puts his arms around me, feels me shivering in the chill. He slides his jacket off and I take it gladly, listening to the

old leather creak as it settles around me, adjusting itself
to the fit of a new body.

"What're you doing up?" he asks, lighting a fresh
cigarette.

"Reading Shakespeare," I answer, and he snorts,
choking on a puff. "What? I've got a test on *The Tempest*
tomorrow. What are you doing up?"

"Not reading Shakespeare," he says, and steps closer
to me, the exhale of smoke surrounding us both.

"You should try it," I say, but I don't know that the
Bard holds any fascination for me in this moment either.
All I want is Isaac, the play of his eyes over mine, the
pull of my body toward his.

"Make me," he says, and I lean forward, whispering a
line into his ear, my hands sliding over his chest to follow the lines of his tattoos up to his mouth.

"'This thing of darkness, I acknowledge mine,'" I
say, sliding my fingers through his hair and pulling his
mouth down to mine.

"Totally yours," he says, right before our lips meet.

Karen wakes me up with dinner, her face the stiff flat
line of a number five on the pain scale.

"I can't get a hold of your case worker," she says.
"Power lines are down everywhere. Your parents will be
coming in the morning."

I poke the straw through my juice box.

"I'm not letting you out of this room," she says.

"Good call," I tell her, and chomp into a granola bar.

I thought she'd leave, but she settles onto my couch, measuring the depth of the snow on the ledge with her hand. It's at least five inches, and that's just what made it under the eaves to my sill.

"Layla's in recovery," Karen says, real quiet, her words almost not reaching me.

"Thanks for telling me."

She doesn't say anything else, so I start eating, trying to fill the empty hole left behind after I dumped everything I had onto Nadine.

"Why'd you do that?"

I don't answer. My logic doesn't need defending, and she would despise my goals in any case. Karen sighs and gets up from the couch, pulling the blood pressure cuff off the wall behind me. "Arm."

I lift it, still eating with the other hand. Karen makes a notation in her laptop, then takes my temperature.

"Fever's going down," she says. "Figures."

"So what was causing it?"

Karen glances at the screen. "Your blood work came back. Doesn't look like you had an infection, so it was likely just a flu bug of some sort."

A flu bug I poured down Nadine's throat out of my own.

"Okay," I say lightly, spearing a strawberry.

Karen's teeth clamp down tight on her lips to keep her from saying all the things she wants to say to me. The Hippocratic oath must be a real bitch. I see the edge of Angela's sleeve as Karen slips out the door, closing it behind her.

From Brandy

News says 2 more inches tonight

County on level 2

B kinda cool to hit level 3

No—3 is total shutdown, emergency vehicles only on

roads.

Brandy doesn't answer, so I assume she understands why a level 3 would be bad. I need people on the roads. I need people losing control. I need screeching metal and failed brakes. I need sirens and panicked, unanswered phone calls.

I need people to die.

And soon.

thirty-six

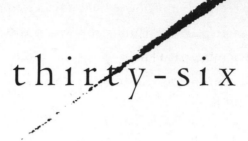

Amanda is not happy with me. I can tell because her eyebrows are tightly knit, which is a poor choice on her part because it's obvious she overplucked one of them when they're together like that. The afternoon sun isn't doing her any favors either, making her squint from the glare off the snow outside.

"Your dad said he thinks it's better to keep distance between you and your mother right now," Amanda says.

"Better for her," I say. It's not a question.

"And he said he'll make the drive once the roads are cleared."

"Are they still that bad?"

Amanda mistakes my interest for a sincere need to see him. "The plows were out all last night and into the

THIS DARKNESS MINE 349

morning," she says. "I'm sure he'll get here as soon as he can."

I'm not sure about that at all, but I let it slide for now.

Amanda has drawn her feet up onto the chair, her knees at her chin. "Do you want to talk about it?"

"No."

"Was this . . ."

She shakes her head quickly, as if to discourage herself from asking the question. Asking if it was Shanna or me who did this, pouring breakfast and bile and salt water into another girl. But asking that would mean I'm not better, that her miraculous microwave box of healing didn't work.

"Karen wants to have your mental condition reevaluated ASAP." Amanda pronounces the acronym phonetically. I wish everyone would start doing that with the American Heart Association. It would make all our conversations so much more spontaneous.

"I don't know if I can really argue against that, at this point," Amanda goes on.

"I was sick. I puked," I say.

"Yeah, I know. But given your past history with Nadine I don't know if I can make it fly." She sighs and rolls one foot, her ankle cracking. "What do you want?"

I want to stay where there's a knife under my mattress and a bottle of Oxy rolled in my sock. I want someone with an O neg heart to die. I want to fill out my jeans again and get plastic surgery on my face. I want Heath standing next to me in our senior prom photo because we fit. I want to see my bedroom again and close the window I should have never gone out of in the first place. I want my life back. I want future Sasha Stone to be a real thing, a real girl, an end goal I can invest in.

"I want to stay here, if I can."

"Okay." Amanda nods. "I'll see what I can do."

She stands up, looking out the window as a gust sends some of the piled snow on the roof eddying off into a spiral.

"Just do me a favor over the next few days."

"What's that?"

"Be good, Sasha Stone."

There's a song in my head, a few bars from freshman band camp that won't stop cycling. It spins and spins, like I did on the field for that show, each step followed by a quarter turn and the desperate need to haul in some air. But breathing is for people who aren't on the outside fringe of a pinwheel, so I stuck it out, red-faced, determined that the field commander was not going to lay into me in front of everyone.

I know I've faded off into something like sleep when I realize the girl in front of me is Layla, and a glance to my left on the next quarter turn reveals Brandy, her prosthetic foot left behind in a divot on the thirty-yard line. My clarinet is humming in my mouth, sending a vibration through my entire face that tickles. I smack at it, waking myself up and knocking my phone to the floor.

I snatch it up to find a missed call from Brandy. Not a text. Weird.

I dial her back.

"Thank God," she says. "I thought I was going to have to fight my way past Angela to get to you."

I glance at the clock. It's ten at night, but I can hear voices in the background.

"What's going on?"

"Everything, just . . . wow. You have no idea."

"Exactly," I confirm. "So tell me."

"So there was a really bad accident. Like, really bad. Car full of college girls went off the bridge next to campus and into the river. There were six of them packed into a Mini Cooper and they sank like a stone."

"Perfect," I say.

And it is. Drowning is an organ recipient's equivalent of a wet dream, no pun intended. There's no organ damage and on a night like tonight, the freezing water lowers body temperature enough that it's already operating like a refrigerator before the lunchbox coolers full of ice even show up tableside. But it also means that the drowning victim has a higher chance of being revived, their systems going into a shock that protects them. For a little while.

"Are they all dead?" I ask.

"I think maybe," Brandy says, her voice down to a whisper now, the voices in the background fading. "They already prepped Jo. She took off in her wheelchair about half an hour ago. Her and one of the littles, too."

"Where are you?"

"I snuck out to the common room to listen in after all the shit hit the fan. So, here's the thing. . . ."

"What, Brandy? Just spit it out."

"One of the girls that went in the water is O neg."

My LVAD keeps going, but I'm not sure the rest of me does, a small caesura where nothing happens inside of me, except a bright flare of hope. I grab my pager from the nightstand, but it stares back with a dead face.

"Nothing on my pager," I tell Brandy.

"That's 'cause she's not dead yet," she says. "She's nonresponsive but not brain dead."

"Right." I try to sound like that's a good thing, but there's a body over in another building with waterlogged skin, full of a chilly heart, eyes, kidneys, lungs that aren't doing her any good anymore.

"I wanted to let you know, so you can get ready."

It's a nice thought. Brandy knows I never packed a go bag, my own little superstition. Like if I didn't prepare, it was more likely to happen for me, everyone else's blood type working for them while they waited with supplies in hand, me with math not on my side and nothing ready to go.

But that's not quite true. I do have something ready. Just not my bag.

"You going to call your parents?" Brandy asks.

"I'll probably hold off," I tell her. "No point in getting hopes up."

"True," she says. "Well, hey, listen. I . . . good luck, okay?"

"Yeah, you too," I say, but I don't know if she hears me because I've already pulled the phone away, already started dialing a number, already have my heart in my throat when he answers.

"Isaac," I say. "I need you here. Now."

thirty-seven

My pager goes off too early.

My bag is packed, sitting on my bed, a note for who-ever finds it first at the top, neatly centered so that it can't be missed. There's a light tap on my door and Karen peeks in.

"Sasha? You're . . . good, you're up."

She's trying hard to be happy for me, and I'm try-ing to appear sane. For the rest of the patients in this moment I'm sure there's a true smile, but the one I'm getting is professional. Now more than ever Karen looks perfect for the cardiac center flier, calm, distant, pos-sibly drugged.

"My pager went off," I tell her, sitting on the edge of the bed with the bag behind me so she can't see that I'm already packed. "How much time do I have?"

She glances at her watch. "Twenty minutes, then I need you in a chair. We'll call your parents, and anyone on your notification list. I—"

"Karen!" I hear a voice yelling from the front desk. "Got another one! Get the little Ries boy ready."

"Jesus," she says under her breath, glancing back at me. "Twenty minutes," she says.

I doubt the ambulance will leave without me. This isn't exactly a city bus route, but I nod like a good girl. "I'll be ready."

She nods and turns to leave, pausing with her hand on the doorframe. "And, Sasha . . . congratulations."

It's a dead word in her mouth, one she's supposed to say. She's trying to make it sound right, like her lips are in a smile even though I know they're not. She's smart enough to keep her back to me when she says it, and I give her credit for trying.

"Thank you," I say, my fingers digging into my palms while I wait for her to get out of my room already.

As soon as the door closes behind her I grab what I need, opening the door a crack to peek outside. Angela looks at me, and I almost slam it closed again. I thought with all the activity she'd be called off, my guard dog assigned other duties.

"What do you need?" she calls through the closed

door as I rifle through my sock drawer for Layla's Oxy.

I'm more composed on the next try, my eyes meeting hers.

"What do you need?" she asks again. "Chair?"

"No, I'm not ready yet," I tell her, and she looks at her watch.

"Then you need to *get* ready," she says. "Ten minutes and you're in the chair, out the door." She doesn't add *good riddance,* but I hear it in her voice.

"Karen said I had twenty."

"Karen's being pessimistic," Angela shoots back.

My whole body starts to sweat, the handle of the knife tucked into the back of my pants sliding down my spine. "Listen, Angela . . ."

She cocks her head to one side and raises an eyebrow, like she's intensely curious to see what I'm going to say next. And honestly, I am too. I've got the Oxy in one hand, but her eyebrow is up there pretty high, so I don't know if that's going to be enough. The last time I snuck out I still had her trust, plus the pills. Now I've only got one of those.

"Listen to what?" she prompts me.

I don't know, but my brain is racing, trying to come up with what I should do. It reminds me of school, and all the nice people wearing their WWJD bracelets. But it's not Jesus I'm worried about. What would a normal girl do? What would someone who hadn't puked down someone else's throat do? What would a girl who didn't have a knife in her pants do? What would Sasha Stone do, if she didn't have Shanna curled inside of her?

"I just want to see the stars again," I blurt out.

It's stupid. It's romantic-comedy, made-for-TV, crap dialogue. So of course it totally works. Angela's eyes soften a little, the wrinkles around her mouth relaxing a smidge.

"There's no reason to think you won't make it," she says.

"Yeah, but . . ." I let tears pool in my eyes. "What if I don't?"

I reach for her hand and squeeze it. It doesn't hurt that five Oxy make an exchange along with the pretense of affection.

She glances down and slides the pills in her pocket. "Five minutes."

"Thanks," I say, slipping out the door and gliding down the dim hallway to the side exit. I zip my jacket closed and jam my hands into the pockets, breath crystallizing in front of me.

It's cold outside, a place I haven't been in weeks. The air hits my lungs in painful bursts, my toes curling against the snow that edges over the tips of my flip-flops. I take my coat off anyway, hanging it on a nearby

tree branch so that Angela will see the sleeve at the edge
of the door, dumbly believing that a dying girl who just
wants to see the stars again would do so right next to a
sodium light.

I head out across the snow, feet punching through
drifts. I lose my left flip-flop in the first thirty seconds,
the right one staying in place a little farther, only giving
up after I fall forward, hands planted in a snowbank up
to my elbows.

A little noise comes out of me, a mix of pain and
annoyance. I haven't hit numbness yet, but I won't wait
on it either. This is nothing compared to what's coming, I tell myself, gritting my teeth as I find a spot I like
beneath a cluster of birches. Their bark is as white as
the snow, the limbs as thin as my arms, which are now
shaking, my skin not even warm enough to melt the
snowflakes that land on me.

I hear his bike before I see it, the sound sending a
jarring mix of chemicals through Shanna's dying heart.
He's looking at his phone as he gets off, kicking the
stand in place casually, a second nature that looks oh so
sexy on him and he doesn't even realize it. I know that
he'll run his hands through his hair twice, shaking out
the snow. I know that he'll hold his phone in his left
hand even though he's right-handed. I know all these
things because I know him.

And I hate that.

I glance back at the cardiac center, gauging the movements of shadows behind the blinds. No one is panicking yet. That's good.

"Isaac," I whisper-yell at him, and he glances up, spotting my waving arms.

"Hey, what . . ." He comes to me, leaving the circle of light he parked his bike under. "What the hell are you doing? Jesus Christ, you're going to freeze out here."

He's taking off his coat, and I kind of hate that too because in the end he's a good guy, maybe even a great guy, and I can't accept that.

"Listen to me, Isaac," I say. "I got a heart."

"You did?" He stops, one shoulder free of his coat, the empty sleeve dragging in the snow. "Holy shit!" he yells. "Holy shit, lady!"

Isaac grabs me, pulling me completely into him, our hearts smashed together. I feel my LVAD protesting the tight space, my lungs crushed by his enthusiasm. I pull away, my feet numb and the coldness working its way up to my knees.

"That's awesome," he says, hands still on my shoulders, eyes brighter than anything I see around me.

"Not for Shanna," I say, my head down, the words falling out like small stones that barely ripple in a pond. But even those ripples reach the far shore, and I feel his hands tighten on me.

"What do you mean? I thought you said that was all bullshit?"

I shake my head, unable to hold his eyes. Because I'm a good girl and I lied to him. Lied to him about ignoring his texts. Lied to him that my heart was his. Lied to get him here, right now.

There are two warm spots on my cheeks, a small trickle of tears that will freeze before they hit the ground. I raise my head. The least I can do is look at him.

"She's always been here, Isaac. And she loves you so much. The way she feels . . . it's . . . I can't even begin to tell you. Her heart swells. I always thought that was a stupid thing they just said in romance novels, but it's real. It's real and she feels it."

I take his hand, now hanging limply at his side, and place it on my chest, right near the scar that peeks out of my tank top.

"She's so in love with you," I say, holding his gaze.

"Right," he says, his voice colder than the air around us. "*She* is. Not you."

He tries to reclaim his hand, but I keep it pressed against my skin. "It's a compliment, Isaac," I try to explain.

He jerks away as I hear the first raised voice from the

cardiac center. Words can't be made out, but I recognize the hint of controlled panic.

"A compliment?" Isaac repeats. "I'm supposed to be happy that you can't admit that you care about me?"

"No," I shake my head, half-frozen tears flying from my face, my lips going numb. "It's not like that. You don't understand."

"You're right, I don't!" Isaac is yelling now, his voice echoing back off the birch trees, my arms, the building behind us.

"Shhhh . . ." I urge him, lifting my finger to my lips, the knife I'd pulled from my waistband coming with it.

"What the fuck is this?" Isaac yells, backing up a few steps, his hands in the air.

"SHHHHH!!!!!" I hiss at him, the sound sliced by the blade, the heat from my lips fogging the metal. "They can't find me. Not yet."

"Who can't find you? Sasha— What—?"

"She loves you," I repeat, pulling the knife away from my face. "Shanna loves you so much and all she wants is to be with you. I can't take that away from her, not when I owe her so much already."

I slip the straps of my tank top down off my shoulders, my chest bare and naked in the moonlight. His eyes follow, even here, even now.

"Sasha . . ."

"I need you to listen to me," I say, raising my voice so he can hear me over what's now a group of people calling my name inside the cardiac center. "Are you listening?"

"Yes," he says, swallowing hard, eyes flickering over my shoulder.

"She's going to come to you now," I tell him. "Once she's with you I'll be okay. I'll be good again."

"Sasha . . . what are you even saying?" Isaac takes a couple of tentative steps toward me, his eyes on the knife and not my face.

"I'm saying what comes next will be disturbing, but I'm going to be okay."

I'm close to numb, but the knife still hurts going in, the tip of the blade barely registering when it cuts through deadened scar tissue, then flaring into a bright streak of pain as it goes deeper, past skin, through nerves to the hard surface of my sternum. It makes a noise when it scrapes across bone as I follow the path of the scar, calmly lifting my breast as I curve underneath it.

"Jesus Christ, what the—help! Somebody! Anybody!"

Isaac is screaming, immobile, torn between running away and stopping me. Blood is pouring from me, running down my torso, soaking my shirt, eating through the snow at my feet and creating steam all around me as my body heat leaves in a cloud, my life evaporating in the night air.

But I am not done yet, and I am determined, I am Sasha Stone. This is mind over matter and my mind is the strongest thing in me and I will not falter, will not hesitate to exorcise my sister from me and reclaim my life, even as I give her what she wants. What she needs.

"Isaac," I say, staggering a little in the snow, tasting blood on my teeth. "Isaac, come here."

And he does, his hands on my shoulders again, now slicked with blood as the weight of my breast pulls the opening I've cut in my chest wider. I reach in, numb fingers warmed by my own body cavity. I find the LVAD, the metal now cold from the night air rushing into me. I clutch it, feeling Shanna, pounding, pulsing, unsure.

And I pull.

She doesn't want to come out, doesn't want to be torn out of the womb of my body. And I understand her fear, understand how hard it is to come face-to-face with someone and show them all your ugliness. Because I've been there, with the scar on my face and wires in my chest, and still I persevered. So I'm taking her out now, tearing out my own ugliness so that I can be new again.

Veins come with it, the connections to my body unwilling to be severed, the cord of my LVAD stretching tight against my stomach as they're pulled out through the hole in my chest. It's still working, spraying blood in a fine mist over my face and his as I cut the cord, cut the veins, cut through everything that holds us together as one.

I give Shanna to Isaac, and she quivers in his hands, happy to be home.

"That's for you," I manage to say, before I fall forward into my own frozen blood.

thirty-eight

And then I died.

For a little while anyway. The numbers are a bit gray, but I think the EMTs in the squad on site to transport me probably have the most accurate data. Typically such things are judged by when the heart stopped beating, but since mine has been replaced with a new one, my time of death is a little fuzzy.

I didn't get the whole heart, to be honest. I didn't even get a decent chunk, I guess. What I actually gave to Isaac was a handful of soft tissue and gristle, the cord from the LVAD and a few bone chips from my sternum. But it did the trick, scared him so badly that he didn't notice that I put the knife in his other hand before I passed out. He ended up in jail for a few days before I cleared his name, but no sane girl would carve herself up like that. So he had to wait there until my new heart was where it belonged. Somewhere they couldn't take it back out of without serious ethical issues and lawsuits.

My new heart likes me, and I like it. It's found a home, burrowed down into the gaping hole I left for others to fix, taking to the reattached arteries as if they were reunited instead of patched together. I could feel it, strong and capable, as soon as I gained consciousness in recovery. It pulsed inside me, flushing all the bad things Shanna brought along with her from my system.

I thumb across my phone, reversing the camera and taking a picture of my chest to send to Brooke, the only person who is returning my texts. I'll never be able to wear a tank or a revealing dress again. What's left of my chest looks like offal from a butcher shop, the bits that end up in the alley Dumpster for the rats. My left breast hangs lower than the other, since I decimated too many pectoral muscles in the attack on my sister.

I slip the phone back under the pillow out of habit, not for secrecy. Mom and Dad were pissed to discover it in my bag, under Layla's favorite coverless paperback and the hospital-issued underwear. But I got to keep it, because as Dad said, "What more can she do?"

Oh, I can do lots more, Dad. Lots and lots more.

But first I need to rest, allow this heart to find its

place in the orchestra of my mind and body. I glance over at Mom, who is on the couch, doing the same.

I told her it was okay when I came out of recovery, that I was good Sasha again and everything was going to be fine now that Shanna was gone. Somehow this made things worse. I saw it in the tightening of the skin around her eyes, almost translucent with stress, saw it in Dad's mouth, now in the constant downturn of three on the pain scale. Mild concern, mixed with discomfort.

There's a knock on my door, all knuckle, the sound of a person who is not asking for permission to come in but letting you know that they are. Mom stirs on the couch as Amanda shuts the door behind her, her face the sort of calm that only comes after a major storm. I've always been impressed with her grim determination, the passive neutral she holds on to by her badly trimmed nails. But right now she's not calm—she's empty. Washed-out. Done. She's been crying, though she tried to hide it.

"That was certainly something, Sasha Stone," she says, ignoring my sleeping mother and plopping into the remaining chair. Mom mutters something in her sleep, then turns her back to us, no doubt aided into serenity by the Xanax her doctor has been giving her.

"It needed to be done," I tell Amanda. "Shanna would have killed me eventually."

She closes her eyes and presses her fingers against her temple and I take the moment to give her a once-over. Something is different, and it's not just the new posture she's taken, a slump that collapses her spine and pulls her shoulders inward.

"You're not wearing your lanyard," I say, finally spotting it. It had been blue, with smiley faces, the effervescent number one. It used to be clipped onto her ID, a picture with too much flash that had illuminated the oil output of each pore for closer inspection.

"I'm not exactly here in a professional capacity," she says. "I got fired."

"What?" I'm honestly surprised. "That's crazy. You're good at your job."

"Yeah, I know," Amanda says. "Then you came along."

I don't have anything to say to that. She tried to heal me with a microwave box and a compact mirror, so I'm not sure this is all on me.

"But it's kind of a relief too, you know?" Amanda goes on, leaning toward me now, elbows on her knees. "Since I'm not your therapist—or anyone's—I can say to you exactly what I think."

"Oh boy," I say.

"You're a terrible person, Sasha Stone," she says, eyes closing down into tiny slits. "There's an ugliness inside of you that can't be dug out, not with the knife you used, not with talk therapy, not with anything I know of. You're so far gone you won't even acknowledge it, claiming it all comes from someone else, somewhere else, never inside of you.

"You take the people who care about you most and manipulate them. You get your friends to lie for you, cut yourself up, and blame it on a boy who will probably never recover from seeing that, send your mother down an unstable path and your father trying to stop her so that he won't get in your way. You got me fired and my license is up for review—do you understand what that means? I worked my whole life to help others and now I'm not going to be able to, because of you."

She's close to me now, the hot breath of another drive-through meal wafting in my face. I sit up, all my cords coming with me, and lean toward her so that we're almost nose to nose.

"And how does that make you feel?" I ask.

thirty-nine

To Isaac

I'm sorry about my sister.

She can't help who she loved.

How are you doing? Do you miss her?

lose my #

To Heath

Thought you might want to know I'm OK.

I really, really don't give a shit.

I open my eyes two weeks later to find Brooke sitting on the only chair in a room I share with another patient, her constant stream of friends needing it more than my dispirited, short-lived visits.

"Hey," I say, pulling myself into a sitting position.

"Hey. So tell me about puking down someone's throat and then cutting your own heart out. I mean . . . I kind of hate you for about forty-five reasons—mostly because your mom totally bitched me out for sneaking you a phone, and your mom is cool and I like her, so that sucked. But you also provide me with front-row seats to the best sickout stories on the planet. I'm like, half Reddit-famous right now because of you."

And there it is, Brooke being unapologetically Brooke. I smile, the action almost normal now, the slashed side of my face nearly matching the other. "Missed you," I say.

"Yeah, no shit," Brooke shoots back. "Wait, let me guess—I'm also your best friend. Which has nothing to do with me being your only friend, right?"

"I wouldn't say you're my only friend. . . ."

"Really? Because, dude, I went through your phone earlier and, yeah, I'm totally your only friend."

"Okay, maybe," I grant her. I wasn't allowed to return to the cardiac center after what Dad has forever dubbed "my little stunt." The last text messages I sent to Layla and Brandy came back as undeliverable, so either they changed their numbers, or they died.

Not sure which option bothers me more.

"So, new heart?" Brooke reaches over and pulls open

my gown without asking, eyes devouring the smooth expanse of scar tissue there, the long, lumpy white path of the knife.

"Yeah." I pull the gown closed again, not wanting to see the slow, steady beat of someone else's heart. Though she would have been the death of me in the end, I've checked my phone once or twice for a message from her.

I miss my sister.

"So what's up at school?" I ask, and Brooke goes off onto a rant about the freshman who thinks he's going to oust her from her spot behind the drum set in the pep band, but how she'll run a flute straight though his eardrum before she lets that happen.

I let her go, closing my eyes and listening to the familiar lilt of her voice, the rise and fall of everything I knew before. If Brooke is still with me, I might be able to find my way back to who I was before Shanna and Isaac, pick my way back through the path to find Sasha Stone.

forty

I walk for graduation, where I accept my GED. There's not the rising swell I was expecting, the resounding affirmation of the entire town at my endurance against all odds. But I understand that the smattering of applause and one long wolf whistle is maybe all a GED deserves anyway, so I'll accept that.

I'm learning to accept a lot of things. Heath and Lilly's long, adoring glances at each other. Isaac's dropping out of school. Brooke's new fascination with a guy she met online who makes GIFs of fishing accidents ending in impalements. Mom and Dad's divorce.

Mom keeps telling me it's not my fault.

I know that.

I also know where that one wolf whistle came from,

a mouth that knows what to do to mine, likes to crush and bite a little. I know because he's her boyfriend, the girl whose heart I have. I found her name with a little research, asked some questions, met her parents. They were nice people who only wanted to hug me, tell me they were glad she could save a life.

Her friends wanted other things, after I pushed a little, worked them past the reservation of speaking ill of the dead. There was a relief for them in saying stuff they weren't supposed to, the dirty things I already knew because I had started doing them myself. I've only slipped a few times, let her have her way—and him have his—in the dark of night once, in a hotel bed Sasha Stone would never dream of sleeping in, let alone doing what they did. And then once, my face in a mirror, a line of white following the pale pink of what remains of my scar. And then it was gone, her heart rejoicing, my nose burning.

I won't let those things happen again, I think as I close my fingers around my GED, shake the principal's hand and return to my seat, ignoring the way her boyfriend's whistle sent a shiver down my spine and made my mouth water for his.

I sit down, cross my legs at the ankle, adjust my mortarboard.

I am Sasha Stone.

I will try to be good.

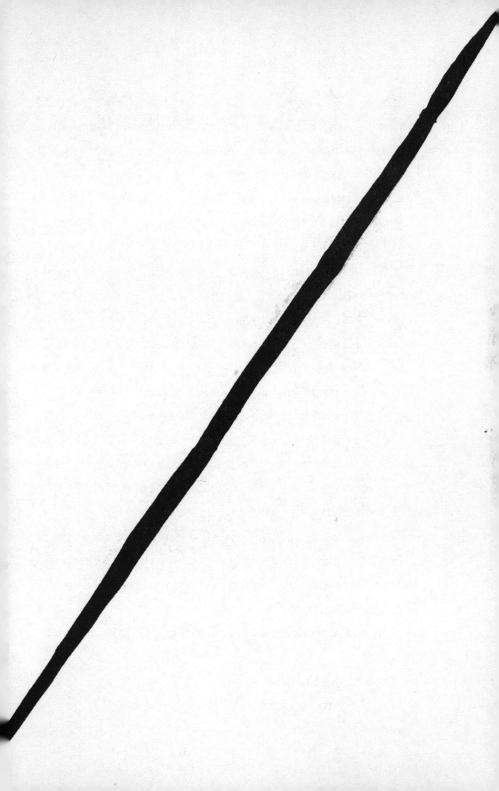

Acknowledgments

Writing may be a solitary endeavor, but the final product of a book has many fingerprints on it. My agent, Adriann Ranta Zurhellen, always takes it in stride when I throw something slightly heinous on the table. The same can be said for my editor, Ben Rosenthal, who appears to be unflappable. As always, Erin Fitzsimmons delivered a beautifully designed cover that also captures the content of the pages.

Many eyes saw this manuscript before it went to my team at Katherine Tegen. Demitria Lunetta and Kate Karyus Quinn deserve much credit for the existence of this book, as they encouraged me to embellish upon a short story that appeared in our anthology *Among the*

Shadows. As usual, R. C. Lewis kept me honest (and possibly sane) while drafting. Thanks to Stephanie Kuehn for a helpful eye, as well as Lydia Kang and Matt Sinclair, who were incredibly patient with my detailed and macabre medical questions.

For a long time I referred to this book in my head as *Fight Club in the Band Room.* This is my band-geek book, written with my band-geek friends in mind: Mel, Erin, Debbie, Amanda, Jeremy, Jim, Joe, Mandy, and Betsy.

We will always walk in step.